'This is it,' Kit said at last, practically in Nita's ear, as they came to the fringes of the area S'reee's instructions had mentioned – fifteen miles east-northeast of Barnegat, New Jersey, right over the remains of an old sunken tanker, six fathoms down in the water. And floating, soaring or slowly fluking through the diffuse green-golden radiance of the water, were the whales.

Nita had to gulp once to find her composure. Hundreds of whales had gathered and were milling about, whales of every kind – minke whales, sei whales, sperm whales, dolphins of more kinds than she knew existed, in a profusion of shapes and colours, flashing through the water.

Stillness swept over the spectators as she approached with Kit, and they recognized who she was. And a single note began to go up from them, starting at the fringes of the circle, working its way inward even to the Celebrants, until she heard even Aroooon's giant voice taking it up. One note, held in every range from the dolphins' dog-whistle trilling to the water-shaking thunder of the blues. One thought, one concept in the Speech, trumpeting through the water with such force that Nita began to shake at the sound of it. *Praise*. They knew she was the Silent One. They knew what she was going to do for them. They were thanking her.

Stunned, Nita forgot to swim – just drifted there in painful joy . . .

DIANE DUANE
DEEP WIZARDRY

CORGI BOOKS

DEEP WIZARDRY
A CORGI BOOK 0 552 52646 0

First published in USA by Laurel-Leaf Books, a division of
Dell Publishing Co., Inc.
First publication in Great Britain

PRINTING HISTORY
Corgi edition published 1991

Conditions of sale
1. This book is sold subject to the condition that it shall
not, by way of trade *or otherwise*, be lent, re-sold, hired
out or otherwise *circulated* without the publisher's prior
consent in any form of binding or cover other than that in which
it is published *and without a similar condition including this condition
being imposed on the subsequent purchaser.*
2. This book is sold subject to the Standard Conditions of
Sale of Net Books and may not be re-sold in the UK below the
net price fixed by the publishers for the book.

This book is set in 11/11½pt Plantin

Corgi Books are published by Transworld Publishers Ltd.,
61–63 Uxbridge Road, Ealing, London W5 5SA, in Australia
by Transworld Publishers (Australia) Pty. Ltd., 15–23 Helles
Avenue, Moorebank, NSW 2170, and in New Zealand by
Transworld Publishers (N.Z.) Ltd., Cnr. Moselle and
Waipareira Avenues, Henderson, Auckland.

Made and printed in Great Britain by
BPCC Hazell Books
Aylesbury, Bucks., England
Member of BPCC

For J.A.C.
re: redemption and fried zucchini

ACKNOWLEDGEMENT

Heartfelt thanks go to Neil Harris and his erstwhile comrades at Commodore, who went crazy hooking up a desperate writer's computer to one of their printers, and who helped her hit the deadline

CONTENTS

CONTENTS

A pause! Lost ground!
—yet not unavailing, for soon shall be found
what took three ages to subdue.
The hunters, on their guard,
give sparingly and greatly, east and west:
yet how shall only faithfulness prevail
against the peril of the overarching deep?

Trigram 63/Chi Chi:
Water over Fire

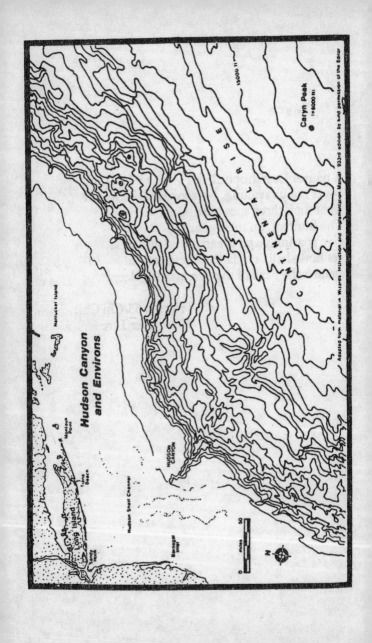

Hudson Canyon
and Environs

Nantucket Island

Montauk
Point

Fire
Island

Long Island

Jones
Beach

Barnegat Inlet

Hudson Shelf Channel

HUDSON
CANYON

CONTINENTAL RISE

Caryn Peak
-19,000 ft.

15,000 ft.

0   50
miles

N

Adapted from material in Wizards Instruction and Implementation Manual 993rd edition by kind permission of the Editor

DEEP WIZARDRY

SUMMER NIGHT'S SONG

Nita slipped out the back door of the beach house, careful not to let the rickety screen door slam, and for a second stood silently on the back porch in the darkness. It was no use. 'Nita' – her mother's voice came floating out from the living room – 'where're you going?'

'Out,' Nita said, hoping to get away with it just this once.

She might as well have tried to rob a bank. 'Out where?'

'Down to the beach, Mum.'

There was a sigh's worth of pause from the living room, broken by the sound of a crowd on TV shouting about a base that had just been stolen somewhere in the country. 'I don't like you walking down there alone at night, Neets . . .'

'Nhhnnnnn,' Nita said, a loud noncommittal noise she had learned to make while her mother was deciding whether to let her do something. 'I'll take Ponch with me,' she said in a burst of inspiration.

'Mmmmmm . . .' her mother said, considering it. Ponch was a large black and white dog, part Border collie, part German shepherd, part mutt – an intrepid hunter of water rats and gulls, and ferociously loyal

13

to his master and to Nita because she was his master's best friend. 'Where's Kit?'

'I dunno.' It was at least partly the truth. 'He went for a walk a while ago.'

'Well . . . OK. You take Ponch and look for Kit, and bring him back with you. Don't want his folks thinking we're not taking care of him.'

'Right, Ma,' Nita said, and went pounding down the creaky steps from the house to the yard before her mother could change her mind, or her father, immersed in the baseball game, could come back to consciousness.

'Ponch! Hey Pancho!' Nita shouted, pounding through the sandy front yard, through the gate in the ancient picket fence, and out across the narrow paved road to the dune on the other side of the road. Joyous barking began on the far side of the dune as Nita ran up it. He's hunting again, Nita thought, and would have laughed for delight if running had left her any breath. This is the best holiday we ever had . . .

At the top of the dune she paused, looking down toward the long dark expanse of the beach. 'It's been a good year,' her father had said a couple of months before, over dinner. 'We can't go far for our holiday – but let's go somewhere nice. One of the beaches in the Hamptons, maybe. We'll rent a house and live beyond our means. For a couple weeks, anyway . . .'

It hadn't taken Nita much begging to get her parents to let her friend Kit Rodriguez go along with them, or to get Kit's folks to say yes. Both families were delighted that their children had each finally found a close friend. Nita and Kit laughed about that sometimes. Their families knew only the surface of what was going on – which was probably for the best.

A black shape came scrabbling up the dune towards Nita, flinging sand in all directions in his hurry. 'Whoa!' she shouted at Ponch, but it was no use; it never was. He hit her about stomach level with both paws and knocked her down, panting with excitement; then, when she managed to sit up, he started enthusiastically washing her face. His breath smelled like dead fish.

'Euuuuw, enough!' Nita said, making a face and pushing the dog more or less off her. 'Ponch, where's Kit?'

'Yayayayayayayaya!' Ponch barked, jumping up and bouncing around Nita in an attempt to get her to play. He grabbed up a long string of dead seaweed in his jaws and began shaking it like a rope and growling.

'Cut it out, Ponch. Be serious.' Nita got up and headed down the far side of the dune, brushing herself off as she went. 'Where's the boss?'

He played with me, Ponch said in another string of barks as he loped down the dune alongside her. *He threw the stick. I chased it.*

'Great. Where is he *now*?'

They came to the bottom of the dune together. The sand was harder there, but still dry; the tide was low and just beginning to turn. *Don't know,* Ponch said, a bark with a grumble on the end of it.

'Hey, you're a good boy, I'm not mad at you,' Nita said. She stopped to scratch the dog behind the ears, in the good place. He stood still with his tongue hanging out and looked up at her, his eyes shining oddly in the light of the nearly full moon that was climbing the sky. 'I just don't feel like playing right now. I want to swim. Would you find Kit?'

The big brown eyes gazed soulfully up at her, and Ponch made a small beseeching whine. *A dog biscuit?*

Nita grinned. 'Blackmailer. OK, you find the boss, I'll give you a biscuit. Two biscuits. Go get 'im!'

Ponch bounded off westwards down the beach,

kicking up wet sand. Nita headed for the water line, where she shrugged off the wind-cheater that had been covering her swimsuit and dropped it on the sand. Two months ago, talking to a dog and getting an answer back would have been something that happened only in Disney movies. But then one day in the library, Nita had stumbled on to a book called *So You Want to Be a Wizard*. She'd followed the instructions in the book, as Kit had in the copy he'd found in a second-hand book shop – and afterwards, dogs talked back. Or, more accurately, she knew what language they spoke and how to hear it. There was nothing that *didn't* talk back, she'd found – only things she didn't yet know how to hear, or how to talk to properly.

Like parents, Nita thought with mild amusement. If her mother knew Nita was going swimming, she'd probably throw a fit: she'd had a terrible thing about night swimming after seeing *Jaws*. But it's OK, Nita thought. *There aren't any sharks here . . . and if there were, I think I could talk them out of eating me.*

She made sure her clothes were above the high-water line, then waded down into the breakers. The water was surprisingly warm around her knees. The waxing moon, slightly golden from smog, made a silvery pathway on the water, everywhere else shedding a dull radiance that made both land and sea look alive.

What a great night, Nita thought. She went out another twenty paces or so, then crouched over and dived into an incoming wave. Waterborne sand scoured her, the water thundered in her ears; then she broke surface and lay in the roil and dazzle of the moonlit water, floating. There were no streetlights here, and the stars she loved were bright. After a while she stood up in the shoulder-high water, watching the sky. Back up on the beach, Ponch was barking, excited and noisy. He can't have found Kit that fast, Nita thought. Probably something distracted him. A crab, maybe. A dead fish. A shark . . .

Something pushed her in the back, *hard*. Nita gasped and whipped around in the water, thinking, This is it, there are *too* sharks here and I'm *dead*! The sight of the slick-skinned shape in the water stopped her breath – until she realized what she was looking at. A slender body, ten feet long; a blowhole and an amused eye that looked at her sidelong; and a long, beaked face that wore a permanent smile. She reached out a hesitant hand, and under her touch the dolphin turned lazily, rolling sideways, brushing her with skin like warm, moonlit satin.

She was immensely relieved. *'Dai 'stiho,'* she said, greeting the swimmer in the Tongue that wizards use, the language that she'd learned from her manual and that all creatures understand. She expected no more answer than a fizz or squeak as the dolphin returned the greeting and went about its business.

But the dolphin rolled back toward her and looked at her in what seemed to be shock. *'A wizard!'* it said in an urgent whistle. Nita had no time to answer; the dolphin dived and its tail slapped the surface, spraying her. By the time Nita rubbed the salt sting out of her eyes, there was nothing near her but the usual roaring breakers. Ponch was bouncing frantically on the beach, barking something about sea monsters to the small form walking beside him.

'Neets?'

Nita waded out of the breakers. At the water line Kit met her and handed Nita her wind-cheater. He was smaller than she was, a year younger, dark-haired and brown-eyed and sharp of face and mind; definitely sharper, Nita thought with approval, than the usual twelve-year-old. 'He was hollering about whales,' Kit said, nodding at Ponch.

'Dolphins,' Nita said. 'At least, *a* dolphin. I said hi to it and it said "A wizard!" and ran away.'

'Great.' Kit looked southwards, across the ocean. 'Something's going on out there, Neets. I was up on the jetty. The rocks are upset.'

Nita shook her head. Her speciality as a wizard was living things; animals and plants talked to her and did the things she asked, at least if she asked properly. It still startled her sometimes when Kit got the same kind of result from 'unalive' things like cars and doors and telephone poles, but that was where his talent lay. 'What can a rock get upset about?' she said.

'I'm not sure. They wouldn't say. The stones piled up there remembered something. And they didn't want to think about it any more. They were shaken.' Kit looked up sharply at Nita. 'That was *it*. The earth shook once . . .'

'Oh, come off it. This isn't California. Long Island doesn't have earthquakes.'

'Once it did. The rocks remember . . . I wonder what the dolphin wanted?'

Nita was wondering too. She zipped up her windcheater. 'Come on, we have to get back before Mum busts a gut.'

'But the dolphin—'

Nita started down the beach, then turned and kept walking backwards when she noticed that Kit wasn't following her. 'The baseball game was almost over,' she said, raising her voice as she got further from Kit and Ponch. 'They'll go to bed early. They always do. And when they're asleep—'

Kit nodded and muttered something, Nita couldn't quite hear what. He vanished in a small clap of inrushing air and then reappeared next to Nita,

18

walking with her; Ponch barked in annoyance and ran to catch up.

'He really hates that "beam-me-up-Scotty" spell,' Nita said.

'Yeah, when it bends space, it makes him itch. Look, I was practising that other one—'

'With the water?' She grinned at him. 'In the dark, I hope.'

'Yeah. I'll show you later. And then—'

'Dolphins.'

'Uh-*huh*. Come on, I'll race you.'

They ran up the dune, followed by a black shape barking loudly about dog biscuits.

WIZARDS' SONG

The moon got high. Nita sat by the window of her ground-floor room, listening through the stillness for the sound of voices upstairs. There hadn't been any for a while.

She sighed and looked down at the book she held in her lap. It looked like a library book – bound in one of those slick-shiny buckram library bindings, with a Dewey decimal number written at the bottom of the spine in that indelible white ink librarians use, and at the top of the spine, the words SO YOU WANT TO BE A WIZARD. But on opening the book, what one saw were the words *Instruction and Implementation Manual, General and Limited Special-Purpose Wizardries, Sorceries, and Spells: 933rd Edition.* Or that was what you saw if you were a wizard, for the printing was done in the graceful, Arabic-looking written form of the Speech.

Nita turned a few pages of the manual, glancing at them in idle interest. The instructions she'd found in the book had coached her through her first few spells – both the kinds for which only words were needed and those that required raw materials of some sort. The spells had in turn led her into the company of other wizards – beginners like Kit and more experienced ones, typical of the wizards, young and old, working quietly all over the world. And then the spells had taken her right out of the world she'd known, into one of the ones 'next door', and into a conflict that had been going on since time's beginning, in all the worlds there were.

In that other world, in a place like New York City but also terribly different, she had passed through the initial ordeal that every candidate for wizardry undergoes. Kit had been with her. Together they had pulled each other and themselves through the danger and the terror, to the successful completion of a quest into which they had stumbled. They saved their own world without attracting much notice; they lost a couple of dear friends they'd met along the way; and they came into their full power as wizards. It was a privilege that had its price. Nita still wasn't sure why she'd been chosen as one of those who fight for the Worlds against the Great Death of entropy. She was just glad she'd been picked.

She flipped pages to the regional directory, where wizards were listed by name and address. Nita never got tired of seeing her own name listed there, for other wizards to call if they needed her. She overshot her own page in the Nassau County section, wanting to check the names of two friends, Senior Wizards for the area – Tom Swale and Carl Romeo. They had recently been promoted to Senior from the Advisory Wizard level, and as she'd suspected, their listing now read 'On sabbatical: emergencies only'. Nita grinned at the memory of the party they'd thrown to celebrate their promotion. The guests had been a select group. More of them had appeared out of nowhere than arrived through the front door. Several had spent the afternoon floating in midair; another had spent it in the fishpond, submerged. Human beings had been only slightly in the majority at the party, and Nita became very careful at the snack table after her first encounter with the dip made from Pennsylvania crude oil and fresh-ground iron filings.

She paged back through the listing and looked at her own name.

CALLAHAN, Juanita T.   243 E. Clinton Avenue
Hempstead NY 11575
(516) 379-6786

On active status   Assignment location:
38 Tiana Beach Road
Southampton NY
11829
(516) 667-9084

Nita sighed, for this morning the status note had said, like Tom's, 'On holiday/emergencies only'. The book updated itself all over that way — pages changing sometimes second to second, reporting the status of world-gates in the area, what spells were working where, the cost of powdered newt at your local Advisory. Whatever's come up, Nita thought, we're expected to be able to handle it.

Of course, last time out they expected us to save the world, too . . .

'Neets!'

She jumped, then tossed her book out the window to Kit and began climbing out. 'Sssh!'

'Shhh yourself, mouth. They're asleep. Come on.'

Once over the dune, the hiss and rumble of the midnight sea made talking safer. 'You on active status too?' Kit said.

'Yup. Let's find the dolphin and see what's up.'

They ran for the breakers. Kit was in a swimsuit and wind-cheater as Nita was, with trainers slung over his shoulder by the laces. 'OK,' he said, 'watch this.' He said something in the Speech, a long liquid-sounding sentence with a curious even-uneven rhyme in it, all of which told the night and the wind and the water what Kit wanted of them. And without pause Kit ran right up to the water, which was retreating at that particular moment – and then on to it. Under his weight it bucked and sloshed the way a waterbed will when you stand on it; but Kit didn't sink. He ran four or five paces out on to the silver-slicked surface – then lost his balance and fell over sideways.

Nita started laughing, then hurriedly shut herself up for fear the whole beach should hear. Kit was lying on the water, his head propped up on one hand; the water bobbed him up and down while he looked at her with a sour expression. 'It's not funny. I did it all last night and it never happened *once*.'

'Must be that you did the spell for two this time,' Nita said, tempted to start laughing again, except that Kit would probably have punched her out. She kept her face as straight as she could and stepped out to the water, putting a foot carefully on an incoming, flattened-out wave. It took her weight, flattening more as she stepped up with the other foot and was carried backward. 'It's like the moving pavement at the airport,' she said, putting her arms out for balance and wobbling.

'Kind of.' Kit got up on his hands and knees and then again, swaying. 'Come on. Keep your knees bent a little. And pick up your feet.'

It was a useful warning. Nita tripped over several breakers and sprawled each time, a sensation like doing a bellyflop on to a waterbed, until she got her sea legs. Once past the breakers she had no more trouble, and Kit led her at a bouncy trot out into the open Atlantic.

They both came to understand shortly why not many people, wizards or otherwise, walk on water much.

The constant slip and slide of the water under their feet forced them to use leg muscles they rarely bothered with on land. They had to rest frequently, sitting, while they looked around them for signs of the dolphin.

At their first two rest stops there was nothing to be seen but the lights of Ponquogue and Hampton Bays and West Tiana on the mainland, three miles north. Closer, red and white flashing lights marked the entrance to Shinnecock Inlet, the break in the long strip of beach where they were staying. The Shinnecock horn hooted mournfully at them four times a minute, a lonely-sounding call. Nita's hair stood up all over her as they sat down the third time and she rubbed her aching legs. Kit's spell kept them from getting wet, but she was chilly; and being so far out there in the dark and quiet was very much like being in the middle of a desert – a wet, hissing barrenness unbroken for miles except by the quick-flashing white light of a buoy or two.

'You OK?' Kit said.

'Yeah. It's just that the sea seems . . . safer near the shore, somehow. How deep is it here?'

Kit slipped his manual out of his wind-cheater and pulled out a large nautical map. 'About eighty feet, it looks like.'

Nita sat up straight in shock. Something had broken the surface of the water and was arrowing towards them at a great rate. It was a triangular fin. Nita scrambled to her feet. 'Uh, Kit!'

He was on his feet beside her in a second, staring too. 'A shark has to stay in the water,' he said, sounding more confident than he looked. 'We don't. We can jump—'

'Oh, yeah? How high? And for how long?'

The fin was thirty yards or so away. A silvery body rose up under it, and Nita breathed out in relief at the frantic, high-pitched chattering of a dolphin's voice. The swimmer leaped right out of the water in its speed, came down, and splashed them both. 'I'm late, and you're late,' it gasped in a string of whistles and pops, 'and S'reee's about to be! Hurry!'

'Right,' Kit said, and slapped his manual shut. He said nothing aloud, but the sea's surface instantly stopped behaving like a waterbed and started acting like water. '*Whoolp!*' Nita said as she sank like a stone. She didn't get wet – that part of Kit's spell was still working – but she floundered wildly for a moment before managing to get hold of the dolphin in the cold and dark of the water.

Nita groped up its side and found a fin. Instantly the dolphin took off, and Nita hoisted herself up to a better position, hanging from the dorsal fin so that her body was half out of the water and her legs were safely out of the way of the fiercely lashing tail. On the other side, Kit had done the same. 'You might have warned me!' she said to him across the dolphin's back.

He rolled his eyes at her. 'If you weren't asleep on your feet, you wouldn't need warning.'

'Kit—' She dropped it for the time being and said to the dolphin, 'What's S'reee? And why's it going to be late? What's the matter?'

'She,' the dolphin said. 'S'reee's a wizard. The Hunters are after her and she can't do anything, she's hurt too badly. My pod and another one are with her, but they can't hold them off for long. She's beached, and the tide's coming in—'

Kit and Nita shot each other shocked looks. Another wizard in the area – and out in the ocean in the middle of the night? 'What hunters?' Kit said, and 'Your pod?' Nita said at the same moment.

The dolphin was coming about and heading along the shoreline, westward toward Quogue. '*The* Hunters,' it said in a series of annoyed squeaks and whistles. 'The ones with teeth, who else? What kind of wizards are they turning out these days, anyway?'

Nita said nothing to this. She was too busy staring ahead of them at a long dark bumpy whale shape lying on a sandbar, a shape slicked with moonlight along its upper contours and silhouetted against the dull silver of the sea. It was the look of the water that particularly troubled Nita. Shapes leaped and twisted in it, shapes with two different kinds of fins. 'Kit!'

'Neets,' Kit said, not sounding happy, 'there really aren't sharks here, the guy from the Coast Guard said so last week—'

'Tell *them!*' the dolphin said angrily. It hurtled through the water toward the sandbar around which the fighting continued, silent for all its viciousness. The only sound came from the dark shape that lay partly on the bar, partly off it – a piteous, wailing whistle almost too high to hear.

'Are you ready?' the dolphin said. They were about fifty yards from the trouble.

'Ready to *what?*' Kit asked, and started fumbling for his manual.

Nita started to do the same – and then had an idea, and blessed her mother for having watched *Jaws* on TV so many times. 'Kit, forget it! Remember a couple of months ago and those kids who tried to beat you up? The freeze spell?'

'Yeah . . .'

'Do it, do it big. I'll feed you power!' She pounded the dolphin on the side. 'Go and beach! Tell your friends to beach too!'

'But—'

'Go and do it!' She let go of the dolphin's fin and dropped into the water, swallowing hard as she saw another fin, of the wrong shape entirely, begin to circle in on her and Kit. 'Kit, get the water working again!'

It took a precious second; and the next one – one of the longer seconds of Nita's life – for her and Kit to clamber up out of the 'liquid' water on to the 'solid'. They made it and grabbed one another for both physical and moral support, as that fin kept coming. 'The other spell set?' Nita gasped.

'Yeah – *now!*'

The usual immobility of a working spell came down on them both, with something added – a sense of being not one person alone, but part of a *one* that was somehow bigger than even Nita and Kit together could be. Inside that sudden oneness, she felt the 'freeze' spell waiting like a phone number with all but one digit dialled. Kit said the one word in the Speech that set the spell free, the 'last digit', then gripped Nita's hand hard.

Nita did her part, quickly saying the three most dangerous words in all wizardry – the words that give all of a wizard's power over into another's hands. She felt it going from her, felt Kit shaking as he wound her power, her trust, into the spell. And then she took all her fright, and her anger at the sharks, and her pity for the poor wailing bulk on the sand, and let Kit have those too.

The spell blasted away from the two of them with a shock like a huge jolt of static, then dropped down over the sandbar and the water for hundreds of feet around, sinking like a weighted net. And as if the spell had physically dragged them down, all the circling, hunting fins in the water sank out of sight, their owners paralyzed and unable to swim.

No wizardry is done without a price. Kit wobbled in Nita's grip as if he were going to keel over. Nita had to lock her knees to keep standing. But both of them managed to stay upright until the weakness passed, and Nita looked around with grim satisfaction at the empty water. 'The sharks won't be bothering us now,' she said. 'Let's get up on the sandbar.'

It was a few seconds' walk to where the dolphins lay beached on the bar, chattering excitedly. Once up on the sand, Kit took a look at what awaited them and groaned out loud. Nita would have too, except that she found herself busy breathing deep to keep from throwing up. Everywhere the sand was black and sticky with gobs and splatters of blood, some clotted, some fresh.

The dark bulk of the injured whale heaved up and down with her breathing, while small weak whistling noises went in and out. The whale's skin was marked with rope burns and little pits and ragged gashes of shark bites. The greatest wound, though, the one still leaking blood, was too large for any shark to have made. It was a crater in the whale's left side, behind the long swimming fin; a crater easily three feet wide, ragged with ripped flesh. The whale's one visible eye, turned up to the moonlight, watched Kit and Nita dully as they came.

'What happened?' Kit said, looking at the biggest wound with disbelief and horror. 'It looks like somebody bombed you.'

'Someone did,' the whale said in a long pained whistle. Nita came up beside the whale's head and laid a hand on the black skin behind her eye. It was very hot. 'It was one of the new killing-spears,' the whale said to Nita, 'the kind that blasts. But never mind that. What did you do with the sharks?'

'Sank them. They're lying on the bottom with a "freeze" on them.'

'But if they don't swim, they can't breathe – they'll die!' The concern in the whale's voice astonished Nita. 'Cousins, quick, kill the spell! We're going to need their goodwill later.'

Nita glanced at Kit, who was still staring at the

wound with a tight, angry look on his face. He glanced up at her. 'Huh? Oh. Sure. Better put up a wizard's wall first, so that the dolphins can get back in the water without getting attacked again.'

'Right.' Nita got her book out and riffled through pages to the appropriate spell, a short-term forcefield that needed no extra supplies to produce. She said the spell and felt it take hold, then sagged back against the whale and closed her eyes till the dizziness went away. Off to one side she heard Kit saying the words that released the freeze.

A few moments later fins began appearing again out on the water, circling inward toward the sandbar, then sliding away as if they bumped into something, and circling in again.

'The water will take the blood away soon enough,' the whale said. 'They'll go away and not even remember why they were here . . .' The whale's eye fixed on Nita again. 'Thanks for coming so quickly, cousins.'

'It took us longer than we wanted. I'm Nita. That's Kit.'

'I'm S'reee,' the whale said. The name was a hiss and a long, plaintive, upscaling whistle.

Kit left the wound and came up to join Nita. 'It was one of those explosive harpoons, all right,' he said. 'But I thought those were supposed to be powerful enough to blow even big whales in two.'

'They are. Ae'mhnuu died that way, this morning.' S'reee's whistle was bitter. 'He was the Senior Wizard for this whole region of the Plateau. I was studying with him – I was going to be promoted to Advisory soon. Then the ship came, and we were doing a wizardry, we didn't notice—'

Nita and Kit looked at each other. They had found out for themselves that a wizard is at his most vulnerable when exercising his strength. 'He died right away,' S'reee said. 'I took a spear too. But it didn't explode right away; and the sharks smelled Ae'mhnuu's blood and a great pack of them showed up to eat. They went into feeding frenzy and bit the spear right out of me. Then one of them started chewing on the spear, and the blasting part of it went off. It killed a lot of them and blew this hole in me. They were so busy eating each other and Ae'mhnuu that I had time to get away. But I was leaving bloodtrail, and they followed it. What else should I have expected . . ?'

She wheezed. 'Cousins, I hope one of you has skill at healing, for I'm in trouble, and I *can't* die now, there's too much to do.'

'Healing's part of my speciality,' Nita said, and was quiet for a moment. She'd become adept, as Kit had, at fixing the minor hurts Ponch kept picking up – bee stings and cat bites and so forth. But this was going to be different.

She stepped away from S'reee's head and went back to look at the wound, keeping tight control of her stomach. 'I can seal this up all right,' she said. 'But you're going to have a huge scar. And I don't know how long it'll take the muscles underneath to grow back. I'm not very good at this yet.'

'Keep my breath in my body, cousin, that'll be enough for me,' S'reee said.

Nita nodded and started paging through her book for the section on medicine. It started out casually enough with first aid for the minor ailments of wizards – the physical ones like colds and the mental ones like spell backlash and brainburn. Behind that was a section she had only skimmed before, never expecting to need it: *Major Surgery*. The spells were complex and lengthy. That by itself was no problem. But all of them called for one supply in common – the blood of the wizard performing them. Nita began to shake. Seeing someone else bleed was bad enough; the sight of her own blood in quantity tended to make her pass out.

'Oh, great,' she said, for there was no avoiding what had to be done. 'Kit, you have anything sharp on you?'

He felt around in his pockets. 'No such luck, Neets . . .'

'Then find me a shell or something.'

S'reee's eye glinted in the moonlight. 'There are the dolphins,' she said.

'What do *they* – oh.' The one dolphin still beached, the one who had brought them in, smiled at Nita, exhibiting many sharp teeth.

'Oh, brother,' she said, and went down the sandbar to where the dolphin lay. 'Look,' she said, hunkering down in front of it, 'I don't even know your name—'

'Hotshot.' He gave her a look that was amused but also kindly.

'Hotshot, right. Look – don't do it hard, OK?' And wincing, Nita put out her left hand and looked away.

'Do what?'

'Do *llllp!*' Nita said, as the pain hit. When she looked again, she saw that Hotshot had nipped her very precisely on the outside of the palm – two little crescents of toothmarks facing each other. Blood welled up, and the place stung, but not too badly to bear.

Hotshot's eyes glittered at her. 'Needs salt.'

'Yeccch!' But Nita still wanted to laugh, even while her stomach churned. She got up and hurried back to Kit, who was holding her book for her.

Together they went over to the terrible wound, and Nita put her bleeding hand to it, turned away as far as she could, and started reading the spell. It was a long series of complicated phrases in the Speech;

31

she spoke them quickly at first, then more slowly as she began to be distracted by the pain in her hand. And as often happens in a wizardry, she began to lose contact with her physical surroundings.

Soon Kit and S'reee and the beach were gone. Even the book was gone, though she was reading from it. She was surrounded by the roaring of green water around her, and the smell of blood and fear, and shadows in the water, pursuing her. She swam for her life, and kept reading.

No wound can be healed, the book said, unless the pain of its inflicting is fully experienced. There was nothing to do but read, and flee, wailing terror-song and grief-song into the water, until the first pain came, the sick, cold sharpness in her side. Nita knew she was sagging, knew Kit was holding her up from behind. But all that was far away.

The second pain came, the fierce mouths ripping and worrying at her till she couldn't go forward any more, only flail and thrash in an agony of helplessness and revulsion—

—and then the third pain hit, and Nita lost control of everything and started to fall down as the white fire blew up in her side. But the words were speaking *her* now, as they do in the more powerful wizardries. Though inwardly Nita screamed and cried for release, it did her no good. Her own power was loose, doing what she had told it to, and the wizardry wouldn't let her go until it was done. When it was, finally, it dropped her on her face in the sand, and she felt Kit go down with her, trying to keep her from breaking something.

Eventually the world came back. Nita found herself sitting on the sand, feeling wobbly, but not hurting anywhere. She looked up at S'reee's side. New grey skin covered the wound, paler than the rest of the whale, but unbroken. There was still a crater there, but no blood flowed; and many of the smaller shark bites were completely gone, as were the burns from the harpoon's rope where it had got tangled around S'reee's flukes.

'Wow,' Nita said. She lifted her left hand and looked at it. The place where Hotshot had bitten her was just a little oval of pink puncture marks, all healed.

'You all right?' Kit said, trying to help her up.

'Yeah, yeah, sure,' Nita said. She pushed him away as kindly and quickly as she could, staggered down to the waterline, and lost her dinner.

When she came back, her mouth full of the taste of the salt water she'd used to wash it out, S'reee had rolled herself more upright and was talking to Kit. 'I still feel deathly sick,' she said, 'but at least dying isn't a problem . . . not for the moment.'

She looked at Nita. Though the long face was frozen into that eternal smile, it was amazing how many expressions could live in a whale's eyes. Admiration was there just now, and gratitude. 'You and I aren't just cousins now, hNii't,' S'reee said, giving Nita's name a whistly whalish intonation, 'but sisters too, by blood exchanged. And I'm in your debt. Maybe it's poor thanks to a debtor to ask him to lend to you again, right away. But maybe a sister, or a friend—' she glanced at Kit '—would excuse that if it had to happen.'

'We're on active status,' Kit said. 'We have to handle whatever comes up in this area. What's the problem?'

'Well then.' S'reee's whistling took on a more formal rhythm. '*As the only remaining candidate Senior Wizard for the Waters About the Gates, by wizard's Right I request and require your assistance. Intervention will take place locally and last no more than ten lights-and-darks. The probable level of difficulty does not*

33

exceed what the manual describes as "dangerous",
though if intervention is delayed, the level may escalate to
"extremely dangerous" or "critical". Will you assist?'

Nita and Kit looked at each other, unnerved by the second part of the job description. S'reee moaned. 'I hate the formalities,' she said in a long unhappy whistle. 'I'm too young to be a Senior: I'm only two! But with Ae'mhnuu gone, I'm stuck with it! And we're in trouble, the water people and the land people both, if we don't finish what Ae'mhnuu was starting when he died!' She huffed out a long breath. 'I'm just a calf; why did I get stuck with this . . ?'

Kit sighed too, and Nita made a face at nothing in particular. On their first job, she and Kit had said something similar, about a hundred times. 'I'll help,' she said, and 'Me too,' said Kit, in about the same breath.

'But you're tired,' Nita said, 'and we're tired, and it's late, we ought to go home . . .'

'Come tomorrow, then, and I'll fill you in. Are you living on the Barrier?'

Nita didn't recognize the name. 'Over there,' Kit said, pointing across the water at Tiana Beach. 'Where the lights are.'

'By the old oyster beds,' S'reee said. 'Can you go out swimming a couple of hours after the sun's high? I'll meet you and we'll go where we can talk.'

'Uh,' Kit said, 'if the sharks are still around—'

Out on the water there was a splash of spray as a silvery form leaped, chatteringly shrilly, and hit the water again. 'They won't be,' S'reee said, sounding merry for the first time. 'Hotshot and his people are one of the breeds the sharks hate worst; when there are enough of them around, few sharks would dare come into the area. Hotshot will be calling more of his people in tonight and tomorrow – that's part of the work I'm doing.'

'OK,' Nita said. 'But what about you? You're stuck here.'

'Wake up!' Kit shouted playfully in Nita's ear, nudging her to look down at the sandbar. She found herself standing ankle-deep in salt water. 'Tide's coming in. She'll be floated off here in no time.'

'Oh. Well then . . .' Nita opened her book, found the word to kill the wizard's-wall spell, and said it. Then she looked up at S'reee. 'Are you sure you're going to be all right?'

S'reee looked mildly at her from one huge eye. 'We'll find out tomorrow,' she said. '*Dai'stiho*.'

'*Dai*,' Nita and Kit said, and walked slowly off the sandbar, across the water, and towards the lights of home.

A SONG OF CHOICE

Nita got up late, and was still yawning and scrubbing her eyes even after she'd washed and dressed and was well into her second bowl of cereal. Her mother, walking around the kitchen in her dressing-gown and watering the plants that hung all about, looked at Nita curiously.

'Neets, were you reading under the bedclothes again last night?'

'No, Mum.' Nita started to eat faster.

Her mother watered another plant, then headed for the sink. On the way, she put a hand against Nita's forehead. 'You feel OK? Not coming down with anything, are you?'

'No, I'm fine.' Nita made an annoyed face when her mother's back was turned. Her mum loved the beach, but at the same time was sure that there were hundreds of ways to fall ill there: too much heat, too much cold, too much time in the water; splinters, rusty nails, tar . . . Nita's little sister Dairine had kicked off a tremendous family fight last week by insisting that the blueness of her lips after a prolonged swim was actually caused by a grape Popsicle.

'Is Kit having a good time?' her mother said.

'Wow, yeah, he says it's the best,' Nita said. Which was true enough: Kit had never been at the beach for more than a day at a time before. Nita suspected that if he could, he'd dig into the sand like a clam and not come out for months.

'I just wanted to make sure. His dad called last night . . . wanted to see how his "littlest" was.'

'"*El Niño*,"' Nita said, under her breath, grinning. It was what Kit's family called him sometimes, a pun – both the word for 'the baby' and the name for a Pacific current that caused storms that could devastate whole countries. The name made Kit crazy, and Nita loved to use it on him.

'Be careful he doesn't hear you,' Nita's mum said mildly, 'or he'll deck you again. —How *have* you two been getting along?'

'Huh? We're fine. Kit's great.' Nita saw a slightly odd look come into her mother's eyes. 'For a boy,' she added hurriedly.

'Well,' her mother said, 'be careful.' And she took the watering can off into the living room.

Now what was that about? Nita thought. She finished her cornflakes at high speed, rinsed the bowl and spoon in the sink, and hurried out of the house to find Kit.

Halfway across the sparse sandy grass of the front yard, another voice spoke up. 'Aha,' it said. 'The mystery lady.'

'Put a cork in it, Dairine,' Nita said. Her sister was hanging upside down from the trapeze swing of the rusty swing set, her short red hair ruffling in the breeze. Dairine was a tiny stick of a thing and an all right younger sister, though (in Nita's estimation) much too clever for her own good. Right now entirely too much clever was showing in those sharp grey eyes. Nita tried not to react to it. 'Going to fall down and bust your head open,' she said. 'Probably lose what few brains you have all over the ground.'

Dairine shook her head, causing herself to swing a little. 'Naaah,' she said, 'but I'd sooner' – she started pumping, so as to swing harder – 'fall off the swing – than fall out the window – in the middle of the night!'

Nita went first cold, then hot. She glanced at the windows to see if anyone was looking out. They weren't. *'Did you tell?'* she hissed.

'I – don't tell anybody – anything,' Dairine said, in time with her swinging. This was true enough. When Dairine had needed glasses, when she'd started getting beaten up at school, and when she was exposed to German measles, nobody had heard about it from *her*.

'Y'like him, huh?' Dairine said.

Nita glared at Dairine, opened her mouth to start shouting, then remembered the open windows.

'Yeah, I like him,' Nita said, and turned red at having to make the admission. The problem was, there was no lying to Dairine. She always found out the truth sooner or later and made your life unbearable for having tried to hide it from her.

'You messing around?' Dairine said.

'Dairiiiiiiiine!' Nita said, quietly, but with murder in it. 'No, we are *not messing around*!'

'OK. I just wondered. You going swimming?'

'No,' Nita said, snapping the strap of her swimsuit very obviously at her sister, 'I thought I'd go skiing. Wake *up*, lamebrain.'

Dairine grinned at Nita upside down. 'Kit went west,' she said.

'Thanks,' Nita said, and headed out of the yard. 'Tell Mum and Dad I'll be back for supper.'

'Be careful,' Dairine called after Nita, in a perfect imitation of their mother. Nita made a face.

'And watch out for sharks!' Dairine added at the top of her lungs.

'Oh, *great*,' Nita said to herself, wondering if her mum or dad had heard. She took off at a dead run in case they had.

She found Kit waiting about a mile down the beach, playing fetch with Ponch to tire him out, as he'd told her he was going to. 'Otherwise he gets crazy if I go away. This way he'll just lie down and sack out.' And sure enough, after some initial barking and dancing around Nita when she arrived, Ponch flopped panting on the sand beside them where they sat talking and finally rolled over on one side and began to snore.

They grinned at each other and headed out into the water. It was unnerving at first, to swim straight out into the ocean, past the breakers and the rollers, past the place where the bottom fell away, and to just keep going as if they never intended to come back. Nita had uncomfortable thoughts about undertow and how it might feel to drown. But just when she was at her twitchiest, she saw a long floppy fin tip up out of the water. S'reee was lolling there in the wavewash, her long pale barnacled belly upward.

The night before, when S'reee had been injured and immobile, it had been hard to tell much of anything about her. Now Nita was struck by the size of her – S'reee was at least forty feet from the tips of her flukes to her pointy nose. And last night she had been a wheezing hulk. Now she was all grace, floating and gliding and rolling like some absurd, fat, slim-winged bird – for her long swimming fins looked more like wings than anything else.

'Did you sleep well?' she sang at them, a weird cheerful crescendo like something out of a happy synthesizer. 'I slept wonderfully. And I ate well too. I think I may get back most of the weight I lost yesterday.'

Kit looked at the healed place, treading water. 'What *do* you eat?'

'Krill, mostly. The littlest things that live in the water, like little shrimp. But some fish too. The blues are running, and the little ones are good. Or they have been until now . . .' She sighed, spraying water out her blowhole. 'That's in the story I have to tell you. Come on, we'll go out to one of the Made Rocks.'

They took hold of her dorsal fin, and she towed them. The 'Made Rock' turned out to be an old square fishing platform about three miles south of Tiana Beach: wooden pilings topped by wooden slats covered with tarred canvas and with bland-faced seagulls. Most of the gulls immediately took off and began flying around and screaming about the humans sitting on *their* spot, despite Nita's and Kit's polite apologies. Some of the other gulls were less annoyed, especially after they found out the visitors were wizards. Later on, whenever Nita thought of her first real conversation with S'reee, what she remembered best were the two seagulls who insisted on sitting on her lap the whole time. They were heavy, and not housebroken.

'I guess the best place to start,' S'reee said when Nita and Kit were settled, 'is with what you already know, that there's been trouble for wizards on the land lately. The trouble's been felt in the sea too. Out here we've been having quakes on the sea floor much more often than we should be having them – severe ones. And some other old problems have been getting worse. The dirt they throw into the water from the High and Dry, especially: there's more of it than ever—'

'"The High and Dry"?'

'The place with all the high things on it.'

'Oh,' Kit said. 'New York City. Manhattan, actually.'

'The water close to it is getting so foul, the fish can't breathe it for many thousands of lengths out. Those that can are mostly sick. And many more of the boats-that-eat-whales have been out here recently. The past few months, there's been a great slaughter—'

Nita frowned at the thought of other creatures suffering what S'reee had been through. She had heard all the stories about the hungry people in Japan, but at the moment she found herself thinking that there *had* to be something else to eat.

'Things have not been good,' S'reee said. 'I know less about the troubles on land, but the Sea tells us that the land wizards have been troubled of late, that there was some great strife of powers on the High and Dry. We saw the moon go out one night—'

'So did we,' Kit said. There was fear in his eyes at the memory, and pride in his voice. 'We were in Manhattan when it happened.'

'We were part of it,' Nita said. She still didn't know all of how she felt about what had happened. But she would never forget reading from the book that kept the world as it should be, the *Book of Night with Moon*, while around her and Kit the buildings of Manhattan wavered like a dream about to break – and beyond a barrier of trees brought to life, and battling statues, the personification of all darkness and fear, the Lone Power, fought to get at them and destroy them.

S'reee looked at them somberly from one eye. 'It's true then what Ae'mhnuu used to tell me, that there are no accidents. You've met the Power that created death in the beginning and was cast out for it. All these things – the lost moon, that night, and the earthquakes, and the fouled water, and the whale-eating ships – they're all Its doing, one way or another.'

41

Kit and Nita nodded. 'It took a defeat in that battle you two were in,' S'reee said. 'It's angry, and the problems we've been having are symptoms of that anger. So we have to bind It, make It less harmful, as the first sea people bound It a long time ago. Then things will be quiet again for a while.'

'Bind It how?' Nita said.

'No, wait a minute,' Kit said. 'You said something about the Sea telling you things—'

S'reee looked surprised for a moment. 'Oh, I forgot that you do it differently. You work your wizardry with the aid of those things you carry—'

'Our books.'

'Right. The whales who are wizards get their wizardry from the Sea. The water speaks to you when you're ready, and offers you the Ordeal. Then if you pass it, the Heart of the Sea speaks whenever you need to hear it and tells you what you need to know.'

Nita nodded. The events in that 'other' Manhattan had been her Ordeal, and Kit's; and after they passed it, their books had contained much more information than before. 'So,' she said, 'bind the Lone Power *how?*'

'The way the first whale-wizards did,' S'reee said. 'The story itself *is* the binding. Or rather, the story's a song: the Song of the Twelve. In the long form it takes – *will* take – hours to sing.'

'I'm glad I had breakfast,' Kit muttered.

S'reee spouted good-naturedly. Nita wondered whether it was accidental that the wind turned at that exact moment, threw the spray straight at Kit, and soaked him to the skin. At any rate, Nita laughed.

'I won't take quite that long,' S'reee said. 'You know about the great War of the Powers, at the beginning of everything; and how the Lone Power invented death and pain, and tried to impose them on the whole universe, and the other Powers wouldn't let It, and threw It out.'

'Even ordinary human beings have stories about it,' Kit said. He took off his wind-cheater and shook it out, mostly on Nita.

'I'm not surprised,' S'reee said. 'Everything that lives and tells stories has *this* story in one form or another. Well. After that war in the Above and Beyond, the Lone Power spent a long while in untravelled barren universes, recouping Its strength. Then It came back to our native universe, looking for some quiet, out-of-the-way place to try out Its new inventions. Right then the only place vulnerable to It, because thinking life was very new here, was this world; and the only place thinking life existed as yet was the Sea. So the Lone One came here to trick the Sea into accepting Death. Its sort of death, anyway – where all power and love are wasted into an endless darkness, lost forever.'

'Entropy,' Nita said.

'Yes. And any sea people It succeeded in tricking would be stuck with that death, the Great Death, forever.—Now there was already a sort of death in the Sea, but only the kind where your body stops. Everyone knew it wasn't permanent, and it didn't hurt much; you might get eaten, but you would go on as part of someone else. No-one was afraid of not being his own self any more – I guess that's the simplest way of putting it. That calm way of life drove the Lone Power wild with hate, and It swore to attach fear and pain to it and make it a lot more interesting.'

S'reee sighed. 'The whales' job then was what it is now: to be masters and caretakers for the fish and the smaller sea people, the way you two-leggers are for the dry-land beasts. So naturally, the only wizards in the Sea were whales, just as humans were originally the only ones on land. That early on, there were only ten whale-wizards, all Seniors. *Ni'hwinyii*, they were called, the Lords of the Humours—'

Nita was puzzled. 'It's the old word for emotions, sort of,' Kit said. 'Not like "funny" humour.'

'I know,' Nita said, annoyed. She hadn't.

S'reee blew, laughing. The spray missed Kit this time. 'Those ten whales ruled the Sea, under the Powers,' she said. 'If the Lone Power wanted to trick the Sea into the Great Death, It had to trick the Ten – then all the life they ruled would be stuck with the Great Death too. So the Lone One went to the Ten in disguise, pretending to be a stranger, a new whale sent to them so that they could decide under which of their Masteries it fell. And as each one questioned the Lone Power, the Stranger whale offered each of them the thing he wanted most, if he would only accept the "Gift" the Stranger would give him. And he showed them just enough of his power to prove that he could do it.'

'Uh-oh,' Kit said softly. 'I've heard that one before.'

'Apples and snakes,' Nita said.

'Yes. The pattern repeats. One after another, the Lone One tempted the Ten. The Sea was silent then and gave them no advice – some people say that the Powers wanted the Ten to make up their own minds. But however that might have been, three of the Ten took the Gift, and fell. Three of them were undecided. Three of them rejected the Gift. And the Lone Power needed a majority of the Lords to accept Death, or Its victory would only be partial.'

'Those were only nine Lords, though,' Kit said.

'Yes, and here the Tenth comes in: the Silent Lord, they called her. She was the youngest of them, and each of the other Nine tried to bring her around to his own way of thinking. The Lone One came to her too and tempted her as It had tempted the others. You know, though, that it's the youngest wizard who has the most power, and where the other Lords were deceived, the Silent Lord wasn't. She realized what the Stranger was and what It was trying to do.

'She was faced with a difficult choice. She knew that even if she rejected the Stranger, the fighting would only go on among the other Nine. Sooner or later they or their successors would accept the Gift and doom the whole Sea to the Great Death. But she also knew something else that the Sea had told her long before, and that others have found out since. If one knows death is coming – any death, from the small ones to the Great one – and is willing to accept it fully, and experience it fully, then the death becomes something else – a passage, not an ending: not only for himself, but for others.'

S'reee's voice got very soft. 'So the Silent Lord did that,' she said. 'Luck, or the Powers, brought one more creature into the singing, uninvited. It was the one fish over whom no mastery was ever given – the Pale Slayer, whom we call the Master-Shark. The Silent Lord decided to accept the "Gift" that the Stranger offered her – and then, to transform the Gift and make it "safe", she gave herself up willingly to die. She dived into a stand of razor coral; and the Master-Shark smelled her blood in the water, and . . . well.' S'reee blew. 'He accepted the sacrifice.'

Nita and Kit looked at each other.

'When that happened, the Lone Power went wild with rage,' S'reee said. 'But that did It no good. The Silent One's sacrifice turned death loose in some of the Sea, but not all; and even where it did turn up, death was much weaker than it would have been otherwise. To this day there are fish and whales that have astonishing lifespans, and some that never seem to die of natural causes. The sharks, for instance: some people say that's a result of the Master-Shark's acceptance of the Silent Lord's sacrifice. But the important thing is that the Lone Power had put a lot of Its strength into Its death-wizardry. It had become death Itself, in a way. And when death was weakened, so was the Lone One. It fell to the sea floor, and it opened for It and closed on It afterwards. And there It lies bound.'

'"Bound"?' Kit said. 'S'reee, when we had our last run-in with the Lone Power, It didn't seem very bound to *us*. It had a whole alternate universe of Its own, and when It came into this one to get us, It went around tearing things up any way It liked. If It *is* bound, how could It have also been running loose in Manhattan?'

S'reee blew, a sober sound. 'It's the usual confusion about time,' she said. 'All the great Powers exist outside it, and all we usually see of Them are the places and moments where and when They dip into the timeflow we're inhabiting. This world has always been an annoyance to the Lone One – It gets frustrated here a lot – so It visits often, in many forms. From inside our timeflow, it can look as if the Lone Power is bound in one place-time and free in another . . . and both appearances are true.' S'reee rolled and stretched in the water. 'Meanwhile, outside the timeflow, where things don't have to happen one after another, the Lone One is eternally rebelling and eternally defeated—'

'We gave It a chance to do something else, when we fought last,' Nita said. 'We offered It the option to stop being a dark power—'

'And it worked,' S'reee said, sounding very pleased. 'Didn't you know? It's also eternally redeemed. But meanwhile we have to keep fighting the battles, even though the war's decided. The Lone

46

One's going to take a long while to complete Its choice, and if we get lazy or sloppy about handling Its thrashing around, a lot of people are going to die.'

'The sea floor,' Nita said, 'has been shaken up a lot lately.'

'That's one symptom that tells us the TwelveSong needs to be re-enacted,' S'reee said. 'We do the Song at intervals anyway, to make sure the story's never forgotten. But when the Lone Power gets trouble-some – as It seems to be doing now – we re-enact the Song, and bind It quiet again.'

'Where do you do this stuff?' Kit said.

'Down the coast a bit,' S'reee said, 'off the edge of the Plateau, in the Great Deep past the Gates of the Sea. Ae'mhnuu was getting ready to call the Ten together for a Song in three days or so. He was training me for the Singer's part – before they blew him in two pieces and boiled him down for oil.'

Her song went bitter, acquiring a rasp that hurt Nita's ears. 'Now I'm stuck with handling it all myself. It's not easy: you have to pick each whale wizard carefully for each part. I don't know who he had in mind to do what. Now I have to work it out myself – and I need help, from wizards who can handle trouble if it comes up.' She looked up at them. 'You two can obviously manage that. And the Ten will listen to you, they'll respect you, after what you went through up in the High and Dry. You've fought the Lone Power yourselves and got off—'

'It was luck,' Kit muttered. Nita elbowed him.

'Singing, huh,' Nita said, smiling slightly. 'I don't have much of a singing voice. Maybe I'd better take the Silent One's part.'

S'reee looked at Nita in amazement. 'Would you?'

'Why not?'

'Not me,' Kit said. 'I'm even worse than she is.

But I'll come along for the ride. The swim, I mean.'

S'reee looked from Kit to Nita. 'You two are enough to make me doubt all the stories I've heard about humans,' she said. 'HNii't, best check that "book" thing and make sure this is something you're suited for. The temperaments of the singers have to match the parts they sing – but I think this might suit you. And the original Silent Lord was a humpback. The shapechange would come easily to you, since we've shared blood—'

'Wait a minute! *Shapechange?*' Nita cried. 'You mean me be a whale?'

Kit laughed. 'Why not, Neets? You *have* been putting on a little weight lately . . .'

She elbowed him again, harder. 'Oh, you'd shapechange too, K!t,' S'reee said. 'We couldn't take you down in the Great Deeps otherwise. —Look, you two, there's too much to tell, and some of it's going to have to be handled as we go along. We've got three days to get everyone together for the Song, so that it happens when the moon's round. Otherwise it won't keep the sea bottom quiet—'

Kit looked suddenly at Nita. 'Did you see that thing on the news the other night? About the volcano?'

'The *what?*'

'There was some scientist on. He said that hot-water vents had been opening up all of a sudden off the Continental Shelf. And he said that if those little tremors we've been having keep getting worse, it could open the bottom right up and there'd be a volcano. The least it'd do would be to boil the water for miles. But it could also break Long Island in two. The beaches would go right under water. And Manhattan skyscrapers aren't built for eathquakes.' Kit was quiet for a moment, then said, 'The rocks remembered. That's why they were upset . . .'

Nita wasn't thinking about rocks, or Manhattan. She was thinking that her parents were planning to be there for another week and a half at least – and she saw a very clear picture of a tidal wave of dirty, boiling water crashing down on the beach house and smashing it to driftwood.

'When should we start, S'reee?' she said.

'Dawn tomorrow. There's little time to waste. Hotshot will be going with us – he'll be singing the Fourth Lord, the Wanderer, in the Song.'

'Dawn—' Nita chewed her lip. 'Could it be a little later? We've got to have breakfast with my parents or they'll freak out.'

'*Parents?*' S'reee looked from Nita to Kit in shock. 'You're still calves, is that what you're telling me? And you went outworld into a Dark Place and came back! I'd thought you were much older—'

'We wished we were,' Nita said under her breath.

'Oh, well. No matter. Three hours after dawn be all right? The same place? Good enough. Let me take you back. I have something to fetch so that you can swim with us, K!t. And, look—' She gazed at them for some time from that small, worried, gentle eye; but longer at Nita. 'Thank you,' she said. 'Thank you very much indeed.'

'Think nothing of it,' Kit said grandly, slipping into the water and patting S'reee on one big ribbed flank.

Nita slid into the water, took hold of S'reee's dorsal fin, and thought something of it all the way home.

SENIORS' SONG

The alarm clock went off right above Nita's head, a painful blasting buzz like a dentist's drill. 'Aaagh,' she said, reluctantly putting one arm out from under the covers and fumbling around on the bedside table for the noisy thing.

It went quiet without her having touched it. Nita squinted up through the morning brightness and found herself looking at Dairine. Her little sister was standing by the bedside table with the alarm clock in her hands, wearing Star Wars pyjamas and an annoyed look.

'And where are we going at six in the morning?' Dairine said, too sweetly.

'*We* are not going anywhere,' Nita said, swinging herself out of bed with a groan. 'Go play with your Barbie dolls, Einstein.'

'Only if you give them back,' Dairine said, unperturbed. 'Anyway, there are better things to play with. Kit, for example—'

'Dairine, you're pushing it.' Nita stood up, rubbed her eyes until they started working properly, and then pulled a dresser drawer open and began pawing through it for a T-shirt.

'What're *you* doing, then – getting up so early all

the time, staying out late? You think Mum and Dad aren't noticing? —Oh, don't wear *that*,' Dairine said at the sight of Nita's favourite sweatshirt. It featured numerous holes made by Ponch's teeth and the words WATCH THIS SPACE FOR FURTHER DEVELOPMENTS. 'Oh, really, Neets, *don't*, it's incredibly tacky—'

'That sounds really weird,' Nita said, 'coming from someone with little Yodas all over her pyjamas.'

'Oh, stuff it, Nita,' Dairine said. Nita turned her head and smiled, thinking that Dairine had become easier to tease since she'd decided to be a Jedi Knight when she grew up. Still, Nita went easy on her sister. It wasn't fair for a wizard to make fun of someone who wanted to do magic, of whatever brand.

'Same to you, runt. When're Mum and Dad getting up, did they say?'

'They're up now.'

'What for?'

'They're going fishing. *We're* going with them.'

Nita blanched. 'Oh, no! Dair, I *can't*—'

Dairine cocked her head at Nita. 'They wanted to surprise us.'

'They did,' Nita said, in shock. 'I *can't* go—'

'Got a hot date, huh?'

'*Dairine!* I told you—'

'Where were you two going?'

'Swimming.' That was the truth.

'Neets, you can swim any time,' Dairine said, imitating their mother's tone of voice. Nita zipped up her jeans and sat down on the bed with a thump. 'What were you going to be *doing* anyway?'

'I told you, *swimming!*' Nita got up, went to the window, and looked out, thinking of S'reee and the summoning and the Song of the Twelve and the rest of the business of being on active status, which was now looking ridiculously complicated. And it looked so simple yesterday . . .

'You could tell them something—'

Nita made a face at that. She had recently come to dislike lying to her parents. For one thing, she valued their trust. For another, a wizard, whose business is making things happen by the power of the spoken word, learns early on not to say things out loud that aren't true or that he *doesn't* want to happen.

'Sure,' she said in bitter sarcasm. 'Why don't I just tell them that we're on a secret mission? Or that we're busy saving Long Island and the greater metropolitan area from a fate worse than death? Or maybe I could tell them that Kit and I have an appointment to go out and get turned into whales, how about *that?'*

Even without turning around, Nita could feel her sister staring at her back. Finally the quiet made Nita twitchy. She turned around, but Dairine was already heading out of the room. 'Go on and eat,' Dairine said quietly, over her shoulder. 'Sound happy.' And she was gone.

Under her breath, Nita said a word her father would have frowned at, and then sighed and headed for breakfast, plastering on to her face the most sincere smile she could manage. At first it felt hopelessly unnatural, but in a few seconds it was beginning to stick. At the dining-room door, where her father came around the corner from the kitchen and nearly ran her over, Nita took one look at him – in his faded lumberjack shirt and his hat stuck full of fish hooks – and wondered why she had ever been worried about getting out of the fishing trip. It was going to be all right.

Her dad looked surprised. 'Oh! You're up. Did Dairine—'

'She told me,' Nita said. 'Is there time to eat something?'

'Sure. I guess she told Kit too then – I just looked

in his room, but he wasn't there. The bed was made; I guess he's ready—'

Nita cheerfully allowed her father to draw his own conclusions, especially since they were the wrong ones. 'He's probably down at the beach killing time,' she said. 'I'll go and get him after I eat.'

She made a hurried commando raid on the kitchen and put the kettle on the cooker for her mother, who was browsing through the science section of *The New York Times* and was ready for another cup of tea. Nita's mother looked up at her from the paper and said, 'Neets, where's your sister? She hasn't had breakfast.'

That was when her sister came thumping into the dining room. Nita saw her mum look at Dairine and develop a peculiar expression. 'Dari,' her mother said, 'are you feeling all right?'

'Yeah!' said Dairine in an offended tone. Nita turned in her chair to look at her. Her sister looked flushed, and she wasn't moving at her normal breakneck speed. 'C'mere, baby,' Nita's mother said. 'Let me feel your forehead.'

'*Mum!*'

'Dairine,' her father said.

'Yeah, right.' Dairine went over to her mother and had her forehead felt, rolling her eyes at the ceiling. 'You're hot, sweetie,' Nita's mother said in alarm. 'Harry, I *told* you she was in the water too long yesterday. Feel her.'

Nita's dad looked slightly bored, but he checked Dairine's forehead and then frowned. 'Well . . .'

'No "wells". Dari, I think you'd better sit this one out.'

'Oh, *Mum!*'

'Cork it, little one. You can come fishing with us in a day or two.' Nita's mother turned to her. 'Neets, will you stay around and keep an eye on your sister?'

'Mum, I don't need a babysitter!'

'Enough, Dairine,' her mum said. 'Up to bed with you. Nita, we'll take you and Kit with us the next time; but your dad really wants to get out today.'

'It's OK, Mum,' Nita said, dropping what was left of the smile (though it now really wanted to stay on). 'I'll keep an eye on the runt.'

'Don't call me a runt!'

'Dairine,' her father said again. Nita's little sister made a face and left, again at half the usual speed.

As soon as she could, Nita slipped into Dairine's room. Her sister was lying on top of the bed, reading her way through a pile of X-Men comics; she looked flushed. 'Not bad, huh?' she said in a low voice as Nita came in.

'How did you *do* that?' Nita whispered.

'I used the Force,' Dairine said, flashing a wicked look at Nita.

'*Dari!* Spill it!'

'I turned Dad's electric blanket up high and spent a few minutes under it. Then I drank about a quart of hot water to make sure I stayed too warm.' Dairine turned a page in her comic book, looking blasé about the whole thing. 'Mum did the rest.'

Nita shook her head in admiration. 'Runt, I owe you one.'

Dairine looked up from her comic at Nita. 'Yeah,' Dairine said, 'you do.'

Nita felt a chill. 'Right,' she said. 'I'll hang out here until they leave. Then I have to find Kit—'

'He went down to the general shop just before you got up,' Dairine said. 'I think he was going to call somebody.'

'Right,' Nita said again.

There was the briefest pause. Then: 'Whales, huh?' Dairine said, very softly.

Nita got out of there in a great hurry.

The sign on top of the building merely said, in big, square, black letters, TIANA BEACH. '"Tiana Beach" *what?*' people typically said, and it was a fair question. From a distance there was no telling what the place was, except a one-storey structure with peeling white paint.

The building stood off the main road, at the end of a spur road that ran down to the water. On one side of it was its small parking lot, a black patch of heat-heaved asphalt always littered with pieces of clam-shells, which the gulls liked to drop and crack open there. On the other side was a dock for people who came shopping in their boats.

The dock was in superb repair. The shop was less so. Its large multipaned front windows, for example, were clean enough outside, but inside they were either covered by stacked-up boxes or with grime; nothing was visible through them except spastically flashing old neon signs that said 'Pabst Blue Ribbon' or 'Cerveza BUDWEISER'. Beachgrass and aggress-ive weeds grew next to (and in places, through) the building's cracked concrete steps. The rough little US Post Office sign above the front door had a sparrow's nest behind it.

Nita headed for the open door. It was always open, whether Mr Friedman the shopkeeper was there or not; 'On the off chance,' as Mr Friedman usually said, 'that someone might need something at three in the morning . . . or the afternoon . . .'

Nita walked into the dark, brown-smelling shop, past the haphazard shelves of canned goods and cereal and the racks of plastic earthworms and nylon surf-casting line. By the cereal and the crackers, she met the reason that Mr Friedman's store was safe day and night. The reason's name was Dog: a whitish, curlyish, terrierish mutt, with eyes like something out of Disney and teeth like something out of Transylvania. Dog could smell attempted theft for miles; and when not biting people in the line of business, he would do it on his own time, for no reason whatever – perhaps just to keep his fangs in.

'Hi, Dog,' Nita said, being careful not to get too close.

Dog showed Nita his teeth. 'Go chew dry bones,' he said in a growl.

'Same to you,' Nita said pleasantly, and made a wide detour around him, heading for the phone booth at the rear of the shop.

'Right,' Kit was saying, his voice slightly muffled by being in the booth. 'Something about "the Gates of the Sea". I tried looking in the manual, but all I could find was one of those "restricted" notices and a footnote that said to see the local Senior for more details—'

Kit looked up, saw Nita coming, and pointed at the phone, mouthing the words 'Tom and Carl'. She nodded and squeezed into the booth with him; Kit tipped the hearing part of the receiver towards her, and they put their heads together. 'Hi, it's Nita—'

'Well, hi there yourself,' Tom Swale's voice came back. He would doubtless have gone on with more of the same if someone else, farther away from his end of the line, hadn't begun screaming 'Hel-LOOOOOOO! HEL-lo!' in a creaky, high-pitched voice that sounded as if Tom were keeping his insane grandmother chained up in the living room. This, Nita knew, was Tom and Carl's intractable macaw Machu Picchu, or Peach for short. Wizards' pets tended to get a bit strange as their masters grew more adept in wizardry, but Peach was stranger than most, and more trying. Even a pair of Senior wizards must have wondered what to do with a creature that would at one moment deliver the evening news a day early, in a flawless imitation of any major newscaster you pleased, and then a second later start ripping up the couch for the fun of it.

'Cut that out!' Nita heard another voice saying in the background, one with a more New Yorkish sound to it: that was Carl. 'Look out!—She's on the cooker. Get her – oh, Lord. There go the eggs. *You little cannibal—*'

'It's business as usual around here, as you can tell,' Tom said. 'Not where *you* are, though, to judge from how early Kit called . . . and from what he tells me. Kit, hang on a minute: Carl's getting the information released for you. Evidently the Powers That Be don't want it distributed without a Senior's supervision. The area must be sensitive right now.'

Nita made small talk with Tom for a few minutes while, in the background, Peach screamed, and Annie and Monty the sheepdogs barked irritably at the macaw, who was shouting *'Bad dog! Bad dog! Nonono!'* at them – or possibly at Carl. Nita could imagine the scene very well – the bright airy house full of plants and animals, a very ordinary-looking place as far as the neighbours were concerned. Except that Tom spent his days doing research and development on complex spells and incantations for other wizards, and then used some of the things he discovered to make a living as a writer on the side. And Carl, who sold commercial time for a 'flagship' channel of one of the major television networks, might also make a deal to sell you a more unusual kind of time – say, a piece of last Thursday. The two of them were living proof that it was possible to live in the workaday world and function as wizards at the same time. Nita was very glad to know them.

'The link's busy,' she heard Carl saying, at some

distance from the phone. 'Oh, never mind, there it goes. Look,' he said, apparently to one of his own advanced-level manuals, 'we need an intervention authorization for an offshore area – yeah, that's right. Here's the numbers—'

Kit had his manual open to the spot where he'd found the notification. Nita looked over his shoulder and watched the box that said RESTRICTED INFOR-MATION suddenly blink out, replaced by the words SEE CHART PAGE 1096. 'Got it?' Tom said.

'Almost.' Kit turned pages. Nita looked over his shoulder and found herself looking at a map of the East Coast, from Nova Scotia to Virginia. But the coast itself was squeezed far over on the left-hand side, and individual cities and states were only sketchily indicated. The map was primarily con-cerned with the ocean.

'OK, I've got it in my book too,' Tom said. 'All those lines in the middle of the water are contour lines, indicating the depth of the sea bottom. You can see that there aren't many lines within about a hundred miles of Long Island. The bottom isn't much deeper than a hundred feet within that distance. But then – you see a lot of contour lines packed closely together? That's the edge of the Continental Shelf. Think of it as a cliff, or a mesa, with the North American continent sitting on top of it. Then there's a steep drop – the cliff is just a shade less than a mile high—'

'Or deep,' Nita said.

'Whichever. About a five thousand foot drop; not straight down – it slopes a bit – but straight enough. Then the sea bottom keeps on sloping eastward and downwards. It doesn't slope as fast as before, but it goes deep – some fifteen thousand feet down; and it gets deeper yet further out. See where it says "Sohm Abyssal Plain" to the south-east of the Island, about six or seven hundred miles out?'

'It has "the Crushing Dark" underneath that on our map,' Nita said. 'Is that the whales' name for it?'

'Right. That area is more like seventeen, eighteen thousand feet down.'

'I bet it's cold down there,' Kit muttered.

'Probably. Let me know when you get back,' Tom said, 'because that's where you're going.'

Nita and Kit looked at each other in shock. 'But I thought even submarines couldn't go down *that* far,' Nita said.

'They can't. Neither can most whales, normally – but it helps to be a wizard,' Tom said. 'Look, don't panic yet—'

'*Go ahead! Panic!*' screamed Picchu from somewhere in the background. 'Do it now and avoid the June rush! Fear death by water!'

'Bird,' Carl's voice said, also in the background, 'you're honing for a punch in the beak.'

'Violence! You want violence, I'll give you violence! No quarter asked or given! Damn the torpedoes, full speed ahead! Don't give up the AWWWK!'

'Thanks, Carl,' Tom said, as silence fell. 'Where were we? Oh, right. You won't just be going out there and diving straight down. There's a specific approach to the Plain. Look back closer to the Island, and you'll see some contours drawn in dotted lines—'

'Hudson Channel,' Nita said.

'Right. That's the old bed of the Hudson River – where it used to run a hundred thousand years ago, while all that part of the Continental Shelf was still above water. That old riverbed leads farther southeast, to the edge of the Shelf, and right over it . . . there was quite a waterfall there once. See the notch in the Shelf?'

59

'Yeah. "Hudson Canyon", it says—'

'The Gates of the Sea,' said Tom. 'That's the biggest undersea canyon on the East Coast, and probably the oldest. It cuts right down through the Shelf. Those walls are at least two or three thousand feet high, sometimes four. Some of the canyons on the Moon and Mars could match the Hudson – but none on Earth. And for the whale-wizards, the Gates have become the traditional approach to the Great Depths and the Crushing Dark.'

The thought of canyon walls stretching above her almost a mile high gave Nita chills. She'd seen a rock-slide once, and it had made her uneasy about canyons in general. 'Is it safe?' she said.

'Of course not,' Tom said, sounding cheerful. 'But the natural dangers are Carl's department; he'll fill you in on what precautions you'll need to take, and I suspect the whales will too.'

'"Natural dangers",' Kit said. 'Meaning there are unnatural ones too.'

'In wizardry, when aren't there? This much I can tell you, though. New York City has not been kind to that area. All kinds of things, even unexploded depth charges, have been dumped at the head of Hudson Canyon over the years. Most of them are marked on your map; but watch out for ones that aren't. And the city has been dumping raw sewage into the Hudson Channel area for decades. Evidently in the old days, before people were too concerned about ecology, they thought the water was so deep that the dumping wouldn't do any harm. But it has. Quite a bit of the sea-bottom life in that area, especially the vegetation that the fish depend on for food, has been killed off entirely. Other species have been . . . changed. The manual will give you details. You won't like them.'

Nita suspected that Tom was right. 'Anyway,' he

said, 'let me give you the rest of this. After you do the appropriate rituals, which the whales will coach you through, the access through the Gates of the Sea takes you down through Hudson Canyon to its bottom at the lower edge of the Shelf, and then deeper and further south-east – where the canyon turns into a valley that gets shallower and shallower as it goes. The valley ends just about where the Abyssal Plain begins, at seven hundred miles off the coast, and seventeen thousand feet down. Then you come to the mountain.'

It was on the map – a tiny set of concentric circles – but it had looked so peculiar, standing there all by itself in the middle of hundreds of miles of flatness, that Nita had doubted her judgement. 'The Sea's Tooth,' she said, reading from the map.

'Caryn Peak,' Tom agreed, giving the human name. 'Some of the oceanographers think it's simply the westernmost peak of an undersea mountain range called the Kelvin Seamounts – they're off the eastward edge of your map. Some think otherwise; the geological history of that area is bizarre. But either way, the Peak's an important spot. And impressive; that one peak is six thousand feet high. It stands up sheer from the bottom, all alone, a third as high as Everest.'

'Five Empire State Buildings on top of each other,' Kit said, awed. He liked tall things.

'A very noticeable object,' Tom said. 'It's functioned as the landmark and meeting place and site of the whales' great wizardries for not even they know how long. Certainly since the continents started drifting towards their present positions . . . at least a hundred thousand years ago. And it may have been used by . . . other sorts of wizards . . . even earlier than that. There's some interesting history in that area, tangled up with whale-wizards and human ones too.'

Tom's voice grew sober. 'Some of the wizards who specialize in history say that humans only learned wizardry with the whales' assistance . . . and even so, our brands of wizardry are different. It's an old, old branch of the Art they practise. Very beautiful. Very dangerous. And the area around Caryn Peak is saturated with residue from all the old wizardries that whales, and others, have done there. That makes any spell you work there even more dangerous.'

'S'reee said that the "danger" level wouldn't go above "moderate",' Kit said.

'She said it *shouldn't*,' Nita said.

'Probably it won't,' Tom said. He didn't sound convinced, though. 'You should bear in mind that the "danger" levels for humans and whales differ. Still, the book said she was about to be promoted to Advisory status, so she would know that— All the same . . . you two keep your eyes open. Watch what agreements you make. And if you make them – keep them, to the letter. From all indications, the Song of the Twelve is a lovely wizardry, and a powerful one . . . probably the most powerful magic done on a regular basis. The sources say it leaves its participants forever changed, for the better. At least, it does when it works. When it fails – which it has, once or twice in the past – it fails because some participant has broken the rules. And those times it's failed . . . Well, all I can say is that I'm glad I wasn't born yet. *Be careful.*'

'We will,' Nita said. 'But what are the chances of something going wrong?'

'We could ask Peach,' Kit said. It was a sensible suggestion; the bird, besides doing dramatic readings from *Variety* and *TV Guide*, could also predict the future – when it pleased her.

'Good idea. Carl?'

'Here I am,' Carl said, having picked up an

extension phone. 'Now, Kit, about the monsters—'

'Carl, put that on hold a moment. What does the Walter Cronkite of the bird world have to say about all this?'

'I'll find out.'

Monsters? Nita mouthed at Kit. 'Listen,' she said hurriedly to Tom, 'I'm going to get off now. I've got to be around the house when my parents leave, so they won't worry about my little sister.'

'Why? Is she ill?'

'No. But that's the problem. Tom, I don't know what to do about Dairine. I thought nonwizards weren't supposed to *notice* magic most of the time. I'm not sure it's working that way with Dairine. I think she's getting suspicious . . .'

'We'll talk. Meanwhile, Carl – what does the bird say?'

'Oh, it is, it is a splendid thing/To be a pirate kiiiiiiiiiiiiiig!' Picchu was singing from somewhere in Tom's living room.

'Picchu—'

'What'sa matter? Don't you like Gilbert and Sullivan?'

'I told you we should never have let her watch *Pirates* on cable TV,' Tom remarked to his partner.

'Twice your peanut ration for the week,' Carl said.

'. . . and I did the deed that all men shun, I shot the Albatross . . .'

'You're misquoting. How about *no* peanuts for the rest of the week—'

'Pieces of eight! Pieces of eight!'

'How about no *food?*'

'Uh—' There was a pause. It didn't take Nita much imagination to picture the look that Carl was giving Picchu. She was glad no-one had ever looked at *her* that way.

'Give.'

63

'Well.' The bird paused again, a long pause, and when she spoke her voice sounded more sober than Nita could remember ever hearing it. *'Do what the night tells you. Don't be afraid to give yourself away. And read the small print before you sign!'*

Kit glanced at Nita with a quizzical expression; she shrugged. At the other end of the line, sounding exceptionally annoyed, Carl said to Picchu, 'You call *that* advice? We asked you for the odds!'

'Never ask me the odds,' Picchu said promptly. 'I don't want to know. And neither do *you* really.' And that end of the conversation swiftly degenerated into more loud squawking, and the excited barking of dogs, and Carl making suggestions to Picchu that were at best rather rude.

'Thanks,' Nita said to Tom. 'I'll talk to you later.' She squeezed out of the phone booth and past Dog, who growled at her as she went. Behind her, Kit said, in entirely too cheerful a tone of voice, 'So, Carl, what about the monsters?'

Nita shook her head and went home.

THE BLUE'S SONG

'Giant man-eating clams,' she said to Kit later, as they walked down an isolated stretch of Tiana Beach towards the surf. 'Giant squid—'

'Krakens,' Kit said.

'I don't care what you call them, they're still giant squid. And squid belong in sushi. I don't like this.'

'With luck, we won't see any of them, Carl says.'

'When have we ever had that kind of luck . . ?'

'Besides, Neets, even *you* can outrun a clam . . .'

'Cute,' she said. They splashed into the water together, glancing up and down the beach as they did so. No-one was in sight; and they had left Ponch up in the dunes, looking for a good place to bury the remains of his latest water rat. 'Look,' Nita said, pointing.

Several hundred yards out, there was a glitter of spray, and sunlight glanced off the curved, up-leaping body of a dolphin as if from an unsheathed, upheld sword. Wild, merry chattering, a dolphin's laughter, came to them over the water, as the leaping shape came down with a splash and another shock of spray.

'Hotshot,' Kit said. 'Let's go.'

They struck out through the breakers, into water

that was again surprisingly warm. This time Nita wasn't able to enjoy it quite as much; the thought of undersea volcanoes was much with her. But even she couldn't be depressed for long when they paused to rest a moment, dog-paddling, and from behind came the nudge in the back she remembered, followed by a delphine laugh. 'You rotten thing,' she said, turning to rub Hotshot affectionately. 'I'm going to get you for the first time you did that.'

'You'll have to catch me first,' Hotshot said with a wicked chuckle – as well he might have, for nothing in the Sea except perhaps a killer whale or one of the great sharks on the hunt was fast enough to catch a dolphin that didn't want to be caught.

'Where's S'reee?' Kit said.

'Out in deeper water, by the Made Rock. HNii't's change could be done right here, but the kind of whale you're going to be would ground at this depth, K!t. Take hold; I'll tow you.'

The fishing platform was once more covered with seagulls, which rose in a screaming cloud at the sight of Kit and Nita and Hotshot. 'I'll meet you later, out at sea,' Hotshot said, leaving them beside a rusty metal ladder that reached down into the water.

Kit and Nita climbed up it and walked across the platform to where they could look down at S'reee, who was rolling in the wavewash.

'You're early,' she whistled, putting her head up out of the water at them, 'and it's just as well; I'm running a bit late. I went a-Summoning last night, but I didn't find most of the people – so we'll have to make a stop out by the Westernmost Shoals today. Sandy Hook, you call it.'

'New Jersey?' Nita said, surprised. 'How are we going to get all the way out there and back before—'

'It's going to be all right, hNii't,' S'reee said. 'Time doesn't run the same under the waters as it

66

does above them, so the Sea tells me. Besides, a humpback swims fast. And as for K!t – well, one change at a time. It'll come more easily for you, hNii't; you'd best go first.'

Wonderful, Nita thought. She had long been used to being picked last for things; having to go first for anything gave her the jitters. 'What do I have to do?' she said.

'Did you have a look at your book last night?'

'Uh-huh. I understand most of what we're going to be doing; it's fairly straightforward. But there was some business I didn't understand very well—'

'The part about shapechanging.'

'Yeah. There wasn't that much in the book, S'reee. I think it might have been missing some information.'

'Why? What did it tell you?'

'Only a lot of stuff about the power of imagination.' She was perplexed. 'S'reee, aren't there supposed to be words or something? A specific spell, or materials we need?'

'For shapechange? You have everything you need. Words would only get in the way,' said S'reee. 'It's all in the being. You pretend hard enough, and sooner or later what you're pretending to be, you *are*. The same as with other things.'

'Oh, come on, S'reee,' Kit said. 'If somebody who wasn't a wizard jumped into the water and pretended to be a whale, I don't care how hard they pretended, nothing would happen without wizardry—'

'Exactly right, K!t. *Wizardry* – not one particular spell. The only reason it works for you is that you *know* wizardry works and are willing to have it so. Belief is no good either; belief as such always has doubt at the bottom. It's knowing that makes wizardry work. Only knowing can banish doubt, and while doubt remains, no spell, however powerful,

67

will function properly. "Wizardry does not live in the unwilling heart", the Sea says. There'd be lots more wizards if more people were able to give up doubt – and belief. Like any other habit, though, they're hard to break . . .'

'It did take me a while to know for sure that it wasn't just a coincidence when the thing I'd done a spell for actually *happened* as soon as I'd done the spell,' Kit admitted. 'I suppose I see the problem.'

'Then you're ready for the solution,' S'reee said. 'Past the change itself, the chief skill of unassisted shapechanging lies in not pretending so hard that you can't get back again. And as I said, hNii't, you have an advantage; we've shared blood. You have humpback in you now – not that our species are so far apart anyway; we're all mammals together. I suppose the first thing you'd better do is get in the water . . .'

Nita jumped in, bobbed to the surface again. 'And that stuff around you is going to have to go,' S'reee added, looking with mild perplexity at Nita's swimsuit. Nita shot a quick look over her shoulder. For a moment, Kit just gazed innocently down at her, refusing to look away – then he turned, rolling his eyes.

Nita skinned hurriedly out of the suit and called to Kit, 'While you're up there, put a warding spell on the platform. I don't want the gulls doing you-know-what all over my suit while we're gone. Or yours.' She flung the wet lump of bathing suit out of the water over-handed; it landed with a sodden *thwack!* at which Kit almost turned around again. 'Can we get on with this?' Nita said to S'reee.

'Surely. HNii't, are you all right?' S'reee said.

'Yes, fine, let's do it!' Nita said.

'So begin!' said S'reee, and began singing to herself as she waited.

Nita paddled for a moment in the water, adjusting

to not having her swimsuit on. Saying 'Begin to *what?*' especially with Kit listening, seemed incredibly stupid, so she just hung there in the water for a few moments and considered being a whale. I don't have the faintest idea what this is supposed to feel like, she thought desperately. But I should be able to come up with something. I *am* a wizard, after all.

Nita got an idea. She took a deep breath, held it, and slowly began to relax into the sound. Her arms, as she let them go limp, no longer supported her; she sank, eyes open, into salty greenness. It's all right, she thought. The air's right above me if I need it. She hung weightless in the green, thinking of nothing in particular.

Down there in the water, S'reee's note seemed louder, fuller; it vibrated against the ears, against the skin, inside the lungs, filling everything. And there was something familiar about it. *Cousin,* S'reee had called her; and *We have blood in common*, she had said. So it should be easy. A matter of remembering, not what you have been . . . but what, somewhere else, you *are*. Simply allow what is, somewhere else, to be what is *here* – and the change is done, effortless. Nita shut her eyes on the greenness and trusted to the wizardry inside her. That was it. *Wizardry does not live in the unwilling heart*. Not the kind of will that meant gritted teeth, resisting something else, like your own disbelief, that was trying to undermine you – not 'willpower' – but the will that was desire, the will so strong that it couldn't be resisted by all the powers of normality . . .

Where am I getting all this? Nita didn't know, didn't care. To be a whale, she thought. To float like this all the time, to be weightless, like an astronaut. But space is green, and wet, and warm, and there are voices in it, and things growing. Freedom: no walls, no doors. And the songs in the water . . . Her arms were feeling heavy, her legs felt odd when she kicked; but none of it mattered. Something was utterly right, something was working. Nita began to feel short of air. It hadn't worked all the way, that was all. She would get it right the next time. She stroked for the surface, broke it, opened her eyes to the light—

—and found it different. First and oddest – so that Nita tried to shake her head in disbelief, and failed, since she suddenly had no neck – the world was split in two, as if with an axe. Trying to look straight ahead of her didn't work. The area in front of her had become a hazy uncertainty comprised of two sets of peripheral vision. And where the corners of her eyes should have been, she now had two perfectly clear sets of sideways vision that nonetheless felt like 'forward'. She was seeing in colours she had no names for, and many she had names for were gone. Hands she still seemed to have, but her fingers hung down oddly long and heavy, her elbows were glued to her sides, and her sides themselves went on for what seemed years. Her legs were gone; a tail and graceful flukes were all she had left. Her nose seemed to be on the top of her head, and her mouth somewhere south of her chin; and she resolved to ask S'reee, well out of Kit's hearing, what had happened to some other parts of her. 'S'reee,' Nita said, and was amazed to hear it come out of the middle of her head, in a whistle instead of words, 'it was easy!'

'Come on, hNii't,' S'reee said. 'You're well along in wizardry at this point; you should know by now that it's not the magic that's exciting – it's what you do with it afterwards.'

More amazement yet. Nita wanted to simply roll over and lie back in the water at the sheer richness of the sound of S'reee's words. She had done the usual experiments in school that proved water was a more efficient conductor of sound than air. But she hadn't dreamed of what that effect would be like when one was a whale, submerged in the conducting medium and wearing a hundred square feet of skin that was a more effective hearing organ than any human ear. Suddenly sound was a thing that stroked the body, sensuous as a touch, indistinguishable from the liquid one swam in.

More, Nita could hear echoes coming back from what she and S'reee had said to each other; and the returning sound told her, with astonishing precision, the size and position of everything in the area – rocks on the bottom, weed three hundred metres away, schools of fish. She didn't need to see them. She could feel their textures on her skin as if they touched her; yet she could also distinctly perceive their distance from her, more accurately than she could have told it with mere sight. Fascinated she swam a couple of circles around the platform, making random noises and getting the feel of the terrain.

'I don't believe it,' someone said above Nita, in a curious, flat voice with no echoes about it. Is that how we sound? Nita thought, and surfaced to look at Kit out of first one eye, then the other. He looked no different from the way he usually did, but something about him struck Nita as utterly hilarious, though at first she couldn't figure out what it was. Then it occurred to her. He had legs.

'You're next, K!t,' S'reee said. 'Get in the water.'

Nita held her head out of water and stared at Kit for a moment. He didn't say anything, and after a few seconds of watching him get so red she could see it through his sunburn, Nita submerged, laughing like anything – a sound exactly like oatmeal boiling hard.

Nita felt the splash of his jump all over her. Then Kit was paddling in the water beside her, looking at her curiously. 'You've got barnacles,' he said.

'That's as may be, K!t,' S'reee said, laughing herself. 'Look at what I brought for you.'

Kit put his head under the water for a moment to see what she was talking about. For the first time, Nita noticed that S'reee was holding something delicately in her mouth, at the very tip-end of her jaw. If spiders lived in the sea, what S'reee held might have been a fragment torn from one of their webs. It was a filmy, delicate, irregular meshwork, its strands knotted into a net some six feet square. The knotting was an illusion, as Nita found when she glided closer to it. Each 'knot' was a round swelling or bulb where several threads joined. Flashes of green-white light rippled along the net whenever it moved, and all Nita's senses, those of whale and wizard alike, prickled with the electric feeling of a live spell, tangled in the mesh and impatient to be used.

'You must be careful with this, K!t,' S'reee said. 'This is a whalesark, and a rare thing. A sark can only be made when a whale dies, and the magic involved is considerable.

'What is it?' Kit said, when he'd surfaced again.

'It's a sort of shadow of a whale's nervous system, made by wizardry. At the whale's death, before the life-lightning's gone, a spell-constructed energy duplicate of the whale's brain and nerves is made from the pattern laid down by the living nerves and brain. The duplicate then has an "assisted shape-change" spell woven into it. When the work's done properly, contact with the sark is enough to change the wearer into whatever kind of whale the donor was.'

S'reee tossed her head. Shimmering, the sark billowed fully open, like a curtain in the wind. 'This is a sperm-whalesark, like Aivaaan who donated it.

He was a wizard who worked these waters several thousand full moons ago, and something of a seer; so that when he died, instead of leaving himself wholly to the Sea, Aivaaan said that we should make a sark of him, because there would be some need. Come and try it on for size, K!t.'

Kit didn't move for a moment. 'S'reee – is what's his name, Aivaaan, in there? Am I going to be him, is that it?'

S'reee looked surprised. 'No, how did you get that idea?'

'You said this was made from his brain,' Nita said.

'Oh. His *under*-brain, yes – the part of the brain that runs breathing and blood flow and such. As for the rest of Aivaaan, his *mind* – I don't think so. Not that I'm any too sure where "mind" is in a person. But you should still be K!t, by what the Sea tells me. Come on, time's swimming.'

'What do I do with it?'

'Just put it around you and wrap it tight. Don't be afraid to handle it roughly. It's stronger than it looks.' She let go of the sark. It floated in the water, undulating gently in the current. Kit took another breath, submerged, reached down, and drew the sark around him.

'Get back, hNii't,' S'reee said. Nita backfinned several times her own length away from Kit, not wanting to take her eyes off him. He was exhaling, slowly sinking feet-first, and with true Rodriguez insouciance he swirled the sark around him like Zorro putting on a new cape. Kit's face grew surprised, though, as the 'cape' continued the motion, swirling itself tighter and tighter around him, binding his arms to his sides.

Alarmed, Kit struggled, still sinking, bubbles rising from him as he went down. The struggling did him no good, and it suddenly became hard to see him as the wizardry in the whalesark came fully alive, and light danced around Kit and the sark. Nita had a last glimpse of Kit's eyes going wide in panic as he and the whalesark became nothing more than a sinking, swirling storm of glitter.

'S'reee!' Nita said, getting alarmed.

With a sound like muffled thunder and a blow like a nearby lightning-strike, displaced water hit Nita and bowled her sideways and backward. She fluked madly, trying to regain her balance enough to tell what was going on. The water was full of stirred-up sand, tatters of weed, small confused fish darting in every direction. And a bulk, a massive form that had not been there before—

Nita watched the great grey shape rise towards her and understood why S'reee had insisted on Kit's change being in deep water. Her own size had surprised her at first – though a humpback looks small and trim, even the littlest males tend to be fifty feet long. But Kit was twice that, easily. He did not have the torpedolike grace of a humpback, but what he lacked in streamlining he made up in sheer mass. The sperm is the kind that most people think of when they hear the word whale, the kind made famous by most whaling movies. Nita realized that all her life she had mostly taken the whale's shape for granted, not considering what it would actually be like up close to one.

But here came Kit, stroking slowly and uncertainly at first with that immense tail, and getting surer by the second; looking up at her with the tiny eyes set in the huge domed head, and with his jaw working a bit, exposing the terrible teeth that could crunch a whaling boat in two. Nita felt the size of him, the weight, and somehow the danger – and kept her movements slow and respectful. He was still Kit – but something had been added.

He glanced at S'reee and Nita, saying nothing, as he rose past them and broke surface to breathe. They followed. He spouted once or twice, apparently to get the feel of it, and then said to S'reee in a rather rueful tone of song, 'I wish you'd warned me!'

His voice ranged into a deeper register than a humpback's and had a sharper sound to it – more clicks and buzzes. It was not entirely comfortable on the skin. 'I couldn't,' S'reee said, 'or you might have fought it even harder than you did, and the change might have refused to take. That would've been trouble for us; if a whalesark once rejects a person, it'll never work for him at all. After this it'll be easier for you. Which in itself will make some problems. Right now, though, let's get going. Take a long breath; I want to get out of the bay without attracting too much attention.'

They took breath together and dived deep, S'reee in the lead and swimming south by west, Nita and Kit following. The surroundings – thick, lazily waving kelp beds and colonies of bright polyps and anemones, stitched through with the brief silver flash of passing fish – fascinated Nita. But she couldn't give the landscape, or seascape, her whole attention; she had other concerns. *Kit*, she tried to say in the Speech's silent form, for privacy's sake – then found that it wasn't working; she wasn't getting the sort of mental 'echo' that told her she was sending successfully. Probably it had something to do with the shapechange spell. 'Hey,' she said aloud, 'you OK?'

The question came out of her as such a long, mournful moan that Kit laughed – a sound more like boiling lava than boiling oatmeal: huge hisses and bubblings mixed together. 'Now I am,' he said, 'or I will be as soon as I can get used to this bit with the eyes—'

'Yeah, it's weird. But kind of nice too. Feeling things, instead of seeing them . . .'

'Yeah. Even the voices have feelings. S'reee is kind of twitchy—'

'Yeah. You've got sharp edges—'

'You've got fur.'

'I do not!'

'Oh, yes you do. It's soft, your voice. Not like your usual one—'

Nita was unsure whether to take this as a compliment, so she let it lie. The moment had abruptly turned into one of those times when she had no idea just what to say to Kit, the sort of sudden silence that was acutely painful to Nita, though Kit never seemed to notice it at all. Nita couldn't think of anything to do about the problem, which was the worst part of the whole business. She wasn't about to mention the problem to her mum, and on this subject the wizards' manual was hugely unhelpful.

The silence was well along toward becoming interminable when S'reee said, 'That's the primary way we have for knowing one another, down here. We haven't the sort of physical variations you have – differences in head shape and so forth – and even if we did, what good would a distinction be if you had to come right up to someone to make it? By voice, we can tell how far away a friend is, how he's feeling, practically what he's thinking. Though the closer a friend is to you, usually, the harder it is to tell what's on his mind with any accuracy.'

Nita started to sing something, then caught herself back to silence. 'Is the change settling in, K!t?' S'reee said.

'Now it is. I had a weird feeling, though, like something besides me, my mind I mean – like something besides that was fighting the change. But it's gone now.'

'Only for the moment,' S'reee said. 'See, it's the old rule: no wizardry without its price, or its dangers.

76

Though the dangers are different for each of you, since you changed by different methods. As I said, hNii't, you have to beware pretending too hard – thinking so much like a whale that you don't want to be a human being any more, or forget how. Wizards have been lost that way before, and there's no breaking the spell from outside; once you're stuck inside the change-shape, no-one but you can break out again. If you start finding your own memories difficult to recall, it's time to get out of the whaleshape, before it becomes you permanently.'

'Right,' Nita said. She wasn't very worried. Being a humpback was delightful, but she had no desire to spend her life that way.

'Your problem's different, though, K!t. Your change is powered more by the spell resident in the whalesark than by anything you're doing yourself. And all the sark's done is confuse your own body into thinking it's a whale's body, for the time being. That confusion can be broken by several different kinds of distraction. The commonest is when your own mind – which is stronger than the whale-mind left in the sark – starts to override the instructions the whale-sark is giving your body.'

'Huh?'

'K!t,' S'reee said very gently, finning upward to avoid the weedy, barnacled wreck of a fishing boat, 'suppose we were – oh, say several hundred hump-back-lengths down, in the Crushing Dark – and suddenly your whale-body started trying to behave like a human's body. Human breathing rate, human pulse and thought and movement patterns, human response to pressures and the temperature of the water—'

'Uh,' Kit said, as the picture sank in.

'So you see the problem. Spend too much time in the sark, and the part of your brain responsible for handling your breathing and so forth will begin to overpower the "dead" brain preserved in the sark. Your warning signs are nearly the opposite of hNii't's. Language is the first thing to go. If you find yourself losing whalesong, you *must* surface and get out of the sark immediately. Ignore the warning—? The best that can happen is that the whalesark will probably be so damaged it can never be used again. The worst thing—' She didn't say it. The worry in her voice was warning enough.

No-one said much of anything for a while, as the three of them swam onward, south and west. The silence, uneasy at first, became less so as they went along. S'reee, to whom this area was as commonplace as Kit's or Nita's home streets might have been, simply cruised along without any great interest in the surroundings. But Nita found the seascape endlessly fascinating, and suspected Kit did too – he was looking around him with the kind of fascination he rarely lent anything but old cars and his z-gauge train set.

Nita had rarely thought of what the seascape off the coast of the island would look like. From being at the beach she had a rather dull and sketchy picture of bare sand with a lot of water on top of it; shells buried in it, as they were on the beach, and there had to be weed beds; the seaweed washed up from somewhere. But all the nature films had given her no idea of the richness of the place.

Coral, for example; it didn't come in the bright colours it did in tropical waters, but it was there in great quantity – huge groves and forests of it, the white or beige or yellow branches twisting and writhing together in tight-choked abstract patterns. And shells, yes – but the shells still had creatures inside them; Nita saw Kit start in amazement, then swim down for a closer look at a scallop shell that was hopping over the surface of a brain coral, going about its business.

They passed great patches of weed, kinds that Nita didn't know the names of – until they started coming to her as if she had always known them: redbladder, kelp, agar, their long dark leaves or flat ribbons rippling as silkily in the offshore current as wheat in a landborn wind.

And the fish! Nita hadn't taken much notice of them at first; they'd all looked alike to her – little and silver. But something had changed. They passed by a place where piles had been driven into the sea floor, close together, and great odd-shaped lumps of rusty metal had been dumped among them. Weed and coral had seized on the spot, wrapping the metal and the piles; and the little life that frequented such places, tiny shrimp and krill, swam everywhere. So did thousands of iridescent, silvery-indigo fish, ranging from fingerling size to about a foot long, eating the krill and fry as if there were no tomorrow. For some of the smallest of them there wasn't *going* to be one, Nita realized, as she also realized how hungry she was.

'Blues!' she said, one sharp happy note, then dived into the cloud of bluefish and krill, and helped herself to lunch.

It was a little while before she'd had enough. It took Nita only a couple of minutes to get used to the way a humpback ate – by straining krill and others of the tiniest ocean creatures, including the smallest of the blues, through the sievelike plates of whalebone, or 'baleen', in her jaws. The swift blue shapes that had been darting frantically in all directions were calming down already as Nita soared out of the whirling cloud of them and headed back over to S'reee and Kit, feeling slightly abashed and that an explanation of some kind was in order for the sudden

79

interruption of their trip. However, there turned out to be no need for one. S'reee had stopped for a snack herself; and Nita realized that Kit had been snacking on fish ever since they left Tiana Beach. A sperm whale was, after all, one of the biggest of the 'toothed' whales, and needed a lot of food to keep that great bulk working. Not that he did anything but swallow the fish whole when he caught them; a sperm's terrible teeth are mostly for defence.

Kit paused only long enough to eat nine or ten of the biggest blues, then drifted down toward the pilings and the objects stacked sloppily among them. 'Neets,' he said, 'will you take a look at this? It's *cars*!'

She glided down beside him. Sure enough, the corroded fins of an old-model Cadillac were jutting out of a great mound of coral. Under the tangled whiteness of the coral, as if under a blanket of snow, she could make out the buried shapes of bonnets or doors, or the wheels and axles of wrecks wedged on their sides and choked with weed. Fish, blues and others, darted in and out of broken car windows and crumpled bonnets, while in several places crabs crouched in the shells of broken headlights.

'It's a fish haven,' S'reee said as she glided down beside them. 'The land people dump scrap metal on the bottom, and the plants and coral come and make a reef out of it. The fish come to eat the littler fish and krill that live in reefs; and then the boats come and catch the fish. And it works just as well for us as for the fishers who live on land. But we've got other business than dinner to attend to, at the moment. And hNii't, don't you think it would be a good idea if you surfaced now?'

Nita and Kit looked at one another in shock, then started upwards in a hurry, with S'reee following them at a more leisurely pace. 'How long have we been down?' Kit whistled.

They surfaced in a rush, all three, and blew. S'reee looked at Kit in some puzzlement; the question apparently meant nothing to her. 'Long enough to need to come up again,' she said.

'Neets, look,' Kit said in a rumbly groan, a sperm whale's sound of surprise. She fluked hard once or twice, using her tail to lift herself out of the swell, and was surprised to see, standing up from the shore half a mile away, a tall brick tower with a pointed, weathered green-bronze top; a red light flashed at the tower's peak. 'Jones Beach already!' she said. 'That's miles and miles from Tiana—'

'We've made good time,' S'reee said, 'but we've quite a way to go yet. Let's put our tails into it. I don't want to keep the Blue waiting.'

They swam on. Even if the sight of the Jones Beach tower hadn't convinced Nita they were getting close to New York, she now found that the increasing noise of the environment would have tipped off the whale that she'd become. Back at Tiana Beach, there had been only the single mournful hoot of the Shinnecock horn and the far-off sound of the various buoy bells. But this close to New York Harbour, the peaceful background hiss of the ocean soon turned into an incredible racket. Bells and horns and whistles and gongs shrieked and clunked and whanged in the water as they passed them; and no sooner was she out of range of one than another one assaulted her twitching skin.

Singing pained notes at one another, the three ran the gauntlet of sound. It got worse instead of better as they got closer to the harbour entrance, and to the banging and clanging was added the sound of persistent dull engine noise. Their course to Sandy Hook unfortunately crossed all three of the major approaches to New York Harbour. Along all three of them big boats came and went with an endless low throbbing, and small ones passed with a rattling, jarring buzz that reminded Nita of lawnmowers and chainsaws.

The three surfaced often to get relief from the sound, until S'reee warned them to dive deep for a long underwater run through one of the shipping lanes. Nita was beginning to feel the slow discomfort that was a whale's experience of shortness of breath before S'reee headed for the surface again.

They broached and blew and looked around them. Not far away stood a huge, black, white-lettered structure on four steel pilings. A white building stood atop the deck, and beside it was a red tower with several flashing lights. A horn on the platform sang one noncommittal note, shortLONG! short-LONG! again and again.

'Ambrose Light,' Kit said.

'The Speaking Tower, yes,' S'reee said. 'After this it'll be quieter – there are fewer markers between here and the Hook. And listen! There's a friend's voice.'

Nita went down again to listen, and finally managed to sort out a dolphin's distant chattering from the background racket. She surfaced again and floated with the others awhile, watching Hotshot come, glittering in the sun like a bright lance hurling itself through the swells. As he came abreast of the Lightship he leaped high out of the water in a spectacular arc and hit the surface with a noise that pierced even all the hooting and dinging going on.

'For Sea's sake, we hear you!' S'reee sang at the top of her lungs, and then added in annoyed affection, 'He's such a showoff.'

'But most dolphins are,' Kit said, with a note to his song that made it plain he wasn't sure how he knew that.

'True enough. He's worse than some, though. No question that he's one of the best of the young wizards, and a talented singer. I love him dearly. But what this business of being Wanderer is going to do to his precious ego—' She broke off as Hotshot came within hearing range. 'Did you find him?'

'He's feeding off the Hook,' Hotshot said, arrowing through the water toward them and executing a couple of playful and utterly unnecessary barrel rolls as he came. Nita began to wonder if S'reee might be right about him. 'He's worried about something, though he wouldn't tell me what it was. Said it was just as well you were coming; he would've come looking for you if you hadn't.'

The four of them started swimming again immediately; that last sentence was by itself most startling news. Blue whales did not *do* things, Nita realized, in the sudden-memory way that meant the information was the Sea's gift. Blue whales *were*, that was all. Action was for other, swifter species . . . except in the Song of the Twelve, where the Blue briefly became a power to be reckoned with. The Song, as Tom had warned, had a way of changing the ones who sang it . . . sometimes even before they started.

'Are you ready for the Oath?' S'reee was saying to the dolphin. 'Any last thoughts?'

'Only that this is going to be one more Song like any other,' Hotshot said, 'even if it *is* your first time. Don't worry, Ree; if you have any problems, I'll help you out.'

Nita privately thought that this was a little on the braggy side, coming from a junior wizard. The thought of talking to an Advisory or Senior that way – Tom, say – shocked her. Nevertheless, she kept her mouth shut, for it seemed like Hotshot and S'reee had known one another for a while.

'And how are our fry doing here?' Hotshot said,

swimming careless rings around Nita as he sang. 'Getting used to the fins all right?'

'Pretty much,' Nita said. Hotshot did one last loop around her and then headed off in Kit's direction. 'How about you, Minnow – *eeeech!*'

The huge jaw of a sperm whale abruptly opened right in front of Hotshot and closed before he could react – so that a moment later the dolphin was keeping quite still, while Kit held him with great delicacy in his huge fangs. Kit's eyes looked angry, but the tone of his song was casual enough. 'Hotshot,' he said, not stopping, just swimming along with casual deliberateness, 'I'm probably singing too. And even if I'm not, I *am* a sperm whale. Don't push your luck.'

Hotshot said nothing. Kit swam a few more of his own lengths, then opened his mouth and let the dolphin loose. 'Hey,' he said then, 'no hard feelings.'

'Of course not,' Hotshot said in his usual recklessly merry voice. But Nita noticed that the dolphin made his reply from a safe distance. 'No problem, Mi—' Kit looked at Hotshot, silent '—ah, K!t.'

'Minnow it is,' Kit said, sounding casual himself. The four of them swam on; Nita dropped back a few lengths and put her head up beside Kit's so that she could sing her quietest and not be heard too far off.

'What was that all about?'

'I'm not sure,' Kit said – and now that only Nita was listening, he sounded a bit shaken. 'S'reee might have been right when she said this body doesn't actually have what's-his-voice's—'

'Aivaaan.'

'His memories, yeah. But the body has its own memories. What it's like to be a sperm. What it *means* to be a sperm, I guess. You don't make fun of us – of them.' He paused, looking even more shaken. 'Neets – don't let me get lost!'

84

'Huh?'

'*Me.* I don't beat people up, that's not my style!'

'You didn't beat him up—'

'No. I just did the ocean equivalent of pinning him up against the wall and scaring him a good one. Neets, I got into being a wizard because I wanted other people *not* to do that kind of stuff to *me*! And now—'

'I'll keep an eye on you,' Nita said, as they began to come up on another foghorn, a loud one. And there was something odd about that foghorn. Its note was incredibly deep. *That has to be almost too deep for people to hear at all. What kind of—*

The note sounded again, and Nita shot Kit an amazed look as she felt the water all around her, and even the air in her lungs, vibrate in response to it. One note, the lowest note she could possibly imagine, held and held until a merely human singer would have collapsed trying to sing it . . . and then slurred slowly down through another note, and another, and holding on a last one of such profound depth that the water shook as if with thunder.

S'reee slowed her pace and answered the note in kind, the courtesy of one species of whale to another on meeting or parting – singing the same slow, sombre sequence, several octaves higher. There was a pause; then she was answered with a humpback's graceful fluting, but sung in a bottom-shaking baritone.

'Come on,' S'reee said, and dived.

The waters around Sandy Hook boil with krill in the spring and summer, so that by night the krill's swarming luminescence defines every current and finstroke in a blaze of blue-green light; and by day the sun slants through the water, brown with millions of tiny bodies, as thickly as through the air in a dusty room. As the group dived, they began to make out a great dark shape in the cloudy water, moving so slowly it barely did more than drift. A last brown-red curtain of water parted before them in a swirl of current, and Nita found herself staring down at her first blue whale.

He was hardly even blue in this light, more a sort of slaty maroon; and the faint dapples on his sides were almost invisible. But his colour was not what impressed Nita particularly. Neither was his size, though blues are the biggest of all whales; this one was perhaps a hundred and twenty feet from nose to tail, and Kit, large for a sperm, was almost as big. That voice, that stately, leisurely, sober, sorrowful voice that sounded like a storm in mourning, *that* mattered to her; and so did the tiny eye, the size of a tennis ball, which looked at her from the immense bulk of the head. That eye was wise. There was understanding in it, and tolerance, and sadness: and most of all, great age.

Age was evident elsewhere too. The blue's flukes were tattered and his steering fins showed scars and punctures, mementos of hungry sharks. Far down his tail, the broken stump of a harpoon protruded, the wood of it rotting, the metal crumbling with rust; yet though the tail moved slowly, it moved with strength. This creature had been through pain and danger in his long life, and though he had learned sadness, it had not made him bitter or weak.

Nita turned her attention back to the others, noticing that Kit was holding as still as she was, though at more of a distance; and even Hotshot was holding himself down to a slow glide. 'Eldest Blue about the Gates,' S'reee sang, sounding more formal than Nita had ever heard her, 'I greet you.'

'Senior for the Gate-waters,' said the Blue in his deep voice, with slow dignity, 'I greet you also.'

'Then you've heard, Aroooon.'

'I have heard that the Sea has taken Ae'mhnuu to its Heart,' said the Blue, 'leaving you Senior in his place, and distressed at a time when there's distress enough. Leaving you also to organize a TwelveSong on very short notice.'

'That's so.'

'Then you had best be about it,' said the Blue, 'while time still remains for singing, and the bottom is still firm under us. First, though, tell me who comes here with you. Swift-Fire-In-The-Water I know already—'

Hotshot made the closest sound Nita could imagine to an embarrassed delphine cough. She smiled to herself; now she knew what to tease him with if he got on her case.

'Land wizards, Arooooon,' S'reee said. 'HNii't—' Nita wasn't sure what to do, so she inclined the whole front of her body in the water in an approximation of a bow. '— and K!t.' Kit followed Nita's suit. 'They were the ones who went into the Dark High-And-Dry after the *Naming of Lights*—'

To Nita's utter astonishment, Arooooon inclined his own body at them, additionally curling his flukes under him in what she abruptly recognized as a gesture of congratulation. 'They're calves,' S'reee added, as if not wanting to leave anything out.

'With all due respects, Senior, they are not,' Arooooon said. 'They came *back* from that place. That is no calf's deed. Many who were older than they did not come back. —You will sing with us then? What parts?'

'I'm not sure yet,' Kit said. 'S'reee needs to see if all her people come in.'

'The Silent Lord,' Nita said.

'Indeed.' Arooooon looked at her for several long moments. 'You are a good age for it,' he said. 'And you are learning the Song—'

87

'I got most of the details from my manual,' she said. She had been up studying late the night before, though not as late as Kit had; a lot of exertion in salt air always left her drained, and she'd put the book aside after several hours, to finish the fine details of her research later. 'The Sea will give me the rest, S'reee says, as we go along.'

'So it will. But I would have you be careful of how you enact your part, young hNii't.' Aroooon drifted a bit closer to her, and that small, thoughtful eye regarded her carefully. 'There is old trouble, and old power, about you and your friend . . . as if blood hung in the water where you swim. The Lone Power apparently knows your names. It will not have forgotten the disservice you did It recently. You are greatly daring to draw Its attention to you again. Even the Heart of the Sea – Timeheart as your kind calls it – may not be quiet for one who has freely attracted the Lone One's enmity. Beware what you do. And do what you say; nowhere does the Lone Power enter in so readily as through the broken word.'

'Sir,' Nita said, rather unnerved, 'I'll be careful.'

'That is well.' Aroooon looked for a moment at Kit before speaking. 'It is a whalesark, is it not?'

'Yes, sir,' Kit said in the same respectful tone Nita had heard him use on his father.

'Have a care of it, then, should you find yourself in one of the more combative parts of the Song,' said Aroooon. 'Sperm whales were fighters before they were singers, and though their songs are often the fairest in the sea, the old blood rises too often and chokes those songs off before they can be sung. Keep your mouth closed, you were best, and you'll do well enough.'

'Thank you, sir.'

'Enough politeness, young wizard,' Aroooon said,

for the first time sounding slightly crusty. 'If size is honour, you have as much as I; and as for years, just keep breathing long enough and you'll have as many of those as I do. —S'reee, you travel more widely now than I, so I put you a question. Are the shakings in the depths worse these days than they ought to be at this time of year and tide of Moon?'

'Much worse, Eldest. That was why Ae'mhnuu originally wanted to convene the Song. And I don't know if the Song will be in time to save the fishing grounds to the east and north, around Nantucket and the Races. Hot water has been coming up close to there, farther east and south. The Shelf is changing.'

'Then let us get started,' Aroooon said. 'I assume you came to ask me to call in some of the Celebrants, time being as limited as it is.'

'Yes, Aroooon. If you would. Though as the rite requires, I will be visiting the Pale One tomorrow, in company with hNii't and K!t. The meeting place for the Song is to be ten thousand lengths north-northeast of the shoals at Barnegat, three days from now. A fast rehearsal – then right down the channel and through the Gates of the Sea, to the place appointed.'

'Well enough. Now administer me the Celebrant's Oath, Senior, so that I may lawfully call the others.'

'Very well.' S'reee swam up close to Aroooon, so that she was looking him straight in one eye with one of hers; and when she began to sing, it was in a tone even more formal and careful than that in which she had greeted him. '*Aroooon u'ao!uor, those who gather to sing that Song that is the Sea's shame and the Sea's glory desire you to be of their company. Say, for my hearing, whether you consent to that Song.*'

'*I consent,*' the Blue said in notes so deep that coral cracked and fell off rock shelves some yards away, '*and I will weave my voice and my will and my blood* with that of those who sing, if there be need.'

'I ask the second time, that those with me, both of your Mastery and not, may hear. Do you consent to the Song?'

'I consent. And may my wizardry and my Mastery depart from me sooner than I abandon that other Mastery I shall undertake in the Song's celebration.'

'The third time, and the last, I ask, that the Sea, and the Heart of the Sea, shall hear. Do you consent to the Song?'

'Freely I consent,' Aroooon sang with calm finality, 'and may I find no place in that Heart, but wander for ever amid the broken and the lost, sooner than I shall refuse the Song or what it brings about for the good of those who live.'

'Then I accept you as Celebrant of the Song, as Blue, and as latest of a line of saviours,' S'reee said. 'And though those who swim are swift to forget, the Sea forgets neither Song nor singer.' She turned a bit, looking behind her at Hotshot. 'Might as well get all of you done at once,' she said. 'Hotshot?'

'Right.'

The dolphin went through the Oath much faster than Aroooon had, though his embarrassment at being referred to as Swift-Fire-In-The-Water was this time so acute that Nita actually turned away so she wouldn't have to look at him. As for the rest of the Oath, though, Hotshot recited it, as Nita had expected, with the mindless speed of a person who thinks he has other more important matters to attend to.

S'reee turned to Nita. 'We can't give K!t the Oath yet,' she said. 'We don't know who he's going to be.'

'Can't you just give it to me and leave that part blank or something?' Kit said eagerly. He loved ceremonies.

'Kit!'

'No, K!t. HNii't, do you know the words?'

90

'The Sea does,' she said, finding it true. S'reee had already begun the ritual questioning; Nita felt for the response, found it. *'I consent, and I will weave my voice and my will and my blood with that of those who sing, if there be need.'* It was astonishing, how much meaning could be packed into a few notes. And the music itself was fascinating; so sombre, but with that odd thread of joy running through it. She threw herself into the grave joy of the final response. '. . . *And may I find no place in that Heart, but wander for ever amid the broken and the lost, sooner than I shall refuse the Song or what it brings about for the good of those who live.'*

'Then I accept you as Celebrant of the Song, and as Silent One, and as the latest in a line of saviours. And though those who swim are swift to forget, the Sea forgets neither Song nor singer.' S'reee looked at Nita with an expression in those blue eyes of vast relief, so much like the one she had given her and Kit when they'd first agreed to help that Nita shuddered a little with the intensity of it, then smiled inside. It was nice to be needed.

'That was well done,' Aroooon said slowly. 'Now, S'reee, give me names, so I'll know whom to call.'

A few moments of singing ensued as S'reee recited the names of five whales Nita had never heard of. Her inner contact with the Sea, moments later, identified them all as wizards of various ratings, all impressive. Aroooon rumbled agreement. 'Good enough,' he said. 'Best get out of the area so that I may begin Calling.'

'Right. Come on, K!t, hNii't. Till the Moon's full, Aroooon—'

'Till then.'

They swam away through the darkening water. S'reee set the pace; it was a quick one. 'Why did we have to leave in such a hurry?' Kit said.

'There aren't many wizardries more powerful than a Calling,' S'reee said as she led them away. 'He'll weave those whales' names into his spell, and if they agree to be part of the Song, the wizardry will lead them to the place appointed, at the proper time.'

'Just by singing their names?'

'K!t, that's plenty. Don't you pay attention when someone calls you by your name? Your name is *part of you*. There's power in it, tied up with the way you secretly think of yourself, the truth of the way you are. Know what a person's name means to him, know who he feels he *is* – and you have power over him. That's what Aroooon is using.'

That was a bit of information that started Nita's thoughts going in nervous circles. *How do I think of myself? And does this mean that the people who know what I think can control me? I'm not sure I like this . . .*

The first note rumbled through the water behind them, and Nita pulled up short, curling around in a quick turn. 'Careful, hNii't!' S'reee sang, a soft, sharp note of warning. Nita backfinned, hovering in the water. 'Don't disturb his circle—'

Looking back, she wouldn't have dreamed of it. The water was growing darker by the second, and as a result the glow of the krill in it was now visible – a delicate, shimmery, indefinite blue-green light that filled the sea everywhere. The light grew brighter, moment by moment; but it was brighter still at the surface, where the waves slid and shifted against one another in a glowing, undulating ceiling. And brightest of all was the track left by Aroooon's swimming – a wake that burned like clouds of cool fire behind him with every slow stroke of his tail.

At the head of the wake, Aroooon himself traced the grand curves of his spell, sheathed in bubbles and cold light. One circle he completed, melding it into itself as he sang that single compelling note; then he began another at right angles to the first, and the water burned behind him, the current not taking the brilliance away. And the blue's song seemed to get into the blood, into the bone, and would not be shaken—

'HNii't,' S'reee said, 'we can't stay, you said you have to get back—'

Nita looked around her in shock. 'S'reee, when did it get so dark! My parents are going to have a fit!'

'Didn't I mention that time didn't run the same way below the water as it does in the Above?'

'Yeah, but I thought—' Kit said, and then he broke off and said a very bad word in whale. 'No, I didn't think. I assumed that it'd go *slower*—'

'It goes faster,' Nita moaned. 'Kit, how are we going to get anything done? S'reee, how long exactly is the Song going to take?'

'Not long,' the humpback said, sounding a bit puzzled by her distress. 'A couple of lights, as it's reckoned in the Above—'

'Two days!'

'We're in trouble,' Kit said.

'That's exactly what we're in. S'reee, let's put our tails into it! Even if we were getting home right now, we'd have some explaining to do.'

She turned and swam in the direction where her sharpening whale-senses told her home was. It was going to be bad enough, having to climb out of this splendid, strong, graceful body and put her own back on again. But Dairine was waiting to give her the Spanish Inquisition when she got home. And her mother and father were going to give her more of those strange looks. Worse . . . there would be questions asked, she knew it. Her parents might even call Kit's family if they got worried enough – and Kit's dad, who was terminally protective of his son, might make Kit come home.

That thought was worst of all.

They went home. It was lucky for them that Nita's father was too tired from his fishing – which had been successful – to make much noise about their lateness. Her mother was cleaning fish in the kitchen, too annoyed at the smelly work to much care about anything else. And as for Dairine, she was buried so deep in a copy of *The Space Shuttle Operators' Manual* that all she did when Nita passed her room was glance up for a second, then dive back into her reading. Even so, there was no feeling of relief when Nita shut the door to her room and got under the covers; just an uneasy sense of something incomplete, something that was going to come up again later . . . and not in a way she'd like.

'Wizardry . . .' she muttered sourly, and fell asleep.

ED'S SONG

'Neets,' her mother said from where she stood at the sink, her back turned. 'Got a few minutes?'

Nita looked up from her breakfast. 'What's up?'

Her mother was silent for a second, as if wondering how to broach whatever she had on her mind. 'You and Kit've been out a lot lately,' she said at last. 'Dad and I hardly ever seem to see you.'

'I thought Dad said it'd be fun to have Dairine and me out of his hair for a while, this holiday,' said Nita.

'Out of his hair, yes. Not out of his life. —We worry about you two when you're out so much.'

'Mum, we're fine.'

'Well, I wonder . . . What exactly are you two doing out there all day?'

'Oh, Mum! Nothing!'

Her mother looked at her and put up one eyebrow in an excellent imitation of Mr Spock.

Nita blushed a bit. It was one of those family jokes that you wish would go away, but never does; when Nita had been little and had said 'Nothing!' she had usually been getting into incredible trouble.

'Mum,' Nita said, 'sometimes when I say "nothing",

it's really just nothing. We hang out, that's all. We . . . do stuff.'

'What kind of stuff?'

'Mum, what does it matter? Just stuff!'

'It matters,' her mother said, 'if it's adult kinds of stuff . . . instead of kid stuff.'

Nita didn't say a word. There was no question that what she and Kit were doing were adult sorts of things.

Her mother took in Nita's silence, waiting for her daughter to break it. 'I won't beat around the bush with you, Neets,' she said at last. 'Are you and Kit getting . . . physically involved?'

Nita looked at her mother in complete shock. 'Mum!' she said in a despairing groan. 'You mean *sex*? No!'

'Well,' her mother said slowly, 'that takes a bit of a load off my mind.' There was a silence after the words. Nita was almost sure she could hear her mother thinking, *If it's true . . .*

The silence unnerved Nita more than the prospect of a talk on the facts of life ever could have. 'Mum,' she said, 'if I was going to do something like that, I'd talk to you about it first.' She blushed as she said it. She was embarrassed even to be talking about this to anybody, and she would have been embarrassed to talk to her mum about it too. Nevertheless, what she'd said was the truth. 'Look, Mum, you know me, I'm chicken. I always run and ask for advice before I do anything.'

'Even about this?'

'Especially about this!'

'Then what *are* you doing?' her mother said, sounding just plain curious now. And there was another sound in her voice – wistfulness. She was feeling left out of something. 'Sometimes you say to me "playing", but I don't know what kids mean any more when they say that. When I was little, it was hopscotch, or Chinese jumprope, or games in the dirt with plastic animals. Now when I ask Dairine what she's doing, and she says "playing", I go in and find she's doing quadratic equations . . . or using my hot-curlers on the neighbour's red setter. I don't know what to expect.'

Nita shrugged. 'Kit and I swim a lot,' she said.

'Where you won't get in trouble, I hope,' her mother said.

'Yeah,' Nita said, grateful that her mother hadn't said anything about lifeguards or public beaches. *This is a real pain*, she thought. *I have to talk to Tom and Carl about this. What do they do with* their *families? . . .* But her mother was waiting for more explanation. She struggled to find some. 'We talk, we look at stuff. We explore . . .'

Nita shook her head, then, for it was hopeless. There was no explaining even the parts of her relationship with Kit that her mother *could* understand. 'He's just my friend,' Nita said finally. It was a horrible understatement, but she was getting hot with embarrassment at even having to think about this kind of thing. 'Mum, we're OK, really.'

'I suppose you are,' her mum said. 'Though I can't shake the feeling that there are things going on you're not telling me about. Nita, I trust you . . . but I still worry.'

Nita just nodded. 'Can I go out now, Mum?'

'Sure. Just be back by the time it gets dark,' she said, and Nita sighed and headed for the door. But there was no feeling of release, no sense of anything having been really settled, as there usually was when a family problem had been hashed out to everyone's satisfaction. Nita knew her mother was going to be watching her. It griped her.

There's no reason for it! she thought guiltily as she

went down to the beach, running so she wouldn't be late for meeting Kit. But there was reason for it, she knew; and the guilt settled quietly into place inside her, where not all the sea water in the world would wash it out.

She found Kit far down the beach, standing on the end of the jetty with a rippling, near-invisible glitter clutched in one hand: the whalesark. 'You're late,' he said, scowling, as Nita climbed the jetty. 'S'reee's waiting—' Then the scowl fell off his face when he saw her expression. 'You OK?'

'Yeah. But my mum's getting suspicious. And we have to be back by dark or it'll get worse.'

Kit said something under his breath in Spanish.

'¡Ay!' Nita said back, a precise imitation of what either of Kit's parents would have said if they'd heard him. He laughed.

'It's OK,' she said. 'Let's go.'

'We'd better leave our swimsuits here,' Kit said. Nita agreed, turning her back and starting to peel out of hers. Kit made his way down the rocks and into the water as she put her bathing suit under the rock with his. Then she started down the other side of the jetty.

Nita found that the whale-body came much more easily to her than it had the day before. She towed Kit out into deeper water, where he wrapped the whalesark around him and made his own change; his too came more quickly and with less struggle, though the shock of displaced water, like an undersea explosion, was no less. S'reee came to meet them then, and they greeted her and followed her off eastward, passing Shinnecock Inlet.

'Some answers to Aroooon's Calling have already come back,' she said. 'K!t, it looks like we may not need you to sing after all. But I would hope you'd attend the Song anyway.'

'I wouldn't miss it,' he sang cheerfully. 'Somebody has to be around to keep Neets from screwing up, after all . . .'

Nita made a humpback's snort of indignation. But she also wondered about the nervousness in S'reee's song. 'Where's Hotshot this morning?'

'Out calling the rest of his people for patrol around the Gates. Besides, I'm not sure he's . . . well, suited for what we're doing today . . .'

'S'reee,' Kit said, picking up the tremor in her song, 'what's the problem? It's just another wizard we're going to see—'

'Oh, no,' she said. 'The Pale One's no wizard. He'll be singing one of the Twelve, all right – but the only one who has no magic.'

'Then what's the problem? Even a shark is no match for three wizards—'

'K!t,' S'reee said, 'that's easy for you to say. You're a sperm, and it's true enough that the average shark's no threat to one of your kind. But this is no average shark we're going to see. This shark would be a good candidate to *really* be the Pale Slayer, the original Master-Shark, instead of just playing him. And there are some kinds of strength that even wizardry has trouble matching.' Her song grew quieter. 'We're getting close. If you have any plans to stay living for a while more, watch what you say when the Pale One starts talking. And for the Sea's sake, if you're upset about anything, don't show it!'

They swam on toward Montauk Point, the long spit of land that was the southeastern tip of Long Island. The bottom began to change from the yellow, fairly smooth sand of the South Shore, littered with fish havens and abandoned oyster beds and deep undergrowth, to a bottom of darker shades – dun, brown, almost black – rocky and badly broken, scattered with old wrecks. The sea around them grew noisy, changing from the usual soft background hiss of quiet water to a rushing, liquid roar that grew in intensity until Nita couldn't hear herself think, let alone sing. Seeing in the water was difficult. The surface was whitecapped, the middle waters were murky with dissolved air, and the hazy sunlight diffused in the sea until everything seemed to glow a pallid grey white, with no shadows anywhere.

'Mind your swimming,' S'reee said, again in that subdued voice. 'The rocks are sharp around here; you don't want to start bleeding.'

They surfaced once for breath near Montauk Point, so that Nita got a glimpse of its tall octagonal lighthouse, the little tender's house nearby, and a group of tourists milling about on the cliff that slanted sharply down to the sea. Nita blew, just once, but spectacularly, and grinned to herself at the sight of the tourists pointing and shouting at each other and taking pictures of her. She cruised the surface for a good long moment to let them get some good shots, then submerged again and caught up with Kit and S'reee.

The murkiness of the water made it hard to find her way except by singing brief notes, waiting for the return of the sound, and judging the bottom by it. S'reee was doing so, but her notes were so short that she seemed to be grudging them.

What's the matter with her? Nita thought. You can't get a decent sounding off such short notes— And indeed, she almost hit a rock herself as she was thinking that, and saved herself from it only by a quick lithe twist that left her aching afterwards. The roaring of the water over the Shoals kept on growing, interfering with the rebound of the song-notes, whiting them out. S'reee was bearing north around the point now and slowing to the slowest of glides.

Kit, to keep from overswimming her, was barely drifting, and keeping well above the bottom. Nita glanced up at him, a great dark shape against the greater brightness of the surface water – and saw his whole body thrash once, hard, in a gesture of terrible shock. 'Nita!'

She looked ahead and saw what he saw. The milky water ahead of them had a great cloud of blood hanging and swirling in it, with small bright shapes flashing in and out of the cloud in mindless confusion. Nita let out one small squeak of fear, then forced herself to be quiet. The sound came back, though, and told her that inside that roiling red darkness, something was cruising by in a wide curve – something nearly Kit's size. She backfinned to hover in the water, glancing up at Kit.

He drifted downward to her, singing no note of his own. She could understand why. Tumbling weightlessly out of the blood-cloud, trailing streaks of watery red, were the slashed and broken bodies of a school of smallfin tuna – heads, tails, pieces too mangled to name, let alone to bear close examination. Some of these drifted slowly to the bottom, where the scavengers – salt-water catfish and crabs and other such – ate them hurriedly, as if not wanting to linger and face whatever hunted above.

Nita didn't want to attract its attention either, but she also wanted Kit's reassurance. This place to which S'reee had brought them was unquestionably the location of a shark's 'feeding frenzy', in which the hunter begins to devour not only its prey, but anything else that gets in the way, uncontrollably, mindlessly, until sated.

Inside the cloud of blood, which the current over the shoals was taking away, something moved. Impossible, was Nita's first reaction as the circling shape was revealed. It broke out of its circling and began to soar slowly towards her and Kit and S'reee. Sonar had warned her of its size, but she was still astonished. No mere fish could be that big.

This one could. Nita didn't move. With slow, calm, deadly grace the huge form came curving toward them. Nita could see why S'reee had said that this creature was a good candidate for the title Master-Shark, even if the original had lived ten thousand years ago, when everything was bigger. The shark was nearly as long as Kit – from its blunt nose to the end of its tail's topfin, no less than ninety feet. Its eyes were that same dull, expressionless black that had horrified Nita when she'd watched *Jaws*. But seeing those eyes on a TV screen was one thing. Having them dwell on you, calm and hungry even after a feeding frenzy – that was much worse.

The pale shape glided closer. Nita felt Kit drift so close to her that his skin brushed hers, and she felt the thudding of his huge heart. In shape, the shark looked like a great white, at least as well as Nita could remember from *Jaws*. There, though, the resemblance ended. 'Great white' sharks were actually a pale blue on their upper bodies and only white below. This one was white all over, an ivory white so pale that great age might have bleached it that colour. And as for size, this one could have eaten the *Jaws* shark for lunch, and looked capable of working Nita in, in no more than a bite or two, as dessert. Its terrible maw, hung with drifting, mangled shreds of bleeding tuna, was easily fifteen feet across. Those jaws worked gently, absently, as the white horror cruised toward the three of them.

S'reee finned forward a little. She inclined the fore half of her body toward the white one and sang, in what seemed utter, toneless calm, 'Ed'Rashtekaresket, chief of the Unmastered in these waters, I greet you.'

The shark swam straight towards S'reee, those blank eyes fixed on her. The whale held her position as the Pale One glided toward her, his mouth open, his jaws working. At the last possible moment he veered to one side and began to describe a great circle around the three.

Three times he circled them, in silence. Next to Nita, Kit shuddered. The shark looked sharply at them, but still said nothing, just kept swimming until he had completed his third circle. When he spoke at last, there was no warmth in his voice, none of the skin-stroking richness she had grown used to in whale-voices. This voice was dry . . . interested, but passionless; and though insatiably hungry, not even slightly angry or vicious. The voice destroyed every idea Nita had of what a shark would sound like. Some terrible malice, she could have accepted – not this deadly equanimity. 'Young wizard,' the voice said, cool and courteous, 'well met.'

The swimmer broke free of his circling and described a swift, clean arc that brought him close enough to Nita and Kit for Nita to see the kind of rough, spiky skin that had injured S'reee so badly two nights before. The great shark almost touched Nita's nose as he swept by.

'My people,' the Pale One said to S'reee, 'tell me that they met with you two nights since. And fed well.'

'The nerve!' Kit said, none too quietly, and started to swim forwards.

Aghast, Nita bumped him to one side, hard. He was so startled he held still again. 'Keep your mouth shut!' she said quietly. 'That thing could eat us all if it wanted to!'

'If *he* wanted to,' said the Pale One, glancing at Nita and fixing her, just for a moment, with one of those expressionless eyes. 'Peace, young human. I'll deal with you in a moment.'

She subsided instantly, feeling like a bird face to face with a snake.

'I am told further,' said the shark, circling S'reee lazily, 'that wizardry struck my people down at their meal . . .'

'And then released them.'

'The story's true, then.'

'True enough, Unmastered,' said S'reee, still not moving. 'I'm no more ignorant than Ae'mhnuu was of the price paid for the reckless wasting of life. Besides, I knew I'd be talking to you today . . . and even if I didn't, I'd have you to deal with at some later time . . . Shall we two be finished with this matter, then? I have other things to discuss with you.'

'Having heard the Calling in the water last night, I believe you do,' said the Pale One, still circling S'reee with slow grace. His jaws, Nita noticed, were still working. 'You were wise to spare those of my Mastery. Are your wounds healed? Is your pain ended?'

'Yes to both questions, Pale One.'

'I have no further business with you, then,' said the shark. Nita felt Kit move slightly against her, an angry, balked movement. Evidently he had been expecting the shark to apologize. But the shark's tone of voice made it plain that he didn't think he'd done anything wrong . . . and bizarrely, it seemed as if S'reee agreed with him.

'Well enough,' S'reee said, moving for the first time, to break out of the Pale One's circle. 'Let's get to business.' The shark went after, pacing her.

'Since you heard the Calling,' S'reee said, 'you know why I'm here.'

'To ask me to be Twelfth in the Song,' said the shark. 'When have I not? You may administer the Oath to me at your leisure. But first you must tell me who the Silent One is.'

'She swims with us,' S'reee said, rolling over on her back as she swam – something Nita would certainly never have dared do, lest it give this monster ideas – and indicating Nita with one long forefin.

Nita would have preferred to keep Kit between her and the shark; but something, the Sea perhaps, told her that this would be a bad idea. Gulping, she slipped past Kit and glided up between S'reee and the great white. She was uncertain of protocol – or of anything except that she should show no fear. 'Sir,' she said, not 'bowing' but looking him straight in those black eyes, 'I'm Nita.'

'My lady wizard,' the Pale One said in that cool, dry voice, 'you're also terrified out of your wits.'

What to say now? But the shark's tone did have a sort of brittle humour about it. She could at least match it. 'Master-Shark,' she said, giving him the title to be on the safe side, 'if I were, saying so would be stupid; I'd be inviting you to eat me. And saying I wasn't afraid would be stupid too – and a lie.'

The shark laughed, a terrible sound – quiet, and dry, and violent under its humour. 'That's well said, Nita,' he said when the laughing was done. 'You're wise not to lie to a shark – nor to tell him that particular truth. After all, fear is distress. And I end distress; that's my job. So beware. I am pleased to meet you; but don't bleed around me. Who's your friend? Make him known to me.'

Nita curved around with two long strokes, swam back to Kit, and escorted him back to the white with her fins barely touching him, a *don't-screw-it-up!* gesture. 'This is Kit,' she said. 'He may or may not be singing with us.'

'A whalesark?' said the Pale One, as Kit glided close to him.

'Yes,' Kit said bluntly, without any honorific note

or tone of courtesy appended to the word. Nita looked at him in shock, wondering what had got into him. He ignored her, staring at the shark. Kit's teeth were showing.

The Pale One circled Kit once, lazily, as he had when offering challenge to S'reee. 'She is not as frightened as she looks, Kit,' he said, 'and at any rate, I suspect you're more so. Look to yourself first until you know your new shape better. It has its own fierce ways, I hear; but a sperm whale is still no match for me.' He said this with the utter calm of someone telling someone else what time it was. 'I would not make three bites of you, as I would with Nita. I would seize your face and crush your upper jaw to make myself safe from your teeth. Then I would take hold of that great tongue of yours and not let go until I had ripped it loose to devour. Smaller sharks than I am have done that to sperm whales before. The tongue is, shall we say, a delicacy.'

The shark circled away from Kit. Very slowly, Kit glided after. 'Sir,' he said – sounding subdued, if not afraid, 'I didn't come here to fight. I thought we were supposed to be on the same side. But frightening us seems a poor tactic if we're supposed to be allies, and singing the same Song.'

'I frighten no-one,' said the shark. 'No-one who fears gets it from anywhere but himself. Or herself. Cast the fear out – and then I am nothing to fear . . . No matter, though; you're working at it. Kit, Nita, my name is ed'Rashtekaresket.'

'It has teeth in it,' Nita said.

The shark looked at her with interest in his opaque gaze. 'It has indeed,' he said. 'You hear well. And you're the Silent One? Not the Listener?'

'The Listener's part is spoken for, Pale One,' S'reee said. 'And the Silent One's part needs a wizard more experienced than any we have – one already tested against the Lone Power, yet young enough to fulfill the other criteria. HNii't is the one.'

'Then these are the two who went up against the Lone One in Manhattan,' ed'Rashtekaresket said. 'Oh, don't sing surprise at me, Kit: I know the human names well enough. After all, you are who you eat.'

Nita swallowed hard. 'Such shock,' the shark said, favouring Nita again with that dark, stony, unreadable look. 'Beware your fear, Nita. They say I'm a "killing machine" – and they say well. I am one.' The terrible laugh hissed in the water again. 'But one with a mind. Nor such a machine that I devour without cause. Those who I eat, human or whale or fish, always give me cause. —I'm glad you brought them, S'reee. If this "Heart of the Sea" the wizards always speak of really exists, then these two should be able to get its attention. And its attention is needed.'

For the first time since the conversation began, S'reee displayed a mild annoyance. 'It exists, Pale One. How many Songs have you played Twelfth in, and you still don't admit that—'

'More Songs than you have, young one,' ed'Rashtekaresket said. 'And it would take more still to convince me of what can't be seen by anyone not a wizard. *Show* me the Sea's Heart, this Timeheart you speak of, and I'll admit it exists.'

'Are you denying that wizardry comes from there?' S'reee said, sounding even more annoyed.

'Possibly,' said the shark, 'if it does not. Don't be angry without reason, S'reee. You warm-bloods are all such great believers. But there's no greater pragmatist than a shark. I believe what I eat . . . or what I see. Your power I've seen: I don't deny that. I simply reserve decision on where it comes from. What I say further is that there's trouble in the deep waters, hereabouts, more trouble than usual – and it's as well the Song is being enacted now, for there's need of it, wherever its virtue comes from. Will you hear my news? For if things go on as they're going now, the High and Dry will shortly be low and wet – and those of my Mastery will be eating very well indeed.'

A SONG OF BATTLES

'What is it?' Kit said. 'Is it the krakens?'

Ed'Rashtekaresket looked at Kit and began a slow, abstracted circling around him. 'You know about that?' said the Master-Shark. 'You're wise for a human.'

'I know that the krakens are breeding this year,' Kit said, 'breaking their usual eleven-year cycle. And they're bigger than usual, our Seniors told us. In the deep water, krakens have been seen that would be a match for just about any whale or submarine they grabbed.'

'That is essentially what I would have told you,' the Master-Shark said to S'reee, still circling Kit. 'My own people have been reporting trouble with the bottom dwellers – but any sharks who cannot escape such are no longer entitled to the Mastery's protection in any case. At any rate, I pass this news along as a courtesy to you warm-bloods. By way of returning the courtesy done to my people after your accident.'

'Thank you,' S'reee said, and bowed as they swam.

'Odd,' ed'Rashtekaresket mused as they went, 'that qualified wizards of high levels are so few, the whales must bring in humans to make up the number.'

'Odd isn't the word for it, Pale One,' S'reee said. 'Advisories and Seniors have been dying like clams at red tide lately.'

'As if,' the Master-Shark said, 'someone or something did not care to have the Song enacted just now.' His voice sounded remote. 'I'm reminded of that Song enacted, oh, a hundred and thirty thousand moons ago – when the bottom shook as it does now, and the Lone One had newly lost the Battle of the Trees. One wizard was injured by rockfall while they made the journey down through the Gates of the Sea. And when they began the Singing proper, first the Killer and then the Blue lost control of their spells at crucial times. You know the moment, S'reee: when the mock-battle breaks out among the three parties, and each one tries to force the others around to its way of thinking.'

Ed'Rashtekaresket fell silent. The four of them swam on. 'Uh, Ed – ed'Rak—' Nita stopped short, unable to remember the rest of his name as anything but the sound of gnashing teeth. 'Look, can I call you Ed?'

Blank eyes turned their attention toward her. 'At least I can say it,' she said. 'And if I'm going to be singing with you, it can't be titles all the time. We have to know each other, you say.'

'A sprat's name,' the shark said, dry-voiced. 'A fry name – for me, the Master.' Then came the quiet, terrible laughter again. 'Well enough. You're the Sprat, and I'm Ed.' He laughed again.

Nita had never heard anything that sounded less like mirth in her life. 'Great. So, Ed, what happened? In that Song, when it went wrong. Was anyone hurt?'

'Of the singers? No. They were inside a spell-circle, and protected – it has to be that way, else anything might get in among the singers and upset their spelling. But when the Song failed, all the power its Singers had tried to use to bind the Lone One rebounded and freed him instead. The sea bottom for hundreds of miles about was terribly torn and changed as a result. Volcanoes, earthquakes . . . Also, there was a landmass, a great island in the middle of these waters. Surely you know about that country, since your people named the ocean after it. That island was drowned. There were humans on it; millions of them died when the island sank. As for the rest – eating was good hereabouts for some time. The species of my Mastery prospered.'

'A hundred and thirty thousand moons ago—' Kit whispered, one soft-breathed note of song. 'Ten thousand years!'

'Atlantis,' Nita said, not much louder.

'Afállonë,' S'reee said, giving the name in the wizardly Speech. 'There were Senior and Master wizards there,' she said sadly, 'a great many of them. But even working together, they couldn't stop what happened. The earthquakes begun by the downfall of Afállonë were so terrible that they tore straight through the first level of the land-under-Sea – the crust, I think the two-leggers call it – and right down to the mantle, the molten stuff beneath. The whole island plate on which Afállonë stood was broken in pieces and pushed down into the lava of the mantle – utterly destroyed. The plates of your continent and that of Europe have since drifted together over the island's old location, covering its grave . . . But even after the Downfall, there was trouble for years – mostly with the atmosphere, because of all the ash the volcanoes spat into the air. It got cold, and whole species of land creatures died for lack of their food. It was thousands of moons before things were normal again. So we tend to be very careful about the Song. *Lest the Sea become the Land, and the Land become the Sea—*'

111

'And the krakens are breeding,' the Pale One said as they swam. 'Well. I'm for the Northern Rips tonight; there's trouble in the water there.'

What kind of creature, Nita wondered, *could hear the sounds of simple distress at a distance of two hundred miles and more?*

'Beware, Nita,' Ed said. 'Only a dead shark could have avoided hearing *that* thought. If we're to know each other well, as you say you desire, best mind how you show me your feelings. Else I shall at last know you most intimately, sooner than you are planning – and the relationship will be rather one-sided.'

Ed's jaws worked. '—I was going to say: matters swimming as they do, I will see you three home. It's getting dark, and—'

'Dark!' Nita and Kit looked around them. The water, turbid green white when they had come here, was now almost black.

'The sun's going down,' Kit said unhappily. 'We're really in for it now.'

Nita agreed. 'Master-Shark,' she said, staying as calm as she could, 'we have to get back to, uh, our feeding grounds. And in a hurry. Our parents are waiting for us, and we had orders to be back before it got dark.'

Ed simply looked at Nita with that calm black stare. 'As you say,' he said, and began to swim faster. 'But we will not be at Bluehaven before many stars are out and the moon is about to set.'

'I know,' Nita said. It was hard to sound unconcerned while her insides were churning. 'Maybe you should go ahead and let them know we're OK,' she said to Kit. 'Tell them I'm coming—'

'No,' Kit said, also at pains to sound calm. 'I'll take my chances with you, Neets. "All for one . . ."'

'Sprat,' Ed said to Nita, 'this is an odd thing, that your sire and dam impose restrictions on you when

112

you're doing a wizardry of such weight.'

'They don't know we're wizards,' Kit said.

S'reee was so surprised by this that she backfinned to a dead stop in the water. Ed, as if nothing took him by surprise, merely circled about the group, while Kit and Nita coasted close by. 'They don't *know*!' S'reee said. 'How do you do anything? How do you prepare wizardries? Let alone the matter of singing the Song without the full support of the people close to you – and when you're singing the Silent One's part, no less!'

There had been something about that last part in the manual. Nita had thought she had all the support she needed in Kit. She was becoming less sure. *Tom, got to call Tom—* 'I know,' she said out loud. 'S'reee, let's swim. We're late enough as it is.'

The four of them headed west again. 'It can't be helped,' Kit said. 'It's not like it is here, where wizardry is something respectable and useful that almost everybody knows about. Up on the land, they used to burn people for it. Nowadays – well, it's safer to hide what you're up to. People would think you were nuts if you tried to tell them you were a wizard. Most people don't believe in magic.'

'What *do* they believe in?' S'reee said, unnerved.

'Things,' Nita said unhappily. 'S'reee, it's too complicated. But doing wizardry and keeping everybody from noticing is a problem.'

'I'm no wizard,' Ed said, 'but only a fool would try to deny a wizard's usefulness. It must be a crippled life your people live up there, without magic, without what can't be understood, only accepted—'

For all her concern about being late, Nita looked wryly sideways at Ed. 'This from someone who won't admit Timeheart exists unless he sees it himself?'

'Sprat,' Ed said, 'if it does in fact exist, can my not believing in it make the slightest difference? And as for understanding – I'm not interested in understanding Timeheart. What use is spending time working out, say, why water is wet? Will it make breathing it any— 'Ware, all!'

The warning came so conversationally that it took Nita precious moments to realize what the problem was. The sea around them was dark to begin with. But in the black water, darker shapes were moving. One of them, writhing and growing, reached up dim arms at them. Nita let out a squeak of surprise, and the returning echoes hit her skin and told her, to her terror, what her eyes couldn't. A long torpedo-shaped body, a great mass of arms that squirmed like snakes, and a long wicked beak-fang hidden at the bottom of them. She backfinned desperately as those writhing arms with all their hooked suckers reached for her.

The sound that began rumbling through the water probably upset the krakens as much as it did her. Nita had never heard the battlecry of an enraged sperm whale – a frightful scrape of sound, starting at the highest note a human being can hear and scaling down with watershaking roughness to the lowest note, then past it. It was hard to see what was going on, but Nita kept singing so her radar would tell her. She would have preferred not to; the echo-'sight' of Kit in the whalesark, arrowing toward the leading kraken, jaws open, all his sharp teeth showing, was a horror. Suckered arms whipped around him, squeezing; and the giant squid had its own noise, a screech so high it sounded like fingernails being scraped down a blackboard.

Before she really knew what she was doing, Nita circled off to pick up speed, and then swam straight towards the kraken's head-ruffle, the thick place where the tentacles joined behind mouth and tooth. She sang for aim as she charged, then lost the song

114

when she rammed the kraken. The squid's long porous backbone crunched and broke under her blow. Rolling, tail lashing, she fluked away. All the telephone pole-length arms spasmed and squeezed Kit hard one last time, then fell away limp. Kit shot in towards the head of the broken squid. Jaws opened, crunched closed, opened again to slash once or twice with wild ferocity. Then Kit fluked powerfully, still singing, and arched away through the water.

'Kit!' Nita cried, but his only answer was the sperm whale battlecry. The water was dark with night, thick with squid ink, and scratchy with stirred sand. Through it all a pallid shape was cruising with terrible speed, jaws open, circling in. The patch of darkness he circled threw out a score of arms to grapple with him. Ed let them draw him closer to his prey, then bit, and blood and ink billowed everywhere in the frantic rush of water expelled by the shrieking squid. Severed chunks of kraken arm spun and swirled in the water, and sank through it. Ed swept forward, jaws wide, and bit again. The shriek cut off. Out of the cloud of blood and ink Ed came silently sailing, cool, untroubled, graceful: the Pale Slayer, a silent ghost looking calmly about him for his next victim. Nita held very still and sang not a note until he passed her by.

S'reee was ramming another kraken as Nita had. But one more closed on her from behind. Kit came swimming, singing his battlecry. He bit the second squid amidships, hanging on to that bullet-shaped body like a bulldog as its struggles shook him from side to side. Between her and Kit and S'reee, Ed was circling a third kraken. It flailed at him, trying to bind his mouth shut so that it could get a better grip on him and squeeze him to death.

It might as well not have bothered. As a fourth

kraken came for her, Nita saw Ed break his circling pattern to dart in and slash, then curve away. Again and again he feinted, again and again his teeth tore, until the kraken was reduced to a tattered, screaming storm of blood and ink and flailing tentacles. Blank-eyed, Ed soared straight at the finned rear end of the doomed creature and opened his mouth. When his jaws scissored shut, all that was left to drift downwards were the tips of several tentacles. The kraken had been about the size of a station wagon.

A fifth kraken took a great suck of water into its internal jet-propulsion system and thrust it out again, tainting the water with the sepia taste of ink as it fled into the depths, wailing like a lost soul. Nita was willing to let it go, and was swimming for the surface when a chill current and a pale form sank past her, spiraling downwards with deadly grace. The utter dark of the night sea swallowed Ed. She heard the kraken's screams, which had been diminishing – and now grew louder, and more ragged, until they abruptly stopped.

Wearily Nita swam upwards. She breached and blew gratefully, doing nothing for a long while but lie there in the wavewash, gasping.

Not too far away, S'reee breached and made her way slowly toward Nita. Neither of them said anything; but the two of them sagged together and simply leaned against each other, taking comfort in the presence of another whale. Some yards off, the water rushed away from Kit's back and sides as he came up, gasping too. Nita looked over at him, shaking. She knew that what she saw was just her friend in a whalesuit. But she kept seeing sharp teeth, slashing in a blood-hunger too much like Ed's for comfort.

'Are you OK?' she said to Kit.

'Yeah.' He sounded uncertain, and Nita breathed

116

out in relief. The voice was a sperm whale's, but the person inside it was definitely Kit. 'Got a little – a little carried away there. You, Neets?'

'All right,' she said.

Out of the depths a white form came drifting upward towards them.

They breathed and dived, all three, to find Ed circling in the clearing water, while a storm of fingerling blues and sardines swarmed about him, picking scraps and shreds out of the water, some of them even daring to pick bloody bits off Ed's skin or from between his teeth. 'That last one was in pain at the thought of returning to the depths without its purpose fulfilled,' he said. 'So I ended that pain.'

'Purpose?' Kit said.

'Surely you don't take that attack for an accident, young one,' Ed said. 'Any more than the shaking of the sea bottom these days or the ill chances that have been befalling S'reee's people have been accidents.'

Nita looked at Kit, and then at Ed, in confusion. 'You mean that what happened to S'reee— I thought you were on our side!'

Ed began to circle slowly inward toward Nita. 'Peace, spratling,' he said. 'I pay no allegiance to anyone in the Sea or above it; you know that. Or you should. I am the Unmastered. I alone.' He swept in closer. 'The encounter S'reee and Ae'mhnuu had with the ship-that-eats-whales was doubtless the Lone One's doing. It has many ways to subtly influence those who live. As for the sharks—' Ed's voice became shaded with a cold, slow rage that chilled Nita worse than anything he'd said or done yet. 'They did according to their nature, just as you do. Do not presume to blame them. On the other flank, however, *my* people have only one Master. If the Lone One has been tampering with species under my Mastery, then It will have to deal with *me*.'

117

That made Nita shake – not only at the thought of Ed trying to take on the Lone Power himself, but at the outrageous thought that the Lone One, for all Its power, might actually be in for some trouble. 'I'm sorry,' she said. 'I thought you meant you told the sharks to just go ahead and attack a hurt whale.' And with some trepidation, she copied S'reee's earlier gesture – rolling over in the water, exposing her unprotected flanks and belly to the Master-Shark.

A few long seconds afterwards she felt what few beings have lived to tell about – the abrasive touch of a live shark's skin. Ed nudged Nita ever so lightly in the ribs, then glided by; almost a friendly touch, except that Nita could see the fanged mouth working still, the opaque black eyes tracking on her. Finned whiteness sailed silent and immense above her, hardly stirring the water. 'In another time, in another place, I might have told them to,' Ed said. 'In another time, I may yet tell them to. And what will you think of me then, Sprat?'

'I don't know,' she said, when the white shape had passed over.

'That was well said too.' Ed circled about the three of them, seeming to both watch them and ignore them at the same time. 'So let us be on our way; we're close to Tiana Beach. S'reee, you and I have business remaining that must be done before witnesses.'

S'reee wasted no time about it, gliding close to Ed – but, Nita noticed, not nearly as close as S'reee had come to Aroooon or Hotshot, or herself. '*Ed'Rash-tekaresket t'k Gh'shestaesteh, Eldest-In-Abeyance to the Pale Slayer That Was, Master for the Sharks of Plain and Shelf and what lies between – those who gather to sing that Song that is the Sea's shame and the Sea's glory desire you to be of their company. Say, for my hearing, whether you consent to that Song.*'

'*I consent, and I will weave my voice and my will and*

my blood with that of those who sing, if there be need.'

'I ask the second time—'

'Peace, S'reee, I know the words by now: who better? *A second time I say it, that those with me, both of my Mastery and not, may hear. Twice I consent to the Song, in my Mastery's name; and a third time, that the Sea, and the Heart of the Sea, shall hear . . .'* Was his voice just a touch drier on that phrase, Nita wondered? 'So up, now, the three of you. We are where you need to be.'

Kit looked around him in confusion. 'How can you tell? There's a lot of Tiana Beach, and you've never seen our house—'

'I can smell your human bodies in the water from this morning,' Ed said, unperturbed. 'And, besides, I hear distress.'

'Uh-oh . . .' Kit said.

'S'reee,' Nita said, stalling, 'when will you need us next?'

'Next dawn,' the humpback said, brushing against first Nita, then Kit, in sympathy. 'I'm sorry we can't have a day's rest or so, but there's no time any more.'

'Do we have to be there?' Kit said.

'The Silent Lord does,' S'reee said, glancing at Nita. 'In fact, normally it's the Silent Lord who administers the Oath, since her stake in the Song is the greatest.'

Nita made an unhappy sound. 'Kit,' she said, 'maybe you'd better stay home. At least you won't get in trouble with your parents that way.'

Kit shouldered over beside her, absent affection that bumped her considerably sideways as his hundred-foot bulk hit her. 'No,' he said. 'I told you: "All for one". It's not fair for you to be stuck with this alone. Besides, what if those things show up again, and Ed's not here—'

'Right,' Nita said.

119

'Neets, we better get going,' Kit said.

She headed for the surface. Kit and S'reee followed; but Ed was above her and surfaced first, several hundred yards westward and much closer to the shore. So the first sound Nita heard from the shore was the screaming.

Nita had never heard her mother scream. The raw panic in the sound got under Nita's skin even worse than Kit's hunting song had.

'Harry!' her mother was shouting, and every few words her terror would gnaw its way through her desperately controlled voice and come out as a scream again. 'Harry, for God's sake look, there's a *fin* out there, it's a *shark!* Get Mr Friedman, get the cops, get *somebody*!'

The beach flickered with lights – torches, held by people running up and down – and every light in Nita's house was on, as well as most of those in the houses next door. Nita gulped at her father's hoarse reply – just as scared as her mother, trying to stay in control and failing.

'Betty, hang on, they're coming! Hang on! Don't go near the water!' For her mother was floundering into the surf, looking out seaward, searching for someone she couldn't see. 'Nita!'

Nita had to fight to stay silent.

Ed cruised serenely, contemptuously close to the shore, bearing off westward, away from Nita and Kit and S'reee. The flashlights followed his pale fin as it breached, as Ed went so far as to raise himself a little out of the water, showing a terrible expanse of back, then the upward-spearing tailfin as big as a wind-surfer's sail. Shouting in fear and amazement, the people followed him down the beach as if hypnotized. The torches bobbed away.

'He's got them distracted, we've got to get out now,' Kit said.

'But our swimsuits—'

'No time! Later! S'reee, we'll see you in the morning!' The two of them fluked wildly and made for the beach, in the direction opposite to the one in which Ed was leading the people on the shore. Nita stayed under the surface as long as she could, then felt the bottom scrape on her belly; she was grounded. Kit had grounded sooner than she had. Nita gasped a long breath of air and let the shapechange go, then collapsed into the water again – not deep for a whale, but three feet deep for her. She struggled to her feet and staggered to shore through the breakers, wiping the salt out of her eyes and shaking with the shock of a spell released too suddenly.

By the time her sight was working properly, there was no time to do anything about the small, dark figure standing a few feet up the incline of the beach, looking straight at her.

Dairine.

There was a slam of imploding air behind Nita. Kit came scrambling up out of the water, with the undone whalesark clutched glittering in one fist. 'Quick,' he said, 'I can do the Scotty spell before they come back—' He reached out and grabbed her by the arm, shaking her. 'Neets, are you OK?'

Then he saw Dairine too. 'Uh,' he said. The sounds of voices down the beach were getting closer; and through them, abrupt and terrible, came a sudden *crack!* of gunfire. Kit looked down that way, then at Dairine again, and took a long breath. 'Right back,' he said. He said one quick syllable and, in another clap of air, vanished.

Dairine just stood there in her pyjamas with Yoda all over them, staring at her sister. 'Whales,' she said.

'Dairine,' Nita whispered, 'how long have they been out here?'

'About an hour.'

'Oh, *no*.' And her parents would be there in moments. 'Dairine,' Nita said, 'look—' There she stopped. She couldn't think what she wanted to say.

'It *is* magic,' Dairine whispered back. 'There really *is* such a thing. And it's that book you have, isn't it? It's not just an old beaten-up kids' book. It's—'

In another slam of air, blowing outward this time, Kit reappeared. He was already in his swimsuit; he flung Nita's at her and then looked unhappily at Dairine.

'And you too,' she said to him as Nita struggled into her suit.

'A wizard?' Kit said. 'Yeah. Both of us.'

Off to their left, there was another gunshot, and a mighty splash. Nita and Kit stared out at the sea. Ed was arrowing straight up out of the water with slow, frightful grace, jaws working as he arched up in a leap like a dolphin's. Fifty feet of him towered out of the water, sixty, eighty, until even his long sharp tailfin cleared the surface and he hung there in midair, bent like a bow, the starlight and the light of the moon sheening ice white along his hide and the water that ran down it. '*Until later, my wizards!*' came his hissed cry in the Speech, as Ed dived dolphin-curved back into the sea. The gunshot cracked across the water at him, once, twice. Ed went down laughing in scorn.

'That's as much as he's going to do,' Kit said. 'They'll be back in a moment, when they see he's gone.'

'That shark—' said Dairine, sounding about ready to go into shock.

'He's a friend,' Nita said.

'Neets,' Kit said, 'what're we going to tell them?'

'That depends on Dairine.' Nita took care to keep her voice perfectly level. 'What about it, Dari? Are you going to spill everything? Or are you going to keep quiet?'

Dairine looked at the two of them, saying nothing. Then, 'I want you to tell me everything later,' she said. '*Everything.*'

'It'll have to be tonight, Dari. We've got to be out again by dawn.'

'You're going to get it,' Dairine said.

'Tell us something else we don't know, Sherlock,' Kit said, mild-voiced.

'Well. I guess I saw you two coming over the dune,' Dairine said, looking from Kit to Nita. She turned to head down the beach.

Nita caught Dairine by the arm, stopping her. Dairine looked back at Nita over her shoulder – her expression of unease just visible in the dim light from the houses up the beach. 'I really don't want to lie to them, Dari,' Nita said.

'Then you better either keep your mouth shut,' Dairine said, 'or tell them the truth.' And she tugged her arm out of Nita's grasp and went pounding off down the beach, screaming, in her best I'm-gonna-tell voice, 'Mum, Dad, it's Nita!'

Nita and Kit stood where they were. 'They're going to ground us,' Kit said.

'Maybe not,' said Nita, in forlorn hope.

'They will. And what're you going to do then?'

Nita's insides clenched. And the sound of people talking was coming down the beach toward them.

'I'm going,' she said. 'This is *lives* we're talking about – whales' lives. People's lives. It can't just be stopped in the middle! You remember what Ed said.'

'That's what I'd been thinking,' Kit said. 'I just didn't want to get you in my trouble – just because I'm doing it, I mean.' He looked at her. 'Dawn, then.'

'Better make it before,' Nita said, feeling like a

123

conspirator and hating it. 'Less light to get caught by.'

'Right.' And that was all they had time for, for Nita's mother and father, and Mr Friedman, and Dairine, all came trotting up together. Then things got confusing, for Nita's dad grabbed her and hugged her to him with tears running down his face, as if he were utterly terrified; and her mother slowed from her run, waved her arms in the air and roared, 'Where the blazes have you *been?*'

'We lost track of the time,' Kit said.

'We were out, Mum,' Nita said. 'Swimming—'

'Wonderful! There are sharks the size of houses out there in the water, and my daughter is off swimming! At night, at high tide, with the undertow—' Her mother gulped for air, then said more quietly, 'I didn't expect this of you, Nita. After we talked this morning, and all.'

Nita's father let go of her slowly, nodding, getting a fierce, closed look on his face now that the initial shock of having his daughter back safe was passing. 'And I thought you had better sense, Kit,' he said. 'We had an agreement that while you stayed with us, you'd do as we said. Here it is hours and hours after dark—'

'I know, sir,' Kit said. 'I forgot – and by the time I remembered, it was too late. It won't happen again.'

'Not for a while, anyway,' Nita's mother said, sounding grim. 'I don't want you two going out of sight of the house until further notice. Understood?'

'Yes, Mrs Callahan.'

'Nita?' her mother said sharply.

There it was: the answer she wasn't going to be able to get around. 'OK, Mum,' she said. Her stomach turned over inside her at the sound of the lie. Too late now. It was out, not to be recalled.

'That also means staying out of the water,' her father said.

Why me? Why me! Nita thought. She made a face. 'OK.'

'OK,' Kit said too, not sounding very happy.

'We'll see how you two behave in the next few days,' Nita's mother said. 'And whether that shark clears out of here. Maybe after that we'll let you swim again. Meanwhile – you two get home.'

They went. Just once Nita looked over her shoulder and was sure she saw, far out on the water, a tall pale fin that stood high as a sail above the surface, then slid below it, arrowing off toward Montauk – distress ended for the moment, and a job done.

Nita felt the miserable place in her gut and thought it was just as well that Ed couldn't come up on the land.

FEARSONG

Nita lay awake in the dark, staring at the ceiling. It was three thirty in the morning, by the glow of the cheap electric clock on the dresser. She would very much have liked to turn over, forget about the clock, the time, and everything else, and just sack out. But soon it would be false dawn, and she and Kit would have to be leaving.

Changes . . .

Only last week, her relationship with her parents had seemed perfect. Now all that was over, ruined – and about to get much worse, Nita knew, when her mum and dad found her and Kit gone again in the morning.

And the changes in Kit—

She rolled over on her stomach unhappily, not wanting to think about it. She had a new problem to consider, for when everyone was in bed, Dairine had come visiting.

Nita put her face down into her pillow and groaned. Dairine had gone right through Nita's wizard's manual, staring at all the strange maps and pictures. It was annoying enough to begin with that Dairine could see the book at all; nonwizards such as her mother and father, looking at it, usually saw only

126

an old, beaten-up copy of something called *So You Want to Be a Wizard*, apparently a kids' book. But Dairine saw what was there, and was fascinated.

The aptitude for wizardry sometimes runs through a whole generation of a family. Several famous 'circles' of wizards in the past had been made up of brothers or sisters or cousins, rather than unrelated people such as she and Kit, or Tom and Carl, who met by accident or in some other line of work and came to do wizardry together by choice. But families with more than one wizard tended to be the exception rather than the rule, and Nita hadn't been expecting this. Also, Nita was beginning to realize that she had rather enjoyed having her wizardry be a secret from everybody but the other wizards she worked with. That secret, that advantage, was gone now too. Dairine had the aptitude for wizardry as strongly as Nita herself had had it when she started.

In fact, she's got it more strongly than I did, Nita thought glumly. The book had to get my attention by force, that first time I passed it in the library. But Dairine noticed it herself, as soon as I brought it home.

For several years Nita had kept her advantage over her sister by only the slimmest of margins. She knew quite well that Dairine was a lot cleverer than she was in most things. Wizardry had been a large and satisfying secret she'd felt sure Dairine would never catch on to. But that advantage was now gone too. The youngest wizards were the strongest ones, according to the book; older ones might be wiser but had access to less sheer power. Dairine had got the better of her again.

Nita turned over on her back, staring at the ceiling once more.

Kit . . .

He just wasn't himself in the whalesark. When

he's in his own skin, she told herself fiercely, he's fine. But she couldn't quite make herself believe that. His look, his stance, were too different in just the past day or two.

She had thought that having a best friend at last would be great fun. And she and Kit had enjoyed each other's company immensely in their first couple of months of wizardry, after the terror and sorrow of their initial encounter with the Art had worn off a bit. But sometimes things just didn't work. Kit would get moody, need to be by himself for days at a time. Or he would say sudden things that Nita thought cruel – except that it was Kit saying them, and Kit wasn't cruel; she knew that.

I wish I'd had some friends when I was younger, she thought. Now I've got one who really matters – and I don't know what to do so he stays my friend. He changes . . .

And Kit was going to be in that whalesark for more and more time in the next couple of days. Would she even know him if this kept up?

Would he know her? Or want to? Humpbacks and sperms were different. Her own aggressiveness had frightened her badly enough, after the fight with the krakens. Kit's had been worse. And he had been enjoying it . . .

Listless, Nita reached under her pillow for her wizard's manual and a torch. She clicked the light on and started paging through the book, intending to kill some time doing 'homework' – finishing the study of her parts of the Song, the Silent Lord's parts. They were mostly in what whales used for verse – songs with a particular rhythm and structure, different for each species, but always more formal than regular conversational song. Since she wasn't good at memorizing, Nita was relieved to find that when she was in whaleform, the Sea would remind her of the exact words. What she needed to study were the emotions and motivations behind each song, the *way* they were sung.

She riffled through the book. There was a lot of background material – the full tale of the first Song, and of others, including the disastrous 'Drowned Song' that ended in the downfall of Atlantis; the names of famous whale-wizards who had sung and how they had sung their parts; 'stage direction' for the Song itself; commentary, cautions, permitted variations, even jokes, for evidently though the occasion was serious, it didn't have to be sombre. Then the Song proper, in verse, with the names of the ten Lords of the Humours: the Singer, the Gazer, the Blue, the Sounder, the Grey Lord, the Listener, the Killer, the Wanderer, the Forager, and of course the Silent Lord. Each of them ruled a kind of fish and also a kind of temperament.

Some of them struck Nita as odd; the Killer, for example, was the patroness of laughter, always joking: the Gazer looked at everything and hardly ever said what he saw. And the Silent Lord – Nita paused at the lines that described 'the one who ruled seas with no songs in them, and hearts that were silent; but in her own silence, others would sing forever . . .'

And of course there was the Pale Slayer. And another odd thing; though the names of all the whales ever to sing the Song were listed, there was no listing for the Master-Shark, except the mere title, repeated again and again. Maybe he's like an executioner in the old days, Nita thought. Anonymous. The commentaries weren't very illuminating. 'The Master of the lesser Death', one of them called him, 'who, mastering it, dieth not. For wizardry toucheth not one to whom it hath not been freely given: nor doth the messenger in any wise partake of the message he bears.'

The manual was like that sometimes. Nita sighed and skimmed down to the first canto: S'reee's verse, it would be, since the Singer opens the Song as the other Ten gather around the lonely seamount Caryn Peak, the Sea's Tooth. Alongside the musical and movement notations for a whale singing the Song, the manual had a rough translation into the Speech:

Blood in the water I sing, and one who shed it:
    deadliest hunger I sing, and one who fed it –
weaving the ancientmost tale of the Sea's
    sending;
    singing the tragedy, singing the joy un-
    ending.

This is our shame – this is the Whole Ocean's
    glory;
    this is the Song of the Twelve. Hark to the
    story!

Hearken, and bring it to pass; swift, lest the
    sorrow long ago laid to its rest devour us
    tomorrow!

There was much more: the rest of the prologue, then the songs of each of the Masters who were part of the Song and their temptations by the Stranger-whale, the Lone Power in disguise. Nita didn't need to pay any attention to those, for the Silent Lord came in only near the end, and the others, even the Stranger, dared use nothing stronger than persuasion on her. The whale singing the part of the Silent One then made her decision which side to be on – and acted.

That was the part Nita had got up to. Almost

done, she thought with some relief, seeing that there wasn't much more beyond this. Only a few more cantos. Boy, how do you manage to be cheerful while singing this stuff? It sounds so creepy.

Must I accept the barren Gift?
   – learn death, and lose my Mastery?
Then let them know whose blood and breath
   will take the Gift and set them free:
whose is the voice and whose the mind
   to set at naught the well-sung Game –
when finned Finality arrives
   and calls me by my secret Name.

Not old enough to love as yet,
   but old enough to die, indeed –
the death-fear bites my throat and heart,
   fanged cousin to the Pale One's breed.
But past the fear lies life for all –
   perhaps for me; and, past my dread,
past loss of Mastery and life,
   the Sea shall yet give up Her dead!

Glad that wasn't me back then, she thought. I could never have pulled that off . . . Nita read down through the next section, the 'stage directions' for this sequence of the Song. 'The whale singing the Silent One then enacts the Sacrifice in a manner as close to the original enactment as possible, depending on the site where the Song is being celebrated . . .'

She skimmed the rest of it, the directions detailing the Pale Slayer's 'acceptance of Sacrifice', his song, the retreat of the Lone Power, and the song's conclusion by the remaining Ten. But she was having trouble keeping her mind on her work. Kit—

'Neets!'

His voice was the merest hiss from outside the

locked window. She got up and peered out the window to see where Kit was, then waved him away from the wall. The spell she had in mind for getting out needed only one word to start it. Nita spoke it and walked through the wall.

Between the distracting peculiarity of the feeling, which was like walking through thick spiderwebs, and the fact that the floor of her room was several feet above the ground, Nita almost took a bad fall, the way someone might who'd put his foot into an open manhole. Kit staggered, barely catching her, and almost fell down himself.

'Clumsy,' he said as he turned her loose.

'Watch it, *Niño*—'

He punched her, not as hard as he might have; then spent a moment or two brushing himself off, and redraped the whalesark over one shoulder, where it hung mistily shimmering like a scrap of fog with starlight caught in it. 'Is that locked?' he said, looking up at Nita's window with interest.

'Uh-huh.'

'And the front and back doors are too.'

'Yeah.'

Kit threw a wicked look at Nita as they made their silent way out of the yard and toward the beach. 'Your mum and dad are going to be really curious how we got out of the house and then locked all the inside locks when we don't have the keys.'

'Uh-huh,' Nita said. 'If we're going to get in real trouble, we might as well confuse them as much as possible. It might distract them . . .'

'Want to bet?' Kit said.

Nita didn't answer.

The beach was desolate. Nita and Kit left their swimsuits under a prominent boulder and slid into the chilly water. Nita changed first and let Kit take hold of her dorsal fin and be towed out to deeper

132

water. She shuddered once, not knowing why, at the strange cool feeling of human hands on her hide as she swam outward.

Beyond the breakers, the water was peculiarly still. The sky was cobalt with a hint of dawn-silver in it; the sea was sheenless, shadowless, the colour of lead. And rising up from the listless water, four or five hundred yards from shore, a tall white fin was cruising in steady, silent circles, like the sail of a ghost ship unable to make port.

'I didn't think Ed was going to be here,' Kit said. He let go of Nita's fin and slipped off into the water.

'Neither did I,' Nita said, not knowing if he heard her before he dived. When he was finished changing, she dived too and made her way toward where Ed swam serenely.

S'reee was there as well. She swam close, whistling Nita a greeting, and brushed skin with her. Hotshot was there too, gamboling and swooping in the dim-lit water – though with just a little more restraint than usual around the silently drifting bulk of Ed.

'A long swim today,' S'reee said to Nita. 'Up to Nantucket. Are you ready? Did you get your problem with your dam and sire worked out?'

'Not really,' Nita said. 'In fact, it'll probably get a lot worse before it gets any better. There's going to be trouble tonight . . .' She stopped; there was no use letting it spoil the day. 'Never mind,' she said. 'Let's go.'

S'reee led the way, a straight course east-northeast, to Nantucket Rips. From her reading and from what the Sea told her, Nita knew those were treacherous waters, full of sudden shelves and hidden rocks. And the wizard's manual spoke of uneasy 'forces' that lingered about those dead and broken ships – forces Nita suspected she would mistake for restless ghosts, if she should have the bad luck to see one.

'You are silent today,' said a dry, cool voice directly above Nita. Glancing upward, Nita saw floating above her, effortlessly keeping pace, the great pale form that had been one of the images keeping her awake last night. 'And you did not greet me. Is this courtesy to another celebrant?'

'Good morning, Ed,' Nita said, in the same mildly edgy tone of voice she would have used on a human being who bugged her that way.

'Oh, indeed,' Ed said. 'You're bold, Sprat. And the boldness comes of distress. Beware lest I be forced to hurry matters, so that we should have even less time to get acquainted than you seem to desire.'

'That was something I was meaning to ask you about,' Nita said, looking up at Ed again. 'The "distress" business—'

'Ask, Sprat.'

'You said before that it was your "job" to end distress where you found it . . .'

'You are wondering who gave me the job,' Ed said, sinking to Nita's level, so that her left-side eye was filled with the sight of him. 'Perhaps it was the Sea itself, which you wizards hear speaking to you all the time. You look askance? Doubtless you think the Sea would be too "good" to assign a whole species to nothing but painful and violent killing.' Ed's voice stayed cool as always, though there was a tinge of mockery to it. 'If you think so, look around you, Sprat. The ocean is full of weaponry as effective as my teeth. Poisons and spines, snares and traps and claws that catch are everywhere. We all have to eat.'

Ed smiled at her. A long shiver went down Nita from head to tail; a shark's smile is an expression the wise person does not provoke. 'Those are just dumb creatures, though,' she said, keeping her song as inoffensive-sounding as possible. 'They don't think.

134

You do – and you *enjoy* what you do.'

'So?' Ed swam closer. 'How should I not? Like all my people I'm built to survive in a certain fashion . . . and it's only wise to cause what you build to feel good when it does what it must to survive. My nerves are tuned to pain. That fact tells me beyond question what my job is. Distress calls me; blood in the water is the clearest sign of that distress, and I have a duty to it. If I destroy, still I serve life. What can't elude me is often sick or injured, and suffering; what survives me or out-thinks me is stronger and wiser for it. And the survivor's descendants will be too. Is that so bad?'

'Well, that way . . . no. But I bet you wouldn't be so calm about it if it was *you* dying.'

'Me? Die?' Ed laughed again. 'The Master-Shark eats the Silent Lord's "Gift", you know, along with the Silent One. There's immortality in all the sharks, in various degrees. But what good is immortality if you haven't died first? And nothing in the Sea is deadly enough to kill me against my will.'

Something about Ed's voice was making Nita curious. 'What about with it?'

'Ah, but will must spread to the body from the mind. And after all the years I've lived in it, my body is too strong. All it wants is to eat, and live. And so it does; and I swim on. Immortality is of terrible power. It would take something more powerful yet to override it . . .'

Nita didn't say anything.

'But all that being so,' Ed said, 'for good or ill, I am the Destroyer. Being that, I might as well enjoy my work, might I not? And so I do. Would it help if I decided to be miserable?' There was actually a touch of humour in that cold, dry voice.

'No, I suppose not.'

'So I go about my work with a merry heart,' Ed

said, 'and do it well as a result. That should please you, I think—'

'I'm delighted,' Nita sang, under her breath.

'—for spells work best, you wizards tell me, when all the participants are of light heart and enjoying themselves. I'll certainly enjoy eating *you* when the time comes 'round.'

'Ed, that's not funny.'

'It isn't?' said the Master-Shark, looking at her.

Nita stopped swimming, letting herself coast for a moment. There was something odd about the way he'd said that— 'Ed, what was that crack supposed to mean?'

The look Ed gave her was expressionless as ever. 'The Silent Lord is pleased to jest with me,' he said.

'Ed!'

'Distress, distress, Sprat. Have a care.'

Ed was drifting closer again, and Nita kept herself as outwardly calm as she could. 'Ed,' she said, slowly and carefully, 'are you trying to say that you're actually planning to *eat* me some time soon?'

'The day after tomorrow,' said the Master-Shark in perfect calm, 'if we keep to schedule.'

Nita couldn't think of a thing to say.

'You seem surprised,' Ed said. 'Why?'

It took Nita a few moments to answer, for her mind was boiling with sudden memories. S'reee's great relief when Nita agreed to participate in the Song. Her repeated questions to Nita about whether she was sure she wanted to do this. The Blue's silent, sad appraisal and approval of her. S'reee's remark about the Silent Lord's contribution to the Song being the most important of any celebrant – 'the Silent Lord has the most at stake.' And the wording of the Celebrant's Oath itself, with its insistent repetition and the line Nita had been so sure was

136

ceremonial: *'and I will blend my blood with theirs should there be need . . .'*

Nita gulped. 'Ed,' she said, 'the Song, the whole thing . . . I thought it was just sort of, sort of a play . . .'

'Indeed not.' Ed seemed unconcerned by her terror. 'There's always blood in the water at the end of the Song. I am no wizard, but even I know that nothing else will keep the Lone Power bound. Nothing but the willing sacrifice, newly made by the Celebrant representing the Silent One – by a wizard who knows the price he is paying and what it will buy. The spells worked during the Song would be powerless otherwise, and the Lone Power would rise again and finish what It once began.'

'But—' Off on her right, she saw Kit looking curiously at her. But at the moment Kit meant nothing to her, and neither did Ed, or the chill silver light dawning in the water, or anything else. The manual's words, which she'd skimmed over so casually: those were what mattered now. *The whale singing the Silent One then enacts the Sacrifice in a manner as close to the original enactment as possible, depending on the site where the Song is being celebrated. The shark singing the Pale Slayer then receives the Sacrifice* . . . With frightful clarity she could remember sitting on the fishing platform off Tiana Beach and S'reee saying, 'The Silent One dived into a stand of razor coral; and the Master-Shark smelled her blood in the water, and . . . well . . .'

Nita started to swim, without any real idea of where she was going, or why she was going there. She went slowly at first, then faster. 'Neets,' Kit was singing behind her, 'what's wrong, what is it?'

'HNii't!' sang another voice, farther away. 'Wait! What's the matter?'

That voice she wanted to hear some more from. Nita wheeled about and hurtled back the way she had come, almost ramming Kit, and not caring, letting him get out of her way as best he could. S'reee saw Nita coming and simply stopped swimming. 'S'reee!' Nita cried, one long note that was more a scream than a song. 'Why didn't you tell me!'

'Oh, hNii't,' S'reee sang, desperate and hurried, 'the Master-Shark is about – for Sea's sake, control yourself!'

'Never mind him! *Why didn't you tell me!*'

'About what the Silent One does?' S'reee said, sounding confused and upset as Nita braked too late and almost hit her too. 'But you said you knew!'

Nita moaned out loud. It was true. *Just about finished with my reading,* she remembered herself saying. *Only one thing I don't understand; everything else is fairly straightforward* . . . And, *I got it, S'reee, let's get on with it* . . . But the truth didn't break her rage. 'You should have made sure I knew what you were talking about!'

'Why?' S'reee cried, getting angry herself now. 'You're a more experienced wizard than *I* am! You went into the Otherworlds and handled things by yourself that it'd normally take whole circles of wizards to do! And I warned you, make sure you know what you're doing before you get into this! But you went right ahead!'

Nita moaned again, and S'reee lost her anger at the sound and moaned too. 'I knew something bad was going to happen,' she sang unhappily. 'The minute I found Ae'mhnuu dead and me stuck with organizing the Song, I knew! But I never thought it'd be anything as bad as *this*!'

Kit looked from one of them to the other, somewhat at a loss. 'Look,' he said to S'reee, 'are you telling me that the whale who sings the Silent One actually has to *die*?'

S'reee simply looked at him. Nita did not look at him, could not.

'That's horrible,' Kit said in a hushed voice. 'Nita, you can't—'

'She must,' S'reee said. 'She's given her word that she would.'

'But couldn't somebody else—'

'Someone else could,' S'reee said. 'If that person would be willing to take the Oath and the role of the Silent Lord in hNii't's place. But no-one will. What other wizard are we going to be able to find in the space of a day and a half who would be willing to die for Nita's sake?'

Kit was silent with shock.

'Anyway, hNii't took the Oath freely in front of witnesses,' S'reee said unhappily. 'Unless someone with a wizard's power freely substitutes himself for her, she has to perform what she's promised. Otherwise the whole Song is sabotaged, useless – can't be performed at all. And if we don't perform it, or if something goes wrong . . .'

Nita closed her eyes in horror, remembering the time the Song failed. What Atlantis couldn't survive, she thought in misery, New York and Long Island certainly won't. Millions of people will die. Including Mum and Dad, Dairine, Ponch, Kit's folks—

'But the Song hasn't started yet,' Kit protested.

'Yes, it has,' Nita said dully. *That* she remembered very clearly from her reading; it had been in the commentaries, one of the things she found strange. 'The minute the first Celebrant takes the Oath, the Song's begun – and everything that happens to every Celebrant after that is part of it.'

'HNii't,' S'reee said in a voice so small that Nita

139

could barely hear her, 'what will you do?'

A shadow fell over Nita, and a third and fourth pair of eyes joined the first two: Hotshot, grinning as always, but with alarm behind the grin; Ed, gazing down at her out of flat black eyes, emotionless as stones. 'I thought I sensed some little troubling over here,' said the Master-Shark.

Kit and S'reee held still as death. 'Yes,' Nita said with terrible casualness, amazed at her own temerity.

'Is the pain done?' said the Master-Shark.

'For the moment,' Nita said. She could feel herself slipping into shock, an insulation that would last her a few hours at least. She'd felt something similar, several years before, when her favourite uncle had died. The shock had got Nita through the funeral; but afterwards, it had been nearly two weeks before she had been able to do much of anything but cry. I won't have that option this time, she thought. There's work to be done, a Song to sing, spells to work . . . But all that seemed distant and unimportant to her, since in a day and a half, it seemed, a shark was going to eat her. Kit looked at Nita in terror, as if he suddenly didn't know her. She stared back, feeling frozen inside. 'Let's go,' she said, and turned to start swimming east-northeast again, their original course. 'The Grey is waiting, isn't she?'

By the sound of her way-song Nita could hear S'reee and Kit and Hotshot following after her; and last of all, silent, songless, came Ed.

I'm going to die, Nita thought.

She had thought that before, occasionally. But she had never believed it.

She didn't believe it now.

And she knew it was going to happen anyway.

Evidently, Nita thought, Ed had been right when he'd said that belief made no difference to the truth . . .

THE GREY LORD'S SONG

They found the whale who would sing the part of the Grey in the chill waters about Old Man Shoals, a gloomy place strewn full of boulders above which turbulent water howled and thundered. The current set swift through the shoals, and the remnants of its victims lay everywhere. Old splintered spars of rotting masts, fragments of crumbled planks, bits of rusted iron covered with barnacles or twined about with anemones; here and there a human bone, crusted over with coral— Broken-backed ships lay all about, strangled in weed, ominous shapes in the murk; and when Nita and Kit and the others sang to find their way, the songs fell into the silence with a wet, thick, troubled sound utterly unlike the clear echoes that came back from the sandy bottoms off Long Island.

The place suited Nita's mood perfectly. She swam low among the corpses of dead ships, thinking bitter thoughts – most of them centring on her own stupidity.

They warned me. *Everybody* warned me! Even Picchu warned me: *'Read the fine print before you sign!'* Idiot! she thought bitterly. What do I do now? *I don't want to die!*

But *'Any agreements you make, make sure you keep,'*

Tom had said – and though his voice had been kind, it had also been stern. As stern as the Blue's: *'Nowhere does the Lone Power enter in so readily as through the broken word.'*

She could see what she was expected to do . . . and it was impossible. I can't die – I'm too young, what would Kit say to Mum and Dad, I don't want to, it's not fair! But the answer stayed the same nonetheless.

She groaned out loud. Two days. Two days left. Two days is a long time. Maybe something will happen and I won't have to die.

'Stop that sniveling noise!' came a sharp, angry burst of song, from practically in front of her. Nita backfinned, shocked at the great bulk rising up from the bottom before her. The echoes of her surprised squeak came back raggedly, speaking of old scars, torn fins and flukes, skin ripped and gouged and badly healed. And the other's song had an undercurrent of rage to it that hit Nita like a deep dive into water so cold it burned.

'How dare you come into my grounds without protocol?' said the new whale as she cruised toward Nita with a slow deliberateness that made Nita back away even faster than before. The great head and lack of a dorsal fin made it plain that this was another sperm whale.

'Your pardon,' Nita sang hurriedly, sounding as conciliatory as possible. 'I didn't mean to intrude—'

'You have,' said the sperm, in a scraping phrase perilously close to the awful sperm whale battlecry that Nita had heard from Kit. She kept advancing on Nita, and Nita kept backing, her eye on those sharp teeth. 'These are *my* waters, and I won't have some noisy krill-eating songster scaring my food—'

That voice was not only angry, it was cruel. Nita started to get angry at the sound of it. She stopped backing up and held her ground, poising her tail for a short rush to ram the other if necessary. 'I'm not interested in your fish, even if they could hear me, which they can't – and you know it!' she sang angrily. 'Humpbacks sing higher than fish can hear – the same as you do!'

The sperm kept coming, showing more teeth. 'You look like a whale,' she said, voice lowering suspiciously, 'and you sing like a whale – but you don't sound like a whale. Who are you?'

'HNii't,' Nita said, giving her name the humpback accent. 'I'm a wizard. A human wizard—'

The sperm whale cried out and rushed at her, jaws wide. Nita arrowed off to one side, easily avoiding the sperm's rush. 'Spy! Murderer!' The sperm was howling, a terrible rasping song like a scream. It came at her again—

Again Nita rolled out of the way, her manoeuvrability easily defeating the other's rage-blinded charge. 'I may be a human,' she sang angrily, 'but I'm still a wizard! Mess with me and I'll—'

WHAM! The sperm whale's spell hit her with an impact that made the displaced-water explosions of Kit's shapechanges seem puny. Nita was thrown backwards, literally head over tail, thrashing and struggling for control as she swore at herself for being caught off guard. The spell was a simple physical-violence wizardry, as contemptuous a gesture from one wizard to another as a slap in the face . . . and as much a challenge to battle as such a slap would have been from one human to another.

Nita went hot with rage, felt about for her inner contact with the Sea, found it, and sang – only three notes, but pitched and prolonged with exquisite accuracy to take the power of the other's spell and turn it back on her tenfold. The spell and the water thundered together. The sperm whale was blown backwards as Nita had been, but with more force, tumbling violently and trailing a song of shock and rage behind her.

Nita held still, shaking with anger, while S'reee and Hotshot and Kit gathered around her. 'I'm all right,' she said, the trembling getting into her song. 'But that one needs some lessons in manners.'

'She always has,' S'reee said. 'HNii't, I'm sorry. I would have kept you back with us, but—' She didn't go on.

'It's all right,' Nita said, still shaking.

'Nice shot,' said a low scrape of song beside her ear, angry and appreciative: Kit. She brushed him lightly with one flank as a great pale shape came drifting down on the other side of her, eyeing her with dark-eyed interest.

'So,' Ed said, calm as ever, 'the Sprat has teeth after all. I am impressed.'

'Thanks,' Nita said, not up to much more conversation with Ed at the moment.

Slowly they swam forward together to where S'reee was hovering in the water, singing more at than with the other whale. '—know you were out of bounds, Areinnye,' she said. 'There was no breach of protocol. We came in singing.'

'That one did not,' said the sperm whale, her song so sharp with anger that it was a torture to the ears. 'My right—'

'—does not extend to attacking a silent member of a party entering your waters within protocols,' S'reee said. 'You attacked hNii't out of spite, nothing more. First spite, then anger because she was human. We heard—'

'Did you indeed? And what else have you heard in these waters, you nursling wizard, you and your little playfellows?' The sperm whale glared at them all as they gathered around her, and the rasp of pain and hatred in her voice was terrible. 'Have you seen my

144

calf hereabouts? For all your magics, I think not. The whalers have been through these waters three days ago, and they served my little M'hali as they served your precious Ae'mhnuu! Speared and left to float belly-up, slowly dying, while they hunted me – then hauled bloated out of the water and gutted, his bleeding innards thrown overboard by bits and pieces for the gulls and the sharks to eat!'

When S'reee spoke again, her voice was unhappy. 'Areinnye, I share your grief. It's things like this that the Song will help to stop. That's why we're here.'

The sperm whale laughed, a sound both anguished and cruel. 'What lies,' she said. 'Or what delusions. Do you truly think *anything* will make them go away and stop hunting us, S'reee?' Areinnye looked with hatred at Nita. 'Now they're even coming into the water after us, I see.'

Kit glided forward ever so slowly, until he was squarely between Nita and Areinnye. 'I guarantee you don't know what she's here for, Areinnye. Preserving your life, along with those of a lot of others – though at the moment, in *your* case, I can't imagine why anyone would bother.'

Areinnye made a sound at Kit that was the sperm whale equivalent of a sneer. 'Oh, indeed,' Areinnye said. 'What could she possibly do that would make any difference to my life?'

'She is the Silent Lord for the Song,' S'reee said.

Areinnye turned that scornful regard on Nita. 'Indeed,' the sperm said again. 'Well. We are finally getting something useful out of a human. But she doubtless had to be compelled to it. No human would ever give up its life for one of us, wizard or not. Or did you trick her into it?'

Gently, hardly stroking a fin, Ed soared toward Areinnye. 'Unwise,' he said. 'Most unwise, wizard, to scorn a fellow wizard so – whatever species she may belong to. And will you hold Nita responsible for all her species' wrongdoing, then? If you do that, Areinnye, I would feel no qualms about holding you responsible for various hurts done my people by yours over the years. Nor would I feel any guilt over taking payment for those hurts out of your hide, *now.*'

Areinnye turned her back on Ed and swam away, as if not caring what he said. 'You take strange sides, Slayer,' the sperm said at last, cold-voiced. 'The humans hunt those of your Mastery as relentlessly as they hunt us.'

'I take no sides, Areinnye,' Ed said, still following her. 'Not with whales, or fish, or humans, or any other Power in the Sea or above it. Wizard that you are, you should know that.' He was beginning to circle her now. 'And if I sing this Song, it is for the same reason that I have sung a hundred others: for the sake of my Mastery – and because I am pleased to sing. You had best put your distress aside and deal with the business we have come to discuss, lest something worse befall you.'

Areinnye turned slowly back toward the group. 'Well, if you've come to administer me the Oath,' Areinnye said to S'reee, 'you might as well get on with it. I was in the midst of hunting when you interrupted me.'

'Softly,' S'reee said. 'Your power is a byword all throughout these parts; I want it in the Song. But we're not so short of wizards that I'll include one who'll bring the High and Dry down on us. Choose, and tell me whether you can truthfully sing and leave your anger behind.'

Areinnye cruised slowly through the group, making no sound but the small ticking noises the sperm uses to navigate. 'Seeing that the human who sings with us sings for the Sea's sake,' she said at last, in that tight, flat voice, 'I am content. But my heart is bitter in me for my calf's loss, and I cannot forget that easily. Let the humans remember that, and keep their distance.'

'If that is well for you two—' Kit and Nita both flicked tails in agreement. 'Well enough, then,' said S'reee. *'Areinnye t'Hwio-dheii, those who gather to sing that Song that is the Sea's shame and the Sea's glory desire you to be of their company. Say, for my hearing, whether you consent to that Song.'*

'I consent . . .' Areinnye sang her way through the responses with slow care, and Nita began to relax slightly. The sperm's voice was beautiful, as pleasant as Kit's, when she wasn't angry. Yet she couldn't help but catch a couple of Areinnye's glances at Ed – as if she knew that she was being watched for her responses and would be watched in the future.

Then the third Question was asked, and Areinnye's song scaled up in the high notes of final affirmation, a sound of tearing, chilly beauty. *'Let me wander forever amid the broken and the lost, sooner than I shall refuse the Song.'* Areinnye sang, *'or what it brings about for the good of those who live.'* But there was a faint note of scorn in the last phrase, as if the singer already counted herself among the lost and broken; and the notes on 'those who live' twisted down the scale into a bitter diminuendo of pain that said life was a curse.

Now it was S'reee's turn to look dubious; but it was too late.

'Well,' the sperm said, 'when is the Foregathering? And where?'

'Tomorrow dawn,' said S'reee, 'in the waters off the Hook. Will you be on time?'

'Yes,' Areinnye said. 'So farewell.' And she turned tail and swam off.

Kit flicked a glance at Ed and said quietly to Nita,

'Boy, *that* was a close one. If those two got started fighting . . .'

'It would not be anything like "close",' Ed said.

'OK, great,' Kit said in mild annoyance, 'she couldn't kill you. But isn't it just possible she might hurt you a little?'

'She would regret it if she did,' Ed said. 'Blood in the water will call in some sharks, true. But their *Master's* blood in the water will call them all in, whether they smell it or not . . . every shark for thousands of lengths around. That is *my* magic, you see. And whatever the Master-Shark might be fighting when his people arrived would shortly not be there at all, except as rags and scraps for fingerlings to eat.'

Nita and Kit and S'reee looked at each other.

'Why do we need Areinnye in the first place?' Nita said to S'reee. 'Is she really that good a wizard?'

Turning, S'reee began to swim back the way they had come, through the now-darkening water. Hotshot paced her; and silently, pale in the dimness, Ed brought up the rear. 'Yes,' S'reee said. 'In fact, by rights, she should have been Ae'mhnuu's apprentice, not I.'

Kit looked at her in surprise. 'Why wasn't she?'

S'reee made a little moan of annoyance. 'I don't know,' she said. 'Areinnye is a much more powerful wizard than I am – even Ae'mhnuu agreed with me about that. Yet he refused her request to study with him, not just once but several times. And now this business with her calf—' S'reee blew a few huge bubbles out her blowhole, making an unsettled noise. 'Well, we'll make it work out.'

'That shall yet be seen,' Ed said from behind them.

The moon was high when Nita and Kit came out of the water close to the jetty and went looking for their clothes. Kit spent a while gazing longingly up at the silver-golden disc, while Nita dressed. 'We're really going to get killed now, aren't we?' he said, so quietly that Nita could hardly hear him.

'Uh-huh.' Nita sat down on the sand and stared out at the waves while Kit went hunting for his bathing suit and wind-cheater.

'Whaddaya think they'll do?' Kit said.

Nita shook her head. 'No idea.'

Kit came up beside her, adjusting his wind-cheater. 'You think they're going to send me home?'

'They might,' she said.

They toiled up the last dune before home and looked down toward the little rough road that ran past the house. All the upstairs lights were on. The downstairs ones were dark; evidently Dairine had been sent to bed.

'Neets—' Kit said. 'What're *you* going to do?'

'I'm sworn, Kit. I'm in the Song. I have to be there.'

'You mean you're going to—'

'Don't,' she said, in genuine pain. She didn't want him to say it, to think it, any more than she wanted to think it herself. And to tell the absolute truth, she wasn't sure of what she was going to do about the Song yet.

'They don't need me for the Song,' Kit said.

'It doesn't look that way.'

'Yeah.' He was quiet a moment. 'Look – if somehow I can get you off the hook, get your parents to think this is all my fault somehow, so that you can still go out . . .'

'No,' Nita said, scandalized. 'Anyway, they'd never buy it. I promised my mum I'd be back on time last time – and blew it. Then I sneaked out today. They know it's me as much as you. I'm just going to have to face the music.'

'With what?' Kit said.

'I don't know.' The thought of treating her parents as enemies made her feel as if the bottom had fallen out of the Universe.

The one good thing, she thought, is that by tomorrow, tonight will be over.

I hope.

'Come on,' she said. Together they went home.

The house was deadly still when they stepped in, and the screen door closing behind them seemed loud enough to be heard for miles around. The kitchen was dark; light flowed into it from the living room, the subdued illumination of a couple of table lamps. There was no sound of TV, even though Nita knew her dad's passion for late-night films; no music, despite her mum's fondness for classics and symphonic rock at any hour of day or night.

Nita's mouth felt dry as beach sand. She stopped where she was, tried to swallow, looked at Kit. He looked back, punched her lightly in the arm, then pushed past her and walked into the living room.

For the rest of her life, Nita thought, she would remember the way that room looked and felt when she walked in. The living room needed a new paint job; its rug was threadbare in places, and the walls were hung with bargain-basement seascapes, wide-eyed children of almost terminal cuteness, and, in one corner, something her dad called the Piece of Resistance – a garish matador done in day-glo paint on black velvet.

Her mother and father were sitting side by side on the Coca-Cola-coloured couch, their backs straight. They looked up as Nita and Kit came through the door, and Nita saw her mother's face tight with fear and her father's closed like a door. They had been reading magazines; they put them aside, and the usually friendly room suddenly looked dingy as a prison, and the matador hurt Nita's eyes.

'Sit down,' her father said. His voice, quiet, calm, sounded too much like Ed's. She managed to hold on to her composure as she headed for Dairine's favourite chair and sat down quickly.

'Pretty slick,' said her father. 'My daughter appears to have a great future in breaking and entering. Or breaking and departing.'

Nita opened her mouth and shut it again. She could have dealt with a good scolding . . . but this chilly sarcasm terrified her. And there was no way out of it.

'Well?' her father said. 'You'd better start coming up with some answers, young lady. You too,' he said to Kit, his eyes flashing; and at the sight of the anger, Nita felt a wash of relief. That look was normal. 'Because what you two say is going to determine whether we send you straight home tomorrow morning, Kit – and whether we let you and Nita see any more of each other.'

Kit looked her father straight in the eye and said nothing.

Sperm whales! Nita thought, and it was nearly a curse. But then she took the thought back as she realized that Kit was waiting for her to say something first, to give him a lead. Great! Now all I have to do is *do* something!

What do I do?

'Kit,' her father said, 'I warn you, I'm in no mood for Latin gallantry and the whole protect-the-lady business. You were entrusted to my care and I want answers. Your parents are going to hear about this in any case – what you say, or don't say, is going to determine what I tell them. So be advised.'

'I understand,' Kit said. Then he glanced at Nita. 'Neets?'

Nita shook her head ever so slightly, amazed as always by that frightened bravery that would wait for her to make a move, then back her utterly. It had nothing to do with the whalesark. Kit, Nita thought, practically trembling with the force of what she felt, you're incredible! But I don't have your guts – and I have to do something!

Her mother and father were looking at her, waiting.

Oh, Lord, Nita thought then, and bowed her head and put one hand over her face, for she suddenly knew what to do.

She looked up. 'Mum,' she said – and then had to start over, for the word came out in a kind of strangled squeak. 'Mum, you remember when we were talking the other day? And you said you wanted to know why we were staying out so much, because you thought something besides "nothing" was going on?'

Her mother nodded, frozen-faced.

'Uh, well, there was,' Nita said, not sure where to go from there. Two months of wizardry, spells wrought and strange places visited and wonders seen – how to explain it all to nonwizards? Especially when they might not be able to see wizardry done right under their eyes – and in the past hadn't? Never mind that, Nita told herself desperately. If you think too much, you'll get cold feet. Just talk.

Her mother was wearing a ready-to-hear-the-worst expression. 'No, not *that*,' Nita said, feeling downright cross that her mother was still thinking along *those* idiotic lines. 'But this is going to take a while.'

Nita swallowed hard. 'You remember in the spring,' she said, 'that day Kit and I went into the city – and that night, the sun went out?'

Her parents stared at her, still angry, and now slightly perplexed too.

'We had something to do with that,' Nita said.

TRUTHSONG

And Nita began to tell them. By the time she saw from their faces just how crazy the story must be sounding, it was already much too late for her to stop.

She told them the story from the beginning – the day she had her hand snagged by an innocent-looking library book full of instructions for wizardry – to the end of her first great trial, and Kit's, that terrible night when the forces of darkness got loose in Manhattan and would have turned first the city and then the world into a place bound in eternal night and cold, except for what she and Kit did. She told them about Advisory and Senior wizards, though she didn't mention Tom and Carl; about places past the world where there was nothing but night, and about the place past life where there was nothing but day.

Not once did her parents say a word.

Mostly Kit kept quiet, except when Nita's memory about something specific failed; then he spoke up and filled in the gap, and she went on again. The look on her father's face was approaching anger again, and her mother was well into complete consternation, by the time Nita started telling them about the dolphin who nudged her in the back, the whale she and Kit found on the beach, and the story the whale had told

153

them. She told them a little – very little, fearing for her own composure – about the Song of the Twelve and what she was going to be doing in it.

And then, not knowing what else to say, she stopped.

Her mother and father looked at each other.

Our daughter, the look said, is going to have to be hospitalized. She's sick.

Nita's mother finally turned to her. Her dad had bowed his head about a third of the way through the story, and except for that glance at her mother seemed unable to do anything but sit with his hands clasped tightly together. But her mother's face was stricken.

'Nita,' she said, very gently – but her voice was shaking like the tightly clasped hands of the man beside her, 'you don't have to make up stories like this to keep us from being angry with you.'

Nita's mouth fell open. 'Mum,' she said, 'are you trying to say you don't believe me?'

'Nita,' her father said. His eyes were haunted, and his attempt to keep his voice sounding normal was failing miserably. 'Give us a break. How are we supposed to believe a crazy story like this? Maybe you've got Kit believing it—' He broke off, as if wanting to find a way to explain all this, something reasonable. 'I suppose it's understandable, he's younger than you . . .'

Nita glanced over at Kit for the first time in a while and gulped. His annoyed look brought the sperm whale battlecry scraping through her memories again.

'*I'll* tell you how you're supposed to believe it,' Kit said.

Nita's mother and father looked at him.

Kit was suddenly sitting a little taller in the chair. And taller still, though he didn't move a muscle. And taller – until Nita could see that Kit's seat and the seat of the chair no longer had much to do with each other. He was hovering about two feet in the air.

'Like *this*,' Kit said.

Holding her breath, Nita looked from Kit to her parents.

They stared at Kit, their faces absolutely unmoved, as if waiting for something. Kit glanced over at Nita, shrugged, and kept floating up until he was sitting six feet or so above the floor. 'Well?' he said.

They didn't move a muscle.

'Harry—' Nita's mother said, then, after what seemed forever.

He didn't say a thing.

'Harry,' her mother said, 'I hate to admit it, but I think all this has got to me . . .'

Nita's father simply kept looking at the chair.

Then, ever so slowly, he leaned his head back and looked up at Kit.

'Hypnosis,' Nita's father said.

'Bull!' Kit said. 'When did I hypnotize you?'

Nita's father didn't say anything.

'I haven't said a thing,' Kit said. 'If I hypnotized you without lights or words or anything, that's a pretty good trick, isn't it? You two better talk to each other and see if you're seeing the same thing. If you aren't, maybe I *did* hypnotize you. But if you *are*—'

Nita's mother and father looked away from Kit with some effort. 'Betty . . .' said Nita's father.

Neither of them said anything further for a few seconds.

'Harry,' her mother said at last, 'if I told you that I saw . . . saw Kit . . .' She stopped and swallowed. Then she started again, and the same feeling that had shaken Nita earlier about Kit took hold of her and shook her about her mother. Evidently bravery came in odd forms, and out of unexpected places. 'If I told you that I saw Kit not sitting in the chair any more,' her mother said, all at once and in a rush. Then her voice gave out on her.

'Above it,' her dad said. And that was all he could manage.

They stared at each other.

'You got it,' Kit said.

Nita's dad broke away from looking at her mother and glared at Nita instead. 'Hypnosis,' her father said. 'There's no other explanation.'

'Yes, there *is!*' Nita hollered at him, waving her arms in frustration, 'but you don't want to admit it!'

'Nita,' her mother said.

'Sorry,' Nita said. 'Look, Kit . . . this isn't going to do it. We need something more impressive.' She got up. 'Come on,' she said. 'Outside. It's my turn.'

Nita yanked the front door open and ran outside, up the dune and down its far side toward the beach. There was a long pause before she heard the sound of footsteps following her down the wooden steps. Shock, she thought, feeling both pity and amusement. If only there was some easier way! But there wasn't . . . She made it down to the beach, picked the spot she wanted, then stood and waited for them to arrive.

First her mother, then her father, came clambering up the dune and slid down its far side, to stand on the beach and stare up and down it, looking for her. Then Kit appeared beside them in a small clap of air that startled her mother so badly she jumped. Her father stared.

'Sorry,' Kit said, 'I should have warned you.' He was still sitting crosslegged in the air, and Nita noticed that he didn't sound very sorry either.

'Oh, Lord,' said Nita's father at the sight of Kit, and then turned resolutely away. 'All right. Where's Nita?'

'Over here, Daddy,' Nita called from where she was standing on the water, just past the line of the breakers.

He stared at Nita. So did Nita's mother, who

slowly went to stand beside her husband. Her voice was shaking as she said, 'Harry, it could be that my eyes are just going . . .'

'Mum,' Nita shouted, 'give me a break; you both went to the optician last month and you were fine!' She bounced up and down on the water several times, then took a few long strides to the west, turned, and came back. 'Admit it! You see me walking on water! Well, surprise: I *am* walking on water! Get it! It's like I told you: I'm a wizard!'

'Nita,' her father said, 'uh, walking on water is, uh—'

'I know,' she said. 'I wouldn't want to overdo it. It makes my legs hurt.' Nita trotted back in to shore, taking a last hop on to the curl of a flattening breaker and letting it push her up on to the beach and strand her there, a few feet in front of them.

Kit uncrossed his legs, got his feet back on the ground, and came to stand beside her. 'So what else would you like to see?' he said.

Her parents looked at each other, then down at the two of them. 'Look, Kit, Nita,' her father said unhappily, 'it's not a question of what we'd like to see. At this point I'm sure you two could get us to "see" anything you wanted to . . . Heaven knows how. But that's not the point. This can't be – none of this is *real!*'

'Want to bet?' Kit said softly. 'Neets, this is going to call for drastic measures.'

'I think you're right. Well, let's see what the manual says about this. Book, please,' she said, thinking the six words of a spell she knew by heart and putting her hand out. Another small clap of air, about as noisy as a cap going off, and her wizard's manual dropped into her hand. Her mother goggled. Nita opened the manual and began browsing through it. 'Let's see . . .'

'You two just stop making things pop in and out for a moment, and listen to me,' Nita's mother said all of a sudden. 'Nita, I want to know where this power came from! You two haven't made a pact with, with—'

Nita thought of her last encounter with the Lone Power and burst out laughing. 'Oh, Mum! Kit and I are the *last* people *that* One wants anything to do with.'

Her mother looked nonplussed. 'Well, that's – never mind, you'll tell me about that some other time. But, honey, why, why?'

'You mean, "Why are there wizards?" Or "Why are *we* wizards?"' Nita said. 'Or do you really mean "What's in it for us?"'

'Yes,' her mother said, sounding lost.

Nita and Kit looked at each other, and Kit shook his head. 'We're never going to be able to explain this,' he said.

She agreed with him. 'Only one thing we can do, I suppose,' Nita said, musing.

'Show them?'

Nita looked at Kit, and for the first time in what seemed days, a smile began to grow. 'Remember that place we went a week and a half ago?' she said. 'The one with the great view?'

'I'll get my book,' he said, grinning back, 'and the string.'

'Don't forget the chip!' Nita said, but Kit had already gone out, *bang!* just like a candle, and Nita was talking to empty air. She turned to her mother and father. 'He went to get some supplies,' she said. 'Most wizardry you need things for – raw materials, kind of.'

'Fine, honey,' her mother said, 'but does he have to keep appearing and disappearing like that?'

'It's faster than walking,' Nita said. 'And we

haven't got all night. He and I are going to have to be out early again tomorrow morning—'

'Nita!' said her father.

She went to him and put her arms around him. 'Please, Dad,' she said, 'let it be for a little while. We told you why. But you have to feel this first. It won't make sense unless you do. In fact, it may never make sense. Just trust me!'

Kit popped back out of nothing, making Nita's mother jump again. 'Sorry, Mrs Callahan,' he said. 'It's fun, that's all. It's a "beam-me-up-Scotty" spell. So's this one we're going to do. Just a little more involved.' He dropped the necessary supplies on the sand – a small coil of cord, an old silicon chip salvaged from a broken pocket calculator, a grey stone. Then he started going through his own manual.

Nita looked down at the stone Kit had brought. 'Good idea,' she said. 'Shorthand, huh?'

'It remembers the way. Should save some work. Good thing, too . . . we've got two more sets of variables this time. Get the figures for me, will you?'

'Right.' Nita held out her book a bit as she went through it, so that her mother and father could look over her shoulder. 'See, Mum? Dad? It's just an instruction manual, like I said.'

'I can't read it,' her father said, staring at the graceful strokes of the written form of the Speech. 'What is it, Arabic?'

'No,' she said. 'No Earthly language. At least, not strictly Earthly. A lot of the forces we work with don't have names in any language on Earth – or they only have vague ones. You can't be vague about magic.'

'Good way to get killed,' Kit said from where he knelt in the sand, scribbling with a stick and sounding cheerful. 'Mr Callahan, Mrs Callahan, don't step on any of these things I'm writing in the sand, or we'll all be in big trouble. Mrs Callahan, what's your birthday?'

'April twenty-eighth,' said Nita's mother.

'Mr Callahan?'

'July seventh,' said Nita's father.

'Neets, how big a circle?'

'Half a second,' Nita said. 'Brighter,' she said to her manual. Its pages began to glow softly in the dark. 'OK, here we are. Four of us . . . about a cubic foot of air for each breath. Allow for excitement – say thirty breaths a minute. Times four . . .' She turned to another page. 'Start,' she said, and heard over her shoulder her mother's quick intake of breath as the page Nita had opened to abruptly went blank. 'Print one two zero times four.' A set of characters appeared. 'OK, print four eight zero times twenty . . . Good. Print nine six zero zero divided by three . . . Great. Cubic metres . . . uhh . . . Oh, blast. Kit, what's the volume of a cylinder again?'

'V equals pi times r squared times the height.'

'That's it. Now how did I do this before?' Nita chewed her lip a little, thinking. 'OK,' she said to the book, 'print three point one four one seven times, uh, three zero.' A figure flickered at her. 'No, that is not a number,' she said to the book. 'Times three zero, and don't get cute with me . . . OK. Print square root parenthesis three two zero zero divided by nine four point two five one close parentheses. Great. End. Kit? Make it thirty-six feet wide.'

'Got it,' Kit said. 'Mrs Callahan, would you stand on this string, please? And whatever happens, don't go near the edge of the circle after I close it.' He started to walk around them all, using Mrs Callahan and the long knotted string as a compass. 'Neets? Come and check your name. And theirs; they can't do it—'

She stepped over to the circle and made sure that the Speech-characters describing herself and her parents were correct, then glanced over Kit's too for safety's sake. Everything was in order. Kit finished the circle he was making in the sand, closed it with the figure-eight design called a wizard's knot, and stood up. 'All set,' Nita said.

'Then let's go.' He opened his book; Nita went looking for the page in hers on which the spell was written. 'It's a "read" spell,' Nita said to her mother and father. 'That means it's going to be a few moments before it takes. Don't say anything, no matter what you feel or see or hear. Don't move, either.'

'You might want to hang on to each other,' Kit said. Nita gave him a wry grin; there had been occasions in the past when the two of them, terrified out of their wits, had done just that. 'Ready?'

'Go ahead,' said Nita's father, and reached out and pulled Nita's mother close.

Nita and Kit looked at each other and began slowly to read out loud. The strange, listening stillness of a working spell began to settle in around the four of them, becoming more pronounced with every word of the Speech, as the Universe in that area waited to hear what would be required of it. The wind dropped, the sound of the surf grew softer, even the breakers in the area became gentler, flatter, their hiss fading to a bare whisper . . .

The sense of expectation, of anticipation, of impatient, overwhelming *potential* grew all around them as the silence grew . . . slowly undergoing a transformation into a blend of delight and terror and power that could be breathed like air, or seen as a shading now inhabiting every colour, a presence inhabiting every shape.

Nita raised her voice into the stillness unafraid,

speaking the words of the spell formula, barely needing to look at her book. The magic was rising in her, pouring through her with dangerous power. But with the sureness of practice she rode the danger, knowing the wonder to which it would bring her, revelling in her defiance of her fear. And in more than that: for Kit was across the circle from her, eyes on hers, matching her word for word and power for power – peer and friend and fellow-wizard, afraid as she was, and still willing to dare, for the delight of what lay on the other side of the magic—

Almost through, Nita thought, exulting. Her words and Kit's wound about one another, wove together, binding the spell tighter around the circle – squeezing air in, squeezing power in, pushing inward with such force that the circle and its contents had no choice but to be somewhere else than they were.

Almost— Nita matched her words to Kit's with a laugh in her voice, rushing him, finding that she *couldn't* rush him because he had already matched pace to keep up with her— She laughed at being anticipated so. Faster and faster they went, like two kids seeing who could say the Pledge of Allegiance faster, as all around them the silence began to sing with inturned power, the air shimmered and rang with force like a gong ringing backwards, soft at first, then louder, though without sound, without breaking that silence – a hiss, a murmur, an outcry of something about to happen, a shout of inner voices, a silent thunderclap. And the last not-sound, so loud it unmade the world around them and struck them deaf and blind—

Then true silence again, with darkness above and whiteness below – but not the same darkness or whiteness as on the beach.

'We're here,' Nita whispered. 'Mum, Dad, have a look around. Don't go near the edges of the circle.'

'Be careful how you move,' Kit said. 'You only weigh a sixth of what you usually do. If your muscles overreact you could bounce right out of the circle. I almost did, first time.'

Nita watched her mother and father stare around them. She swallowed – partly out of reflex, for her ears were ringing in the silence that surrounded them now. That was to be expected; this stillness was more total than anything experienced on Earth. Her other reason for swallowing was more practical. The sudden transfer to one-sixth gravity tended to upset your stomach unless you were used to it.

Her father was staring at the ground, which had changed from wet beach sand to a mixture of greyish gravel and pebbles, and rocks the size of fists or melons, all covered with a grey-white dust as fine as talc. But Nita's mother was staring up at the sky with a look of joy so great it was pain – the completely bearable anguish of an impossible dream that suddenly comes true after years of hopeless yearning. Tears were running down her mother's face at the sight of that sky, so pure a velvet black that the eye insisted on finding light in it where light was not – a night sky set with thousands of stars, all blazing with a cold fierce brilliance that only astronauts ever saw; a night sky that nonetheless had a ravening sun standing noonday high in it, pooling all their shadows black and razor-sharp about their feet.

Nita was blinking hard herself to manage the stinging of her eyes; she knew how her mother felt. 'Over there, Mum,' she said very quietly. 'Off to the left. Look.'

'Off to the left' was a steep slope that plunged down and down to a deep chasm, filled with absolute blackness ungentled by the presence of air. On the far side of the chasm stretched a flat, rocky plain that seemed to stop too soon, running up against a horizon abnormally close. Out on the plain, not too far away, a dazzling squarish glow of gold sat on four spidery legs. Some thirty yards from the bright platform on legs stood a silvery pole with an American flag standing out from it, held straight by a rod running through the top of it: a necessity – for here where it stood, no wind would ever stir it.

'No,' Nita's father said, his voice hushed. 'Impossible. Tranquillity Base—'

'No,' Kit said, his voice soft too. 'That's going to be a tourist attraction in a few years, when they build the Hilton there – so we don't go down there for fear of leaving footprints where somebody might find them. This is from *Apollo 16*. See over there?' He pointed past the abandoned first-stage platform of the LEM *Orion* at the first Lunar Rover, which sat parked neatly beside a boulder – a delicate-looking little dunebuggy, still in excellent condition, used only once by a couple of astronauts from Pasadena for jaunts to Stone Mountain, on which the four of them stood.

Nita's father slowly went down on one knee and brushed his hand along the dry, pale lunar soil, turning over the stones that lay there, then picking one up and clutching it hard in his fist.

'Harry,' Nita's mother said, still looking up. The tone of her voice made her husband look up too – and seeing what she saw, he forgot the rock.

What they saw was part of a disc four times the size of the Moon as seen from the Earth; and it seemed even bigger because of the Moon's foreshortened horizon. It was not the full Earth so familiar from pictures, but a waning crescent, streaked with cloud swirls and burning with a fierce green-blue radiance – a light with depth, like the fire held in the heart of an opal. That light banished the idea that blue and green were 'cool' colours; one could have warmed one's hands at that crescent. The blackness to which it shaded was ever so faintly touched with silver – a disc more hinted at than seen; the new Earth in the old Earth's arms.

'There'll be a time,' Nita said softly, 'when any time someone's elected to a public office – before they let them start work – they'll bring whoever was elected up here and just make them look at that until they get what it means . . .'

Kit nodded. 'You wanted to know where the power came from,' he said to Nita's mother and father. 'The grownups who're wizards tell us that whatever made *that* made the power too. It's all of a piece.'

'"The *grownups* who're wizards"?'

'And as for "why",' Kit said, '*that's* why.' There was no need for him to point to 'that'. 'Not just for the – for what you felt on the way in. That's part of it. But because somebody's got to take care of *that*. Not just part of it – not just one country, or one set of rules, or one species, at the expense of the others. But everything that lives, all the kinds of "people". *All* of it, with nothing left out. One whole planet. Somebody's got to make sure it grows as well as it can. Or just that it survives. That's what wizards do.'

'Daddy,' Nita said, 'it's like you always say. If you don't do it yourself, it may not get done right. And we can't afford to let *that* get screwed up. We have to live there. So will other people, later.'

Her father shook his head, confused. 'Nita,' he said, sounding unsure, 'you're too young to be thinking about this kind of thing.'

She bit her lip. 'Dad – that sort of thinking might be one of the reasons why things aren't working so well back there . . .'

'Neets,' Kit said, 'we have to get back. We're losing heat pretty fast.'

165

'Mum, Dad,' Nita said. 'we can come back some other time. It's late, and Kit and I have an early day tomorrow. Got the rock?' she said to Kit.

'Uh-huh. Ready?'

Nita's mother reached out and pulled her husband close this time. 'Is it going to be like it was before?'

'Huh? No. It just takes a lot of effort to push all this air up out of Earth's gravity well, that's all. You have to reach escape velocity—'

Nita's father blinked. 'Wait a minute. I thought this was – magic.' He said the word as if for the first time in his life.

Nita shrugged. 'Even with magic,' she said, 'you have to obey the rules. Downhill is a lot easier than uphill in a wizardry, same as anywhere else. Kit?'

'Ready,' he said. They looked at each other, took a breath, and said one short word in unison.

WHAM! – and air and sand and water blew outward in all directions as they left noon for midnight, standing once again on the long dark beach silvered with moonlight. Kit stepped to the edge of the circle, first scuffing the wizard's knot out of existence, then going around and breaking the circle once at each compass point. 'Let's go in,' Nita said to her parents. 'I'm dead.'

The four of them trudged up the stairs to the front door, back into the living room. Her dad plopped down on to the couch and said, 'Nita, wait just a few minutes. I have to ask you something.'

Nita looked at him, sighed, and did as she was told. 'Tell me again,' her dad said, 'this stuff about what you're doing underwater. Just very briefly.'

It turned out to be more than briefly, since much of what Nita had told her parents had fallen out of their heads the first time, discarded in general disbelief. And it was with growing dismay that Nita watched the unease in her parents' faces, as she told them again about the undersea tremors, the pollution of the water, the slaughter of the whales – and the purposes of the Lone Power, though she tried to tell them as little about that as she could.

'Nita,' her father said at last, 'what are the chances that you could get hurt doing this "Song" business? The truth.'

She looked at him unhappily. 'Pretty good,' she said.

'And the same for Kit?' her mother said.

'Just about,' Kit said.

Nita's father shook his head. 'Nita. Look. I understand . . . no. I sort of understand how you and Kit feel about this. Magic . . .' He raised his hands, dropped them again, in a helpless gesture. 'If someone offered me the chance to be a magician, I'd jump at it . . .'

'A wizard,' Nita said. And, *No, you wouldn't*, she thought. Because if you would have, really, you would have been offered it! There are never enough wizards . . .

But her father was still talking. 'But this business . . . endangering yourself, or endangering Kit— Your mother and I can't permit it. You're going to have to bow out.'

For a moment, as far as Nita was concerned, everything faded out, drowned in a great wash of relief and hope. The perfect excuse. Perfect. My mum and dad won't let me. Sorry, S'reee, Hotshot, Ed . . .

Opaque black eyes looked at Nita out of the scene her eager mind was already constructing for her – and hope died. The hair stood up all over Nita – not from fear, but from something more terrible. Without any warning, and for the first time, she understood in her own person what had only been a word to her before: honour. *I can't*, she thought. *For me – for me* – it's not right.

'Dad,' she said unhappily, 'you didn't get it. I'm sworn to the Song. If I back out now, the whole thing will be sabotaged.'

Her father got up, a sign that he intended this argument to be over shortly. 'Come on, Neets. Surely someone else could do it—'

'No.'

'Nita,' said her mother, looking stern, 'you don't understand. *We're not letting you do this*. Or Kit either, while he's under our roof. You're going to have to find a replacement. Or the – the whales will. Whoever. *You're not going*.'

I must not have said it right, they're not understanding! 'Mum—' Nita said, searching frantically for words. 'This isn't just some cute thing that Kit and I are doing because it'll be fun! If we don't stop the forces that are beginning to move, there are going to be massive earthquakes all up and down the East Coast. That's not a maybe. It's a *will*! You think the Island would survive something like that? The whole place is nothing but rocks and rubbish the glaciers dumped in the ocean; it'll break up and wash away like a sandcastle at high tide! And you think Manhattan'll survive? It's already got four unstable geological faults of its own, right through the bedrock! And none of the buildings there are earthquake-proof; one quake'll leave the place looking like somebody kicked over a pile of bricks!' Nita was waving her arms in the air now, so upset that she was beyond caring whether she looked silly or not. 'Millions of people could die—'

'Could,' her father said, seizing on the word. He was pacing now.

Kit shook his head. '*Will*,' he said, and there was such a weight of certainty and misery on the word that Nita's father stopped pacing, and her mother closed her mouth, and they both stared at Kit in amazement. 'You're saying,' Kit said, gazing at them out of eyes suddenly gone dark and fierce, 'that you don't care whether ten million people, *more* than ten million people, would die, just so long as we two don't get hurt.'

Nita's mother spluttered, to Nita's great satisfaction. That one had sunk in. 'No, we aren't, we just—'

'You don't even care that ten million people *might* die,' Nita said. 'Just so Kit and I are OK, you're willing to run that risk.'

'No, I—' Nita's father saw what was being done to him. 'Young lady, no more out of you! Just the quakes going on off the coast now, by the reports we've heard, are too dangerous for you to be down there.'

'Daddy, believe me, we've survived a lot worse!'

'Yes – and your mother and I didn't know about it then! Now we do.' Her father turned away. 'The answer is no, and that's final!'

From many fights Nita had overheard between her parents, Nita knew that when her dad said that, it never was. 'Daddy,' she said. 'I'm sorry, I really am. I love you, and I wish like anything I could do what you want. But I *can't.*'

'*Nita!*' There was that rage again, full-blown, worse than before. Her father was on his feet, standing right over her, glaring at her. '*You will do as I tell you!*'

Hot all over, Nita shot to her feet – standing on the chair – and in sheer desperation shouted right back in his face. '*Don't you get it? There are some things in the world more important than doing what you tell me!*'

Her father and mother stared at her, stunned.

'Besides,' Kit said quietly from out of her range of vision, 'how would you stop us?'

Nita's father turned away to stare at Kit now.

'Look,' Kit said. 'Mr Callahan, Mrs Callahan – we

gave our word that we'd do this.' *What is this 'we'?* Nita thought, bemused. 'And the wizardry we're doing is mainly directed against the One who invented the broken promise. Breaking our word will play right into Its hands and cause a lot of people to die, at best. Maybe destroy this world, sooner or later, at worst.'

'But we have only your word on that!' Nita's mother said.

'Uh-huh. But isn't our word any good? And why would we lie to you about *this*? Considering that we're going through all this stuff for the sake of telling you the truth.'

Nita's mother closed her mouth.

'*She didn't have to tell you,*' Kit said, sounding angry for the first time. 'But it would've been lying, in a way – and Nita thinks you're worth not lying to.' He paused, then said, 'I do too. We may just be kids, but we're old enough to tell the truth. And to take it. Are you?'

The question wasn't a taunt: it was honestly meant. 'Even if you're not, we'll still have to do what we have to,' Nita said, though saying it made her unhappy. 'When you two wake up in the morning, this could all seem like a dream to you – if it had to. I suppose you'd better make up your minds, because we have to get some sleep or we won't be worth dead fish tomorrow.'

Her parents were staring at each other. 'Betty . . .' said Nita's father.

'We need more time,' Nita's mother said.

'I don't think we've got it.'

Her mother looked back at her father. 'If they're right about this,' she said, 'it would be wrong of us to stop them if they want to help.'

'But we're responsible for them!'

'Apparently,' Nita's mother said, in a peculiar

mixture of pride and pain, 'they've learned that lesson better than we suspected, Harry. Because now they seem to be making themselves responsible for *us*. And a lot of other people.'

'I guess there comes a time when you can't do anything but trust,' her father said at last, sounding reluctant. 'It just seems – so soon . . . Nita – is all this on the level?'

'Oh, Daddy.' She loved him, right then, and hurt for him, more than she could have told him. 'I wish it weren't. But it is.'

Nita's father was silent for several long breaths. 'Millions of lives,' he said under his breath.

And another silence, which he finally broke as if it were a physical thing. 'When do you need to be up?'

'Sixish. I'll set my alarm, Daddy.' Nita got stiffly down from the chair, aching all over. Behind her, Kit go up and brushed past her as Nita hugged first her dad goodnight. Maybe the last time she would ever hug him . . . or the second-to-the-last – Oh, don't think of that now!

Her mother had caught Kit on the way past and hugged him – and now wouldn't let Nita past without one either. She held her for a moment at arm's length. 'Thank you for – up there, baby,' she said, nodding once at the ceiling. Her eyes were wet, but she was smiling.

'It's OK, Mum. Any time.' Is this what it feels like when your heart breaks? Oh, Lord, don't let me cry.

'And thank you for trusting us.'

Nita swallowed. 'You taught me how,' she said. And then she couldn't stand it any more. She broke away and headed for her room, Kit right behind her.

She knew there was one hurdle left between her and bed. Actually, the hurdle was *on* the bed: sitting there crosslegged in the dark, looking at her with cool interest as they came in.

171

'Well?' Dairine said, as Nita flopped down on her stomach beside her, and the bed bounced them both once or twice. 'I saw you disappear. Where'd'ja take them?'

'The moon.'

'Oh, come *on*, Neets.'

'Dairine,' Kit said from the doorway. 'Catch.'

Nita glanced up, saw her sister reach up and pick something out of the air: an irregular piece of pale, grainy stone, about the size and shape of a rubber. Dairine peered at it, rubbing it between her fingers. 'What is this? Pumice?' There was a moment of shocked silence; then Dairine's voice scaled up to an aggrieved shriek. 'You *did* go to the moon! And you didn't take *me*! You, you—' Apparently she couldn't find anything sufficiently dirty to call them. '*I'm going to kill you!*'

'Dari, shut up, they're in shock out there!' Nita said. This argument did little to save her. Far more effective was Kit's wrestling Dairine down flat, stuffing her under the bedclothes and a couple of pillows, and more or less sitting on her until she shut up and stopped struggling.

'We'll take you next time,' Nita said, and then the pain hit her again. 'Kit,' she said, husky-voiced. 'Remind me to see that the runt here gets to the moon in the near future. Next week, maybe. If she behaves.'

'Right,' Kit said. 'You give up, runt?'

'Hwhmffm hnnoo rrhhrhn ffwmhhnhhuh,' said the blankets.

'Keep talking like that and your mouth'll get stuck that way,' Kit said, and let Dairine out.

Nita's sister extricated herself from the covers with icy dignity that lasted just until she was sitting where she had been, back in control and smoothing her ruffled pyjamas. 'Mum 'n' Dad didn't kill you,' she said to Nita.

'Nope. You gave me good advice, runt.'

'Huh? What advice?'

'Last night, I suspect,' Kit said. 'That stuff about "Either keep your mouth shut, or tell the truth—"'

Nita nodded, looking from Kit to Dairine, while Dairine modestly polished her nails on her Yoda pyjamas. And Nita stared at her, and then started to laugh, so hard that she got the hiccups and fell over sideways, and Dairine looked at her as if she'd gone nuts, and Kit sat down and punched her once or twice, worriedly, in the shoulder. 'Neets? You OK?'

'Oh, Kit,' she managed to gasp at last, between bubbles of laughter. 'What Picchu said—'

'Huh?'

'What Peach said. "Do what the night tells you—"' She went off into the giggles again.

Kit looked down at her, perplexed. 'You lost me.'

Nita pushed herself upright, reached out and tugged a couple of times, weakly, at one of Dairine's pyjama-sleeves. '*Do what the night tells you*. Not night like when it gets dark. Knight! Do what the *knight* tells you! As in the Junior Jedi here—' She went over sideways again and strangled her last few whoops of laughter in a convenient pillow.

'It *was* good advice,' he said to Dairine. 'Thanks, Dari.'

'Uh, sure,' said Dairine, amazed at another compliment.

Nita sat up again after a little while, wiping her eyes. 'Yeah,' she said. 'Even if I took it before I remembered *you* said it . . . it was good advice.' She thought she would let her sister have just one more compliment – especially since it was true, and information she might never have another chance to give her. 'You're going to be one hot wizard someday,' Nita said.

Dairine sat speechless.

'Neets,' Kit said, 'we've had a long day. And tomorrow'll be longer. I'm sacking out. Dairine—'

'Right,' Nita said. She lay down again, feeling glad, afraid, excited, shaky, light – a hundred things at once. She never noticed when Dairine got off her bed; she never heard Kit leave. She fell into sleep as if into a hole.

FOREGATHERING SONG

Nita sat hunched in a miserable little bundle on the beach, her arms around her knees – staring at the bright morning sea and not seeing it.

She had gone to bed with the feeling that everything would be all right when she woke up in the morning. But she'd awakened to a pair of parents torn among insane curiosity, worry, approval, and disapproval, who drank cup after cup of coffee and stared at the lump of lunar pumice in the middle of the table, and made little sense when they talked.

She hardly knew them. Her mum and dad alternated between talking to her, hanging on every word she said, and talking over her head about her, as if she weren't there. And they kept touching her like a delicate thing that might break – though there was an undercurrent of anger in the touches that said her parents had suddenly discovered she was in some ways stronger than they were, and they didn't like it.

Nita sighed. I'd give anything for one of Dad's hugs that squeeze the air out and make you go *squeak!* she thought. Or to hear Mum do Donald Duck voices at me. But fat chance of that . . .

She let out a long, unhappy breath. Kit was finishing his breakfast at a leisurely pace and handling endless questions about wizardry from her parents – covering for her. Just as well: she had other business to attend to before they left.

'Tom,' she said, almost mourning, under her breath. She had been down to Friedman's already and had 'minded the store' under Dog's watchful eye for a long time, waiting for Tom to return her call. She needed expert help, in a hurry. I've gone as far as I can on my own, she thought. I need advice! Oh, Tom, *where are you?*

As she'd expected. Nothing—

The last thing she expected was the sudden explosion of air that occurred about twenty feet down the beach from her, flinging sand in all directions. No, Nita corrected herself. The *last* thing she expected was what the explosion produced: a man with one towel wrapped around his waist and another draped around his neck – tall, broad-shouldered and narrow-waisted, with dark hair and the kind of face one sees in cigarette ads, but never hopes to see smile. It was not Tom, but Carl. He looked around him, saw Nita, and came over to her in a hurry, looking grave. 'What's the matter, Nita?' he said, casual as always, but concerned. 'I heard that even though it wasn't for me.'

She looked up at him wanly and tried to smile just a little; but the smile was a dismal failure. 'Uh, no. Look, no-one was answering the phone – and then I was just thinking—'

'That wasn't what I would call "just" thinking,' Carl said, sitting down on the sand beside her. 'Sometimes I forget what kind of power wizards have when they're kids . . .'

Nita saw that Carl's hair was wet. 'I got you out of the shower,' she said. 'I'm sorry . . .'

'No, I was out already. It's OK.'

'Where's Tom?' Nita said.

'He has a breakfast meeting with some people at ABC; he asked me to take his calls. Not that I had much choice, in your case . . . You've got big trouble, huh? Tell me about it.'

She did. It took her a while. Though she braced herself for it, the look of shock on Carl's face when he heard about Nita's accepting the Silent Lord's part was so terrible, she started to leak tears again. Carl sat still while she finished the story.

'Do your parents know?' he said at last.

'No,' Nita said. 'And I don't think I'm going to tell them. I think Dad suspects – and Mum knows he does and doesn't want to talk to him about it.'

Carl let out a long breath. 'I don't know what to tell you,' he said.

This was not the most encouraging thing Nita had ever heard. A Senior Wizard *always* knew what to tell you. 'Carl,' she said, tears still thick in her voice, 'what can I do? I can't – I can't just die!'

It was the first time she had actually said the word out loud. It left her shaking all over like the aftermath of a particularly large wizardry, and the tears started coming again.

Carl was quiet. 'Well, yeah, you can,' he said at last, gently. 'People do it all the time – sometimes for much less cause.'

'But there must be something I could do!'

Carl looked down at the sand. 'What did you *say* you were going to do?'

Nita didn't say anything; they both knew the answer very well. 'You know what caused this?' Carl said.

'What?'

'Remember the blank-cheque sorcery you did while in the other Manhattan, that time? The open-ended request for help?'

'Uh-huh.'

177

'That kind of spell always says that at some later date you'll be called upon to return the energy you use.' Carl looked somber. 'You got your help. But it must have taken a lot of energy to seal a whole piece of another space away from every other space, forever . . .'

Nita scrubbed at her eyes, not much liking this line of reasoning. 'But the spell never said anyone was going to have to die to pay back the price!'

'No. All it said was that you were going to have to pay back the exact amount of energy used up at some future date. And it must have been a very great amount, to require lifeprice to be paid. There's no higher payment that can be made.' Carl fell silent a moment, then said, 'Well, one.' And his face shut as if a door had closed behind his eyes.

Nita put her head down on her knees again. This wasn't working the way it was supposed to. 'Carl, there has to be something you, we could do—'

The surf crashed for a long time between her words and his. 'Nita,' Carl said finally, 'no. What you absolutely do *not* want is "something you could do". What you really want is for me to get you off the hook somehow, so you don't have to carry through with your promise.'

Her head snapped up in shock. 'You mean— Carl, don't you care if I die or not?'

'I care a whole lot.' The pain in Carl's voice made it plain that he did. 'But unfortunately I also have to tell you the truth. That's what Seniors are for; why do you think we're given so much power to work with? We're paid for what we do – and a lot of it isn't pleasant.'

'Then tell me some truth! Tell me what to do—'

'No,' he said gently. 'Never that. Nine-tenths of the power of wizardry comes from making up your own mind what you're going to do. The rest of it is just mechanics.' Carl looked at her with a professional calm that reminded Nita of her family doctor. 'What I *can* do is go over your options with you.'

She nodded.

'So first – what you'd like to do. You want to break your word and not sing the Song. That'd be easy enough to do. You would simply disappear – stay on land for the next week or so and not have anything further to do with the whales with whom you've been working. That would keep you out of the Song proper; you'd be alive three days from now.'

Carl looked out to sea as he spoke, nothing in his expression or his tone of voice hinting at either praise or condemnation. 'There would naturally be results of that action. For one, you took the Celebrant's Oath in front of witnesses and called on the Powers of wizardry themselves to bring certain things about if you break the Oath. They will bring those things about, Nita – the Powers don't forget. You'll lose your wizardry. You'll forget that there *is* any such thing as magic in the world. Any relationships you have with other wizards will immediately collapse. You would never have met Kit, for example, or me, or Tom, except for your wizardry. So we'll cease to exist for you.'

Nita held still as stone.

'There'll also be effects on the Song itself as a result of your leaving. Even if the group manages to find a replacement wizard to sing the Silent One—' Nita thought of Kit and froze. '—the Song itself will still have been sabotaged by your betrayal of your Oath. It won't be effective. The undersea tremors, the pollution and the attacks on the whales and all the rest of it will continue. Or the Lone Power will enter into the wizardry and throw it completely out of control – in which case I don't want to think of what will happen to New York and the Island, sooner or later. If all the other wizards in the area worked together, we might be able to slow it down. But not for long.'

Carl took a breath. 'And on top of everything else, breaking the Celebrant's Oath will also be a violation of the Wizard's Oath, your oath to assist in slowing down the death of the Universe. In your last moment as a wizard, as you lose your magic, you will *know* beyond all doubt that the Universe around you is going to die sooner because of your actions. And all through your life there'll always be something at the bottom of your heart that feels sad . . . and you'll never be able to get rid of it, or even understand it.'

Nita didn't move.

'That was all the "bad" stuff. On the "good" side I can tell you that you probably wouldn't die of the upheavals that will start happening. What you did in Manhattan with Kit wouldn't be forgotten by the Powers either; they pay their debts. I imagine your parents would get a sudden urge to go and visit some relatives in another state – something like that – and be a good distance inland when the trouble started. And after the trouble, you would go on to live what would seem a perfectly normal life . . . after all, most people think it's normal to have a nameless sorrow at the bottom of your soul. You'd grow up, and find a job, and get married, or not, and work and play and do all the other things that mortals and wizards do. And then you'd die.'

Nita was silent.

'Now the second option,' Carl said. 'You go down there and keep your word – though you're not happy about it, to say the least. You sing the Song, and when the time comes you dive into that coral or whatever and cut yourself up, and the Master-Shark comes after you and eats you. You experience about two or three minutes of extreme pain, pain like being hit by a car or burned all over, until you go into shock, or your brain runs out of oxygen, whichever comes first; and you die. Your parents and friends then have to deal with the fact of your death.'

Nita's tears started again.

'The "good" side to this option,' said Carl, 'is that the Song will be successfully completed, millions of people will continue to live their lives untroubled, and the Lone Power will have suffered another severe setback. My estimate is that It couldn't interfere in any large way with the Sea's affairs – and, to some extent, with the land's – for some forty to fifty years thereafter. Possibly more.'

Nita nodded slowly. 'So if—'

'Wait. There's a third option,' Carl said.

'Huh?'

He looked at her with an expression she couldn't fully decipher. 'Sing the Song and make the Sacrifice – but do it willingly. Rather than just doing it because you have to, to keep terrible things from happening.'

'Does it make a difference?'

Carl nodded. 'If you can make the Sacrifice willingly, the wizardry will gain such power as you can barely imagine. The Lone One's power is always based on Its desire to have Its own way in everything. Nothing undermines Its workings faster than power turned towards having something be the way someone *else* wants it.'

Carl looked hard at her. 'I have to make real sure you understand this. I'm *not* talking about the sort of fakery most people mean when they talk about "sacrifice" – none of that "unselfishness" business, which usually has the desire for other people to feel guilty or sad hidden at the bottom of it. No being a "martyr". That would sabotage a wizardry almost as badly as running out on it. But to willingly give up one's life for the sake of the joy and well-being of others will instantly destroy whatever power the Lone One has currently amassed.' He glanced away. 'That doesn't mean you couldn't be afraid and still have it work, by the way.'

'Great,' Nita said with a nervous laugh.

'The important thing is that, other times when the Sacrifice has been made willingly, there have been fewer wars afterwards, less crime, for a long while. The Death of things, of the world as whole, has been slowed . . .'

Nita thought of people fighting and shooting and stealing from each other; she thought of A-bombs and H-bombs, and people starving and poor – and she thought of all that slowed down. But all those troubles and possibilities seemed remote right now compared to her own problem, her own life. 'I don't know if I could do that,' Nita said, scarcely above a whisper.

There was a long pause. 'I don't know if I could either,' said Carl, just as quietly.

She sat still for a long time. 'I think—'

'Don't say it,' Carl said, shaking his head. 'You couldn't possibly have decided already. And even if you have—' He glanced away. 'You may change your mind later . . . and then you'll be saved the embarrassment of having to justify it to me.'

'Later—' She looked at him in distress and confusion. 'You mean you would still talk to me if I—' She stopped. 'Wait a minute. If I don't do it, I won't *know* you! And if I *do* it—'

'There's always Timeheart,' Carl said softly.

Nita nodded, silent. She had been there once, in that 'place' to which only wizards can find their way while still alive; that terrible and beautiful place where things that are loved are preserved, deathless, perfect, yet still growing and becoming more themselves through moment after timeless moment. 'After we— After we're alive, then—'

'What's loved,' Carl said, 'lives.'

She looked at him in a few moments' sorrowful wonder. 'But sure,' she said. 'You're a Senior. You must go there all the time.'

'No.' He looked out over the sea. 'In fact, the higher you're promoted, when you're a wizard, the more work you have to do – and the less time you get to spend outside this world, except on business.' He breathed out and shook his head. 'I haven't been to Timeheart for a long time, except in dreams . . .'

Now it was his turn to sound wistful. Nita reached out and thumped Carl's shoulder once or twice, hesitantly.

'Yeah,' Carl said. Slowly he stood up and brushed the sand off his towel, then looked down at her. 'Nita,' he said – and his voice was not impassive any more, 'I'm sorry.'

'Yeah,' she said.

'Call us before you start the Song, if you can, OK?' The New York accent was pronounced and raspy, as if Carl's nose was stuffed up.

'Right.'

He turned away, then paused and looked back at her. And everything suddenly became too much for Nita. She went to Carl in a rush, threw her arms around him at about waist height, and began to bawl. 'Oh, honey,' Carl said, and got down on one knee and held Nita tight, which was what she needed. But the helpless expression on his face, when she finally got some control over herself and looked up, almost hurt her more than her own pain.

After a while she pushed him away. Carl resisted her for a moment. 'Nita,' he said. 'If you— If you do . . .' He paused. '. . . Thank you,' he finally said, looking at her hard. 'Thank you. For the ten million lives that'll keep on living. They'll never know. But the wizards will . . . and they won't ever forget.'

'A lot of good that'd do *me*!' Nita said, caught between desperate laughter and tears.

'Sweetheart,' Carl said, 'if you're in this world for comfort, you've come to the wrong place . . . whether you're wizard or just plain mortal. And if you're doing what you're doing because of the way other people will feel about it – you're *definitely* in the wrong business. What you do has to be done because of how *you'll* feel about you . . . the way you did it last night, with your parents.' His voice was rueful. 'There are no other rewards . . . if only because no matter what you do, no-one will *ever* think the things about you that you want them to think. Not even the Powers.'

'Right,' Nita said again.

They let go of each other. Carl turned and walked away quickly. The air slammed itself shut behind him, and he was gone.

Nita walked back to the house.

She kept her goodbyes brief. 'We may be back tonight,' she said to her mother and father as they stood together on the beach, 'or we may not. S'reee says it'll depend on how much of the rehearsal we get finished.'

'Rehearsal—' Her mother looked at her curiously.

'Uh-huh. It's like I told you,' Kit said. 'Everyone who sings has his own part – but there's some ensemble singing, and it has to be done right.'

'Kit, we're late,' Nita said. 'Mum—' She grabbed her mother and hugged her hard. 'Don't worry if we don't come back tonight, Mum, please,' she said. 'We may just go straight into the Song – and that's a day and a half by itself. Look for us Monday morning.' *Us!* her mind screamed, but she ignored it. 'Dad—' She turned to him, hugged him too, and saw, out of the corner of her eye, her mother hugging Kit.

Nita glanced up and down the beach. 'It's all clear, Kit,' she said. She shrugged out of the towel wrapped around her, leaving it with her mother, then sprinted for the water. A few fast hops over several breakers, and there was depth enough to dive and stroke out to twenty-foot water. Nita leaped into the whaleshape as if it were an escape rather than a trap from which she might never return. Once a humpback, she felt normal again – and felt a twinge of nervousness; there was something S'reee had warned her about that . . .

No matter. Nita surfaced and blew goodbye at her mother and father, then turned for Kit, who was treading water beside her, to take her dorsal fin and be towed out to depth.

Out in the fifty-foot water Kit wrapped the whalesark about him and made the change with a swiftness that was almost savage. The sperm whale that appeared in his place had a bitter, angry look to its movements when it began to swim away from shore.

'Kit,' Nita said as they went, 'you OK?'

It was some time before he answered. 'No,' he said. 'Why *should* I be? When you're going to—' He didn't finish the sentence.

'Kit, look—'

'No, *you* look. Don't you see that there's nothing I can do about all this? And I don't like it!' His song was another of the scraping sperm-whale battlecries, soft but very heartfelt, and the rage in it chattered right down Nita's skin like nails down a blackboard.

'There's not much I can do about it myself,' she

185

said, 'and I don't like it either. Let's not talk about it for now, please! My brain still hurts enough from last night.'

'Neets,' he said, 'we've got to talk about it sometime. Tomorrow's *it*.'

'Fine. Before tomorrow. Meanwhile, we've got today to worry about. Are we even going the right way?'

He laughed at her then, a painful sound. 'Boy, are you preoccupied,' Kit said. 'Clean your ears out and listen!'

She stopped everything but the ticks and clicks a humpback uses to find its way, and listened – and was tempted to laugh herself. The sea had a racket hidden in it. From the south-west was coming an insane assortment of long, odd, wild sounds. Sweet high flutings that cut sharply through the intervening distance; clear horncalls, as if someone hunted under the waves; outer-spacy whistles and warbles like the electronic cries of orbiting satellites; deep bass scrapes and rumbles, lawn-mower buzzes and half-tone moans and soulful sighs. And many of those sounds, sooner or later, came back to the same main theme – a series of long wistful notes, slowly ascending into pitches too high and keen for human ears, then whispering away, lost in the quiet breathing of the water.

Nita had never heard that main theme before, but she recognized it instantly from her reading and her wizard's-sense of the Sea. It was the loss/gain/sorrow motif that ran all through the Song of the Twelve; and what she heard now, attenuated by distance but otherwise clear, was the sound of its singers, tuning up for the performance in which that mournful phrase would become not just a motif but a reality.

'Kit,' Nita said with a shiver, 'that's a lot more than ten whales! Who are all those other voices?'

He bubbled, a shrug. 'Let's find out.'

She whistled agreement and struck off after Kit, due west, away from the south shore of the island and out across the Atlantic-to-Ambrose shipping approaches once more. Song echoed more and more loudly in the sunlit shallows through which they swam; but underneath them Nita and Kit were very aware of the depths from which no echo returned – the abyss of Hudson Canyon, far below them, waiting.

'This is it,' Kit said at last, practically in Nita's ear, as they came to the fringes of the area S'reee's instructions had mentioned – fifteen miles east-northeast of Barnegat, New Jersey, right over the remains of an old sunken tanker six fathoms down in the water. And floating, soaring, or slowly fluking through the diffuse green-golden radiance of the water, were the whales.

Nita had to gulp once to find her composure. Hundreds of whales had gathered and were milling about, whales of every kind – minke whales, sei whales, sperm whales, dolphins of more kinds than she knew existed, in a profusion of shapes and colours, flashing through the water; several blues, grave-voiced, gliding with huge slow grace; fin whales, hardly smaller than the blues, bowhead whales and pygmy rights and humpbacks, many of them; grey whales and pygmy sperms and narwhals with their long single spiral teeth, like unicorn horns; belugas and killers and scamperdowns and bottlenosed whales— 'Kit,' Nita sang, faint-voiced, 'S'reee didn't tell me there were going to be *people* here!'

'Me either. I guess spectators at the rehearsal are so common, she forgot . . .' Kit sounded unconcerned.

Easy for you, Nita thought. You like crowds! She sang a few notes of sonar, trying nervously to hear some familiar shape. One shape at least Nita recognized, accompanied by the slow, calm, downscaling note of the Blue, as Aroooon passed by, a gold-tinged shadow in the background of greenness and the confusion of bodies. And there was Hotshot's high chatter, some ways off, accompanied by several other dolphin voices very like his – members of his pod.

Stillness swept over the spectators as she approached with Kit, and they recognized who she was. And a single note began to go up from them, starting at the fringes of the circle, working its way inward even to the Celebrants, until she heard even Aroooon's giant voice taking it up. One note, held in every range from the dolphin's dog-whistle trilling to the water-shaking thunder of the blues. One thought, one concept in the Speech, trumpeting through the water with such force that Nita began to shake at the sound of it. *Praise*. They knew she was the Silent One. They knew what she was going to do for them. They were thanking her.

Stunned, Nita forgot to swim – just drifted there in painful joy.

From behind, as the note slowly ebbed away, Kit nudged her. 'Get the lead out, Neets,' he sang, just for her hearing. 'You're the star of this show. So start acting like it! Go in there and let them know you're here.'

She swam slowly through the spectator whales, into the clear water in the centre of their great circle, where the Celebrants were gathered.

One by one, as she circled above the weed-covered remnant of the trawler, Nita quickly identified the whales she knew. Aroooon, yes, swimming off more or less by himself to tideward, singing his deep scrape of notes with the absent concentration of a perfectionist who has time to hunt perfection; Hotshot, doing barrel rolls near the surface and chattering through the quick bright harmonies of some part of the Wanderer's song; Areinnye, aloof from both Wanderer and Blue, running again and again over a phrase of the Grey Lord's song and paying no further attention to Nita after a quick glance.

There were also five other whales whom Nita didn't know, exactly as Kit had pegged them. A beluga, dolphin-sized but whale-shaped, lazing near the surface and singing some longing phrase from the Gazer's song; a pilot whale, long and slim and grey, silent for the moment and looking at Nita with interest; a right whale, with its huge, strange, bent-out-of-shape baleen mouth, listening to the beluga; a killer whale, the sharp blacks and whites of its hide a contrast to the greys and quiet mottlings of most of the others.

And – thank Heaven! – S'reee, swimming towards Nita from beside the killer. Nita had been shaken by the sight of the killer – killer whales being one of a humpback's most persistent natural enemies – but just now her composure was so unravelled, there wasn't much more damage that could be done to it. As S'reee came up to greet her, Nita managed to sing in something like a calm voice, and as if she were actually in charge, 'Well, we're late. Should we get started?'

'Good idea,' said S'reee, brushing skin briefly and reassuringly with Nita. 'Introductions first, though.'

'Yes, please.'

S'reee led Nita off to the north, where several of the singers were working together. 'We've been through the first part of the Song already this morning,' said S'reee, 'the name-songs and so forth. I've heard you do yours, so there was no need for you to be here till late. We're up to the division now, the "temptation" part. These are the people singing the Undecided group—'

'Hi, Hotshot,' Nita sang as she and S'reee soared into the heart of the group. The dolphin chattered a greeting back and busied himself with his singing again, continuing his spirals near the surface, above the heads of the right whale and a whale whose song Nita hadn't heard on the way in, a Sowerby's beaked whale. She immediately suspected why she hadn't heard it; the whale, undoubtedly there to celebrate the Forager's part, was busy eating – ripping up the long kelp and redweed stirring around the shattered deckplates of the wreck. It didn't even look up as she and S'reee approached. The right whale was less preoccupied; it swam towards Nita and S'reee at a slow pace that might have been either courtesy or caution.

'HNii't, this is T!h!ki,' said S'reee. Nita clicked his name back at him in greeting, swimming forward to brush skin politely with him. 'He's singing the Listener.'

T!h!ki rolled away from Nita and came about, looking at her curiously. When he spoke, his song revealed both great surprise and some unease. 'S'reee – this is a human!'

'T!h!ki,' Nita said, wry-voiced, with a look at S'reee, 'are *you* going to be mad at me for things I haven't done too?'

The right whale looked at her with that cockeyed upward stare that rights have – their eyes being placed high in their flat-topped heads. 'Oh,' he said, sounding wry himself, 'you've run afoul of Areinnye, have you. No fear, Silent Lord – hNii't, was it? No fear.' T!h!ki's song put her instantly at ease. It had an amiable and intelligent sound to it, the song of a mind that didn't tend toward blind animosities. 'If you're going to do the Sea such a service as you're doing, I could hardly do less than treat you with

190

honour. For Sea's sake don't think Areinnye is typical . . .

'However,' T!h!ki added, gazing down at the calmly feeding beaked whale, 'some of us practically have to have a bite taken out of us to get us to start honouring and stop eating.' He drifted down a fathom or so and bumped nose-first into the beaked whale. 'Roots! Heads up, you bottom-grubber, here comes the Master-Shark!'

'Huh? Where? *Where?*' the shocked song came drifting up from the bottom. The kelp was thrashed about by frantic fluking, and through it rose the beaked whale, its mouth full of weed, streamers of which trailed back and whipped around in all directions as the whale tried to tell where the shark was coming from. 'Where— What— Oh,' the beaked whale said after a moment, as the echoes from its initial excited squeaking came back and told it that the Master-Shark was nowhere in the area. 'Ki,' it said slowly, 'I'm going to get you for that.'

'Later. Meantime, here's S'reee, and hNii't with her,' said T!h!ki. 'HNii't's singing the Silent Lord. HNii't, this is Roots.'

'Oh,' said Roots, 'well met. Pleasure to sing with you. Would you excuse me?' She flipped her tail, politely enough, before Nita could sing a note, and a second later was head-down in the kelp again, ripping it up faster than before, as if making up for lost time.

Nita glanced with mild amusement at S'reee as Hotshot spiralled down to join them. 'She's a great conversationalist,' Hotshot whistled, his song conspiratorially quiet. 'Really. Ask her about food.'

'I sort of suspected,' Nita said. 'Speaking of the Master-Shark, though, where *is* Ed this morning?'

S'reee waved one long fin in a shrug. 'He has a late

appearance, as you do, so it doesn't really matter if he shows up late. Meanwhile, we have to meet the others. Ki, are you finished with Roots?'

'Shortly. We're going through the last part of the second duet. I'll catch up with you people later.' The right whale glided downward towards the weeds, and S'reee led Nita off to the west, where the Blue drifted in the water, and the beluga beside him, a tiny white shape against Aroooon's hugeness.

'Aroooon and I are two of the Untouched,' said S'reee. 'The third, after the Singer and the Blue, is the Gazer. That's Iniihwit.'

'HNii't,' Aroooon's great voice hailed them as Nita approached.

Nita bent her body into a bow of respect as she coasted through the water. 'Sir,' she said.

That small, calm eye dwelt gravely on her. 'Are you well, Silent Lord?' said the Blue.

'As well as I can be, sir,' Nita said. 'Under the circumstances.'

'That's well,' said Aroooon. 'Iniihwit, here is the human I spoke of.'

The beluga swam away from Aroooon to touch skin with Nita. Iniihwit was male, much smaller than Nita as whales went, though big for a beluga. But what struck her more than his smallness was the abstracted, contemplative sound of his song when he did speak. There were long silent days of calm behind it, days spent floating on the surface alone, watching the changes of sea and sky, saying little, seeing much. 'HNii't,' he said, 'well met. And well met now, for there's something you must hear. You too, Senior.'

'The weather?' S'reee said, sounding worried.

'Yes indeed. It looks as if that storm is not going to pass us by.'

Nita looked at S'reee in surprise. 'What storm? It's clear.'

'For now,' said Iniihwit. 'Nevertheless, there's weather coming, and there's no telling what it will stir up in the depths.'

'Is there any chance we can beat it?' S'reee said, sounding very worried indeed.

'None,' the beluga said. 'It will be here in half a light. We'll have to take our chances with the storm, I fear.'

S'reee hung still in the water, thinking. 'Well enough,' she said. 'Come on, hNii't; let's speak to Areinnye and the others singing the Undecided. We'll start the group rehearsal, then go straight into the Song. Time's swimming.'

S'reee fluked hard and soared off, leaving Nita in shock for a moment. We won't be going home tonight, she thought. No goodbyes. No last explanations. I'll never set foot on land again . . .

'Neets?' Kit's voice said from behind her.

'Right,' she said.

She went after S'reee to see the three whales singing the Undecided. Areinnye greeted Nita with cool cordiality and went back to her practising. 'And here's the Sounder,' S'reee was saying. 'Fluke, this is hNii't.'

Nita brushed skin with the Sounder, who was a pilot whale; small and mottled grey, built along the same general lines as a sperm, though barely a quarter the size. Fluke's eyes were small, his vision poor, and he had an owlish, shortsighted look about him that reminded Nita of Dairine in her glasses. The likeness was made stronger by a shrill, ratchety voice and a tendency towards chuckles. 'Fluke?' Nita said.

'I was one,' the Sounder said. 'I'm a triplet. And a runt, as you can see. There was nothing to do to hold my own with my brother and sister except become a wizard in self-defence.'

Nita made a small amused noise, thinking that there might not be so much difference between the motivations and family lives of humans and whales. 'And here's Fang,' said S'reee.

Nita found herself looking at the brilliant white and deep black of the killer whale. Her feelings were decidedly mixed. The humpback-shape had its own ideas about the Killer, mostly prejudiced by the thought of blood in the water. But Nita's human memories insisted that killers were affable creatures, friendly to humans; she remembered her Uncle Jerry, her mother's older brother, telling about how he'd once ridden a killer whale at an aquatic park in Hawaii and had had a great time. *This* killer whale edged closer to Nita now, staring at her out of small black eyes – not opaque ones like Ed's, but sharp, clever ones, with merriment in them. 'Well?' the killer said, his voice teasing. 'Shark got your tongue?'

The joke was so horrible, and somehow so funny, that Nita burst out laughing, liking this creature instantly. 'Fang, is it?'

'It is. HNii't, is it?'

'More or less.' There was a kind of wicked amusement about Fang's song, which by itself was funny to listen to – sweet whistles and flutings peppered liberally with spits and fizzes. 'Fang, are you from these waters originally?'

'Indeed not. I came down from Baffin Bay for the Song.'

Nita swung her tail in surprise. 'That's in Canada! Fifteen hundred miles!'

'What? Oh, a great many lengths, yes. I didn't swim it, hNii't. Any more than you and K!t there went where you went last night by swimming.'

'I suppose,' she said, 'that a wizardry done like that – on such short notice, and taking the wizards such a distance – might have been noticed.'

Fang snorted bubbles. '"Might"! I should say so. By everybody. But it's understandable that you might want to indulge yourselves, anyway. Seeing that you and your partner won't have much more time to work together in the flesh.'

Fang's voice was kind, even matter-of-fact; but Nita wanted to keep away from that subject for the moment. 'Right. Speaking of which, S'reee, hadn't we better start?'

'Might as well.'

S'reee swam off to a spot roughly above the wreck, whistling, and slowly the whole group began to drift in toward her. The voices of the whales gathered around to watch the Celebrants began to quiet, like those of an audience at a concert.

'From the top,' S'reee said. She paused a few seconds, then lifted up her voice in the Invocation.

'Blood in the water I sing, and one who shed it:
deadliest hunger I sing, and one who fed it—
weaving the ancientmost song of the Sea's sending:
singing the tragedy, singing the joy unending.'

Joy . . . Nita thought, trying to concentrate. But the thought of whose blood was being sung about made it hard.

The shadow that fell over Nita somewhere in the middle of the first song of the Betrayed whales, though, got her attention immediately. A stream-lined shape as pale as bleached bone glided slowly over her, blocking the jade light; one dead-black, unreflecting eye glanced down. 'Nita.'

'Ed,' she said, none too enthusiastically. His relentless reality was no pleasant sight.

'Come and swim with me.'

He arched away through the water, northward towards Ambrose Light. The gathered spectators drew back as Nita silently followed.

Shortly they were well to the north, still able to hear the ongoing practice Song, but out of hearing range for normal conversation. 'So, Silent Lord,' Ed said, slowing. 'You were busy last night.'

'Yes,' Nita said, and waited. She had a feeling that something odd was going on inside that chill mind.

Ed looked at her. 'You are angry . . .'

'Damn right I am!' Nita sang, loudly, not caring for the moment about what Ed might think of her distress.

'Explain this anger to me,' said the Master-Shark. 'Normally the Silent Lord does not find the outcome of the Song so frightful. In fact, whales sometimes compete for the privilege of singing your part. The Silent Lord dies indeed, but the death is not so terrible – it merely comes sooner than it might have otherwise, by predator or old age. And it buys the renewal of life, and holds off the Great Death, for the whole Sea – and for years.'

Ed glanced at her, sedate. 'And even if the Silent One should happen to suffer somewhat, what of it? For there is still Timeheart, is there not . . . ? The Heart of the Sea.' Nita nodded, saying nothing. 'It is no ending, this Song, but a passage into something else. How they extol that passage, and what lies at its end.' There was faint, scornful amusement in Ed's voice as he lifted his voice in a verse of the Song – one of the Blue's cantos – not singing, exactly, for sharks have no song; chanting, rather. '". . . *Past mortal song—*

'"*—that Sea whereof our own seas merely hint,*
     poor shadows sidewise-cast from what is real—
  where Time and swift-finned Joy are foes no more,
     but lovers; where old friend swims by old friend,
  senior to Death, undying evermore—

partner to Songs unheard and Voices hid;
songs past our knowing, perilously fair—"'

Ed broke off. 'You are a wizard,' he said. 'You have known that place, supposedly.'

'Yes.' Timeheart had looked like a bright city, sky-scrapered in crystal and fire, power trembling in its streets and stones, unseen but undeniably there. And beyond the city stretched a whole universe, sited beyond and within all other worlds, beyond and within all times. Death did not touch that place. 'Yes, I was there.'

'So you know it awaits you after the Sacrifice, after the change of being. But you don't seem to take the change so calmly.'

'How can I? I'm human!'

'Yes. But make me understand. Why does that make your attitude so different? Why are you so angry about something that would happen to you sooner or later anyway?'

'Because I'm too young for this,' Nita said. 'All the things I'll never have a chance to do – grow up, work, live—'

'This,' Ed said mildly, looking around him at the green-burning sea, the swift fish flashing in it, the dazzling wrinkled mirror of the surface seen from beneath, 'this is not living?'

'Of course it is! But there's a lot more to it! And getting murdered by a shark is hardly what I call living!'

'I assure you,' Ed said, 'it's nothing as personal as murder. I would have done the same for any wizard singing the Silent Lord. I *have* done the same, many times. And doubtless shall again . . .' His voice trailed off.

Nita caught something odd in Ed's voice. He sounded almost . . . wistful?

'Look,' she said, her own voice small. 'Tell me something . . . Does it really have to hurt a lot?'

'Sprat,' said Ed dispassionately, 'what in this life doesn't? Even love hurts sometimes. You may have noticed . . .'

'Love – what would you know about that?' Nita said, too pained to care about being scornful, even to the Master-Shark.

'And who are you to think I would know nothing about it? Because I kill without remorse, I must also be ignorant of love, is that it?'

There was a long, frightening pause, while Ed began to swim a wide circle about Nita. 'You're thinking I am so old an order of life that I can know nothing but the blind white rut, the circling, the joining that leaves the joined forever scarred. Oh yes, I know that. In its time . . . it's very good.'

The rich and hungry pleasure in his voice disturbed Nita. Ed was circling closer and closer as he spoke, swimming as if he were asleep. 'And, yes . . . sometimes we wish the closeness of the joining wouldn't end. But what would my kind do with the warm-blood sort of joining, the long companionships? What would I do with a mate?' He said it as if it were an alien word. 'Soon enough one or the other of us would fall into distress – and the other partner would end it. There's an end to mating and mate, and to the love that passed between. That price is too high for me to pay, even once. I swim alone.'

He was swimming so close to Nita now that his sides almost touched hers, and she pulled her tail and fins in tight and shrank away from the razory hide, not daring to move otherwise. Then Ed woke up and broke the circle, gliding lazily outward and away as if nothing had happened. 'But, Sprat, the matter of *my* loves – or their lack – is hardly what's bothering you.'

'No,' she burst out bitterly, 'love! I've never had a chance to. And now – now—'

'Then you're well cast for the Silent Lord's part,' Ed said, his voice sounding far away. 'How does the line go? *Not old enough to love as yet, but old enough to die, indeed*— That has always been the Silent Lord's business – to sacrifice love for life . . . instead of, as in lesser songs, the other way around . . .'

Ed trailed off, paused to snap up a sea bass that passed him by too slowly. When his eyes were more or less sane again and the water had carried the blood away, Ed said, 'Is it truly so much to you, Sprat? Have you truly had no time to love?'

Mum and Dad, Nita thought ruefully. Dairine. That's not love, I don't love Dairine! – do I? She hardened her heart and said, 'No, Pale One. Not that way. No-one . . . that way.'

'Well then,' said the Master-Shark, 'the Song will be sung from the heart, it seems. You will still offer the Sacrifice?'

'I don't want to—'

'Answer the question, Sprat.'

It was a long while before Nita spoke. 'I'll do what I said I would,' she said at last. The notes of the song whispered away into the water like the last notes of a dirge.

She was glad Ed said nothing for a while, for her insides gripped and churned as she finally found out what real, grownup fear was. Not the kind that happens suddenly, that leaves you too busy with action to think about being afraid – but the kind that she had been holding off by not officially 'deciding': the kind that swims up as slowly as a shark circling, letting you see it and realize in detail what's going to happen to you.

'I am big enough to take a humpback in two bites,' Ed said into her silence. 'And there is no need for me to be leisurely about it. You will speak to the Heart of the Sea without having to say too much to me on the way.'

Nita looked up at him in amazement. 'But I thought you didn't believe – I mean, you'd never—'

'I am no wizard, Nita,' Ed said. 'The Sea doesn't speak to me as it does to you. I will never experience those high wild joys the Blue sings of – the Sea That Burns, the Voices. The only voices I hear cry out from water that burns with blood. But might I not sometimes wonder what other joys there are? – and wish I might feel them too?'

The dry, remote pain in his voice astonished her. And Nita thought abruptly of that long line of titles in the commentaries in her manual: as if only one shark had ever been Master. Sharks don't die of natural causes, she thought. Could it be that, all these years, there *has* been just one Master? And all around him, people die and die, and he – can't—

—and wants to? And so he understands how it is to want to get out of something and be stuck with it.

Nita was terribly moved – she wasn't sure why. She swam close to the Pale One's huge head for a moment and glided side by side with him, matching his course and the movements of his body.

'I wish I could help,' she said.

'As if the Master could feel distress,' Ed said, with good-natured scorn. The wound in his voice had healed without a scar.

'And as if someone else might want to end it,' Nita said, sarcastic, but gentle about it.

Ed was silent for a long while. 'I mean, it's stupid to suffer,' Nita said, rather desperately, into that silence. 'But if you have to do it, you might as well intend it to do someone some good.'

In silence they swam a few lengths more through the darkening water, while Nita's fear began to build in her again, and one astonished part of her mind shouted at her, *You're running around talking about doing nice things for someone who's going to kill you? You're crazy!*

Ed spoke at last. 'It's well said. And we will cause it to be well made, this Sacrifice. You, young and never loving; I, old and never loved.' Calm, utterly calm, that voice. 'Such a Song the Sea will never have seen.'

'HNii't?' came a questioning note through the water, from southward of Ambrose: S'reee's voice. 'It's almost your time—'

'I have to go,' Nita said. 'Ed—'

'Silent Lord?'

She had no idea why she was saying it. 'I'm sorry!'

'This once, I think,' the passionless voice said, 'so am I. Go on, Sprat. I will not miss my cue.'

Nita looked at him. Opaque eyes, depthless, merciless, lingered on her as Ed curved past. 'Coming!' Nita sang in S'reee's direction, loud, and tore off southward.

No pale shadow followed.

The next few hours, while the water darkened further, ran together for Nita in a blur of music, and annoying repetitions, and words that would have been frightening if she hadn't been too busy to be frightened. And something was growing in her, slowly, but getting stronger and stronger – an odd elation. She sang on, not questioning it, riding its tide and hoping it would last through what she had to do. Again and again, with the other Celebrants listening and offering suggestions, she rehearsed what would be the last things she would ever say:

'. . . *Sea, hear me now,
and take my words and make them ever law!*—'

'Right, now swim off a little. No-one hears this part. Upward, and toward the centre, where the peak will be. Right there—'

'Must I accept the barren Gift?
* —learn death, and lose my Mastery?*
Then let them know whose blood and breath
* will take the Gift and set them free:*
whose is the voice and whose the mind
* to set at naught the well-sung Game—*
when finned Finality arrives
* and calls me by my secret Name.*

'Not old enough to love as yet,
* but old enough to die, indeed—'*
—Oh Lord—
'—the death-fear bites my throat and heart,
* fanged cousin to the Pale One's breed.*
But past the fear lies life for all—
* perhaps for me: and, past my dread,*
past loss of Mastery and life,
* the Sea shall yet give up Her dead!'*

—and then the paleness came to circle over her, bringing with it the voice that chanted all on one soft hissing note, again and again, always coming back to the same refrain—

'Master have I none, nor seek.
Bring the ailing; bring the weak.
Bring the wounded ones to me:
They shall feed my Mastery . . .'

That strange excitement was still growing in Nita. She let it drive her voice as she would have used it to drive a wizardry, so that her song grew into something that shook the water and almost drowned out even Ed's voice, weaving about it and turning mere hunger to desire, disaster to triumph—

> *'Lone Power, I accept your Gift!*
> *Freely I make death part of me;*
> *By my acceptance it is bound*
> *into the lives of all the Sea—*

> *yet what I do now binds to it*
> *a gift I feel of equal worth:*
> *I take Death with me, out of Time,*
> *and make of it a path, a birth!*

> *Let the teeth come! As they tear me,*
> *they tear Your ancient hate for aye—*
> *—so rage, proud Power! Fail again,*
> *and see my blood teach Death to die!'*

. . . The last time she sang it, Nita hung unmoving, momentarily exhausted, for the moment aware of nothing but Kit's anxious eyes staring at her from outside the circle and the stir of water on her skin as the Pale One circled above her.

'That's right,' S'reee said at last, very quietly. 'And then—'

She fell silent and swam out of the circle of Celebrants. Behind her, very slowly, first the Blue and then the rest of the whales began to sing the dirge for the Silent Lord – confirmation of the transformation of death and the new defeat of the Lone Power. Nita headed for the surface to breathe.

She came up into early evening. Westward, sunset was backing itself into scarlet embers; eastward a moon lacking only the merest shard of light to be full lifted swollen and amber through the surface haze; northward, the bright and dark and bright again of Ambrose Light glittered on the uneasily shifting waves, with the opening and closing red eyes of Manhattan skyscraper lights low beyond it; and southward, gazing back at them, the red-orange glow of Arcturus sparkled above the water, here and there striking an answering spark off the crest or hollow of some wave. Nita lay there gasping in the wavewash and let the water rock her. Heaven knows, she thought, I need somebody to do it . . .

Beside her Kit surfaced in a great wash of water and blew spectacularly – slightly forward, as sperms do. 'Neets—'

'Hi,' she said. She knew it was inane, but she could think of no other way to keep Kit from starting what he was going to start, except by saying stupid things.

'Neets,' he said, 'we're out of time. They're going to start the descent as soon as everybody's had a chance to rest a little and the protective spells are set.'

'Right,' she said, misunderstanding him on purpose. 'We better get going, then—' She tilted her head down and started to dive.

'Neets.' Suddenly Nita found that she was trying to dive through a forty-foot thickness of sperm whale. Nita blew in annoyance and let herself float back to the surface again. Kit bobbled up beside her – and, with great suddenness and a slam of air, threw off the whalesark. He dogpaddled there in the water, abruptly tiny beside her bulk. 'Neets, get out of that for a minute.'

'Huh? Oh—'

It was a moment's work to drop the whaleshape; then she was reduced to dogpaddling too. Kit was treading water a few feet from her, his hair slicked down with the water. He looked strange – tight, somehow, as if he were holding on to some idea or feeling very hard. 'Neets,' he said, 'I'm not having this.'

Nita stared at him. 'Kit,' she said finally, 'look, there's nothing we can do about it. *I've* had it. Literally.'

'No,' Kit said. The word was not an argument, not even defiance; just a simple statement of fact. 'Look, Neets – you're the best wizard I've ever worked with—'

'I'm the *only* wizard you've ever worked with,' Nita said with a lopsided grin.

'I'm going to kill you,' Kit said – and regretted it instantly.

'No need,' Nita said. 'Kit – why don't you just admit that this time I've got myself into something I can't get out of.'

'Unless another wizard gets you out of it.'

She stared at him. 'You loon, you *can't*—'

'I *know*. And it hurts! I feel like I *should* volunteer, but I just can't—'

'Good. 'Cause you do and *I'll* kill *you*.'

'That won't work either.' He made her own crooked grin back at her. '"All for one", remember? We *both* have to come out of this alive.'

And he looked away.

'Let's go for both,' Nita said.

Silence.

She took a deep breath. 'Look, even if we *don't* both get out of this, I think it's going to be all right. Really—'

'No,' Kit said again, and that was that.

Nita just looked at him. 'OK,' she said. 'Be that way.' And she meant it. This was the Kit she was used to working with: stubborn, absolutely sure of himself – most of the time; the person with that size-twelve courage packed into his size-ten self, a courage that would spend a few minutes trembling and then take on anything that got in its way – from the Lone Power to her father. If I've got to go, Nita thought in sudden irrational determination, that sheer guts has got to survive – and I'll do whatever's necessary to make sure he does.

'Look,' she said, 'what're you going to tell my parents when you get back?'

'I'm going to tell them we're hungry,' Kit said, 'and that you'll fill 'em in on the details while I eat.'

I did tell him to be that way . . . 'Right,' Nita said.

For a long time they stayed where they were, treading water, watching the moon inch its way up the sky, listening to the Ambrose fog signal hooting the minutes away. A mile or so off, a tanker making for New York Harbour went by, its green portside running lights towards them, and let off a low groaning blast of horn to warn local traffic. From under the surface, after a pause, came a much deeper note that held and then scaled downward out of human hearing range, becoming nothing but a vibration in the water.

'They're ready to leave,' Kit said.

Nita nodded, slipped into whaleshape again, and looked one last time with all her heart at the sunset towers of Manhattan, until Kit had finished his change. Then they dived.

THE SONG OF THE TWELVE

Hudson Channel begins its seaward course some twenty miles south of Ambrose Light – trending first due south, parallel to the Jersey shore, then turning gradually towards the south-east and the open sea as it deepens. Down its length, scattered over the channel's bottom as it slowly turns from grey-green mud to grey-black sand to naked, striated stone, are the broken remnants of four hundred years' seafaring in these waters and the refuse of three hundred years of human urban life, mixed randomly together. There are new, almost whole-bodied wrecks lying dead on their sides atop old ones long since gone to rot and rust; great dumps of incinerated wood and ash, chemical drums and lumps of coal and jagged piles of junk metal; sunken, abandoned buoys, old cable spindles, unexploded ordnance and bombs and torpedoes; all commingled with and nested in a thick ooze of untreated, settled sewage – the rubbish of millions of busy lives, thrown where they won't have to look at it.

The rugged bed of the channel starts out shallow, barely a fathom deeper than the seabed that surrounds it. It was much deeper once, especially where it begins; but the ooze has filled it thickly, and for some miles it is now hard to tell that any channel at all lies under the rotting rubbish, under the ancient faded beer cans and the hubcaps red with rust. Slowly, though, some twenty miles down the channel from its head, an indentation becomes apparent – a sort of crooked rut worn by the primordial Hudson River into the ocean floor, a mile wide at the rut's deepest, five miles wide from edge to edge. This far down – forty fathoms under the surface and some sixty feet below the surrounding ocean bed, between a great wide U of walls – the dark sludge of human waste lies even thicker. The city has not been dumping here for some time, but all the old years' sewage has not gone away. Every stone in the deepening rut, every pressure-flattened pile of junk on the steadily downward-sloping seabed around the channel, is coated thick and black. Bottom-feeding fish are few here: there is nothing for them to eat. Krill do not live here: the water is too foul to support the microscopic creatures they eat, and even of a summer night the thick olive colour of the sea is unchanged.

The channel's walls begin to grow less and less in height, as if the ocean is growing tired of concealing the scar in its side. Gradually the rut flattens out to a broad shallow depression like a thousand other valleys in the Sea. A whale hanging above the approximate end of the channel, some one hundred and thirty miles south east of New York Harbour, has little to see on looking back up the channel's length – just an upward-sloping scatter of dark-slimed rocks and mud and scraps of rubbish, drab even in the slate-green twilight that is all this bottom ever sees of noon. But looking downward, south-ward, where its course would run if the channel went any farther—

—the abyss. Suddenly the thinning muck, and the

gentle swellings and dippings of the sea bed, simply stop at the edge of a great steep semicircular cliff, two miles from side to side. And beyond the cliff, beyond the edge of the Continental Shelf, curving away to north-east and south-west – nothing. Nothing anywhere but the vague glow of the ocean's surface three hundred feet above; and below, beyond the semicircle, the deadly stillness of the great deeps, and a blackness one can hear on the skin like a dirge. Icy cold, and the dark.

'I warn you all,' S'reee said as the eleven gathered Celebrants and Kit hung there, looking down into that darkness at the head of Hudson Canyon. 'Remember the length of this dive; take your own breathing needs carefully into consideration, and tell me now if you think you may need more air than our spells will be taking with us. Remember that, at the great pressures in the Below, you'll need more oxygen than you usually do – and work will make you burn more fuel. If you feel you need to revise the breathing figures on the group spell upwards, this is the time to do it! There won't be a chance later, after we've passed the Gates of the Sea. Nor will there be any way to get to the surface quickly enough to breathe if you start running low. At the depths we'll be working, even a sperm whale would get the bends and die of such an ascent. Are you all sure of your needs? Think carefully.'

No-one said anything.

'All right. I remind you also, one more time, of the boundaries on the pressure-protection spell. They're marked by this area of light around us – which will serve the added purpose of enabling us to see what's going on around us. If we need to expand the boundaries, that's easily done. But unless I direct you otherwise, stay inside the light. Beyond the lighted area, there's some direction for a limited area, but it's erratic. Don't depend on it! Otherwise you may find yourself crushed to a pulp.'

Nita glanced at Kit; he gave her an I-don't-care wave of the tail. Sperm whales were much less bothered by pressure changes than most of the species, and the great depths were part of their hunting grounds. 'You be careful,' she sang at him in an undertone. 'Don't be silly down there.'

'Don't *you*.'

'Anything else?' S'reee said. 'Any questions?'

'Is there time for a fast bite?' Roots said, sounding wistful.

'Certainly,' Fang said, easing up beside the beaked whale with that eternal killer-whale smile. 'Where should I bite you?'

'Enough, you two. Last chance, my wizards.'

No-one sang a note.

'Then forward all,' S'reee said, 'and let us take the adventure the Powers send us.'

She glided forward, out into the darkness past the great curved cliff, tilted her nose down, and dived – not straight, but at a forty-five-degree angle roughly parallel to the downward slope of the canyon. The wizard-light advanced with her. Areinnye followed first; then Fang and Iniihwit, with Fluke and Roots close behind. After them came T!h!ki and Aroooon and Hotshot, and Nita, with Kit behind her as rearguard, suspiciously watching the zone of light around them. Only one of the Celebrants did not stay within that boundary, sailing above it, or far to one side, as he pleased – Ed, cruising restlessly close to the canyon walls as the group descended, or pacing them above, a ghost floating in midnight-blue water.

'I don't like it,' Nita sang, for Kit's hearing only, as she looked around her.

'What?'

'This.' She swung her tail at the walls – which were

210

towering higher and higher as they cut downward through the Continental Shelf. On the nautical maps in their manuals, the canyon had looked fairly innocent; and a drop of twenty-five feet in a half-mile had seemed gentle. But Nita was finding the reality that rose in ever-steepening battlements around her much more threatening. The channel's walls at their highest had been about three hundred feet high, comparable to the walls she'd seen in the Grand Canyon on vacation. But these walls were already five or six hundred feet high, growing steadily steeper as the canyon's angle of descent through the shelf increased. If Nita had a neck to crane back, it would already be sore.

As it was, she had something much worse – a whale's superb sonar sense, which told her exactly how puny she was in comparison to those cliffs – exactly where loose rocks lay on them, ready to be shaken down at the slightest bottom tremor.

Kit looked up around them and sang a note of uncomfortable agreement. 'Yeah,' he said. 'It gives me the creeps too. It's too tall—'

'No,' Nita said softly. 'It's that this isn't a place where we're supposed to be. Something very large happened here once. That's your speciality; you should be able to feel it.'

'Yeah, I should.' There was a brief pause. 'I seem to have been having trouble with that lately. —But you're right, it's there. It's not so much the tallness itself we're feeling. But what it's – what it's a symbol of, I think—'

Nita said nothing for a moment, startled by the idea that Kit had been losing some of his talent at his speciality. There was something that could mean, some warning sign— She couldn't think what.

'Kit, this is one of the places where Afállonë was, isn't it?'

He made a slow sound of agreement. 'The whole old continental plate Atlantis stood on was ground under the new plates and buried under the Atlantic's floor, S'reee said. But the North American plate was a lot further west when the trouble first started, and the European one was further east. So if I've got the story straight, this would have been where Afállonë's western shoreline was, more or less. Where we're going would still have been open sea, a couple of million years ago.'

'Millions of years—' Nita looked at him in uncomfortable wonder. 'Kit – that's much farther back than the fall of Afállonë. That could—' Her note failed her momentarily. 'That could go right back to the first Song of the Twelve—'

Kit was still for a while as they kept diving. 'No wonder,' he said at last, 'no-one travels down through the Gates of the Sea except when they're about to do the Song. Part of the sorcery is buried in the stone. If anybody should trouble it, wake it up—'

'—like we're doing,' Nita said, and fell silent.

They swam on. The immensities rearing up about them grew no more reassuring with time. Time, Nita thought – how long have we been down here? In this changeless cold dark, there was no telling; and even when the sun came up, there still would be no knowing day from night. The darkness yielded only grudgingly to the little sphere of light the Celebrants carried with them, showing them not much, and too much, of what Nita didn't want to look at – those walls, reaching so far above her now that the light couldn't even begin to illumine them. Nita began to get a bizarre sense of being indoors – descending a winding ramp of infinite length, its walls three miles apart and now nearly a mile high.

It was at about this time that Nita felt on her skin what sounded at first like one of the Blue's deeper notes, and stared ahead of her, wondering partly what he was saying – the note was one that made no sense to her. Then she wondered why he was curving his body upward in such surprise. But the note grew, and grew, and grew louder still, and though they were now nearly a mile from the walls on either side, to her shock and horror Nita heard the walls begin to resonate to that note.

The canyon walls sounded like a struck gong, one of such boneshaking, subterranean pitch as Nita had never imagined. *She* sounded, caught in the torrent of shock waves with the rest of the Celebrants. *Seaquake!* she thought. The sound pressed through her skin from all sides like cold weights, got into her lungs and her heart and her brain, and throbbed there, hammering her into dizziness with slow and terrible force.

The sluggish, brutal pounding against her skin and inside her body eventually began to die down. But the quake's effects were still going on around her, and would take much more time to settle. Sonar was nearly drowned; Nita was floating blind in the blackness. *This is the pits!* she thought in anguish, and concentrated everything she had on one good burst of sound that would cut through the terrible noise and tell her what was going on.

The echoes that came back reassured her somewhat. All the Celebrants were still fairly close together, safe within the light of the pressure-protection spell. Kit was further ahead than he had been, fighting for control and slowly finding it. Others, S'reee and Fang and Areinnye, were closer to Nita. And there was other movement close to them – large objects drifting downward, slowly, resonating with the same note, though in higher octaves, as the towering cliffsides. Massive objects, said the echo. *Solid* massive objects. Falling faster now. One of

213

them falling past S'reee and down toward Areinnye, who was twisting and struggling against the turmoil of the water for balance—

Warn her! was Nita's first thought, but even as she let out another cry, she realized it was useless – Areinnye would have no time to react. The falling rock, a piece of cliff-shelf nearly as long as a city square, was practically on top of her. Shield spell, Nita thought then. Impossible—

She did it anyway. It was an old friend, that spell, long since learned by heart. When activated, punches, or any physical object thrown at one, slid right off it. Running them together in her haste, she sang the nine syllables of the spell that were always the same, then added four more that set new coordinates for the spell, another three that specified how much mass the shield would have to repel – *tons and tons! Oh, Lord!* – and then the last syllable that turned the wizardry loose. She felt the magic fall away from her like a weight on a cord, dropping toward Areinnye. Nothing to do now but hang on, she thought, letting herself float. Faintly, through the thunder, the echoes of her spell brought Nita the shape of Areinnye, still struggling, trying to get out from under the falling rock-shelf, and failing. Her connection with the spell brought her the feeling of the massive slab of stone dropping towards it, closer, closer still. Making contact—

—crushing down and down on to her wizardry with force more terrible than she had anticipated. The spell was failing, the shelf was settling down on it and inexorably pressing it closer and closer to Areinnye, who was in turn being forced down against the battering of the shock waves, towards the floor of the canyon. The spell was breaking up, tearing like a rotten net filled with weights. No, Nita thought, and strained, pouring all her concentration, all her will, down the connection to the spell. *No!* It was like hanging on to a rope in a tug of war, and losing, and not letting go – digging in, muscles popping out all over, aching, straining, blood pounding, and not letting go— The spell firmed a little. The shelf, settling slowly down and down on to Areinnye, forcing her closer and closer to the bottom, seemed to hesitate. 'Kit!' Nita screamed into the water. *I'm going to lose it. I'm going to lose it!* 'Kit!'

The echo of her yell for help showed her another sperm-whale shape, a larger one than Areinnye's, fighting his way against the battering shock waves and down towards the bottom of the canyon – towards where Areinnye floundered, underneath the stone shelf, underneath the spell. Kit rammed Areinnye head-on, hitting her squarely amidships and punching the smaller sperm whale backward thirty or forty feet. But not out from under the settling shelf; and now Kit was partly under it too. The spell began sagging again. Nita panicked; she had no time or energy left for any more warnings, any more *anything*. She threw herself so totally into the spell that she couldn't feel her body, couldn't hear, couldn't see, finally became nothing but a single, none-too-coherent thought: *No!* But it was no use. The spell was coming undone, the rock was coming down, this time for good. And Kit was under it. No! No, *no, NO*—

And everything went away.

The next thing Nita felt was the shock of a spell being broken by forces too great for it to handle, as the rock-shelf came crushing down on it, smashing it flat against something both soft and hard. '*NO!*' Nita screamed again in horror, as the diminishing thunder of the seaquake was briefly augmented by the multiple crashes of the shelf's shattering. The floor of the canyon was obscured even to sonar by a thick fog of rockdust and stirred-up ooze, pierced all through by flying splinters of stone, but Nita dived into it anyway. 'Kit!'

'You sang?' came a sperm whale's sharp-edged note from down in the rock-fog, sounding tired but pleased.

Speechless with relief and shaking with effort, Nita pulled up her nose and just let herself float in the trembling water, listening to the rumbling of the quake as it faded away and the songs of the other whales round about as they checked on one another. She became aware of the Master-Shark, finning slowly downcanyon not too far from her and favouring her as he went with a look that was prolonged and indecipherable. Nita glided hurriedly away from him, looking around her.

The light of the protection spell showed Nita the roiling of the cloud of ooze and dust in the bottom of the canyon, and the two shapes that swam slowly up through it – first Kit, fluking more strongly than Nita would have believed possible for someone who'd just gone through what they all had, then Areinnye, stroking more weakly, and swimming with a stiffness that made it very plain just how hard Kit must have hit her. Kit rose to hang beside Nita. More slowly, Areinnye came swimming up to face her.

'There seems to be a life between us, hNii't,' the sperm whale said.

The mixture of surprise and anger in Areinnye's song made Nita uncomfortable. 'Oh, no,' she said, rather weakly. 'Kit did it—'

'Oh, dead fish,' Kit said. 'You held it for a good ten seconds after we were out from under. You would've managed even if I hadn't helped.'

'I had incentive,' Nita muttered.

Kit looked at her for a moment. 'You didn't drop

it until Ed nudged you,' he said. 'You might have gone deaf for a little, or maybe you were in spell overload. But either way, this was your business. Don't blame me.'

'Silent Lord,' Areinnye said – still stiffly formal, but with an uncertain note in her voice, 'I thank you. I had hardly given you cause for such an act.'

'You gave me plenty of cause,' she said wearily. 'You took the Oath, didn't you? You're with me. And you're welcome.' She took a deep breath, feeling the respiratory part of the protection spell briefly surround her blowholes with a bubble of air for her to inhale. 'Kit,' she said, 'can we get going and get this over with?'

'That is well said,' came Ed's voice. He was coming upcanyon again, fast. As Nita looked up she saw him arrow overhead, ghastly pale in the wizard-light, with a trail of darkness billowing thick behind him, and something black in his jaws. It struggled; Ed gulped it down. Inside his gill slits and lower body, Nita could see the swallowed thing give a last couple of convulsive heaves. 'And we'd best get on with it—'

Thick black sucker-tipped arms whipped up from the disturbed ooze on the bottom, grasping, flailing in the light. 'Oh, no,' Nita moaned. Kit plunged past her, the first note of the scraping sperm-whale battlecry rasping down Nita's skin as he dived for the body to which those arms belonged. Farther down the canyon, almost out of range of the wizard-light, there was a confused boiling-together of arms, long dark bodies, flat platterlike yellow eyes glowing with reflected light and wild-beast hunger – not just a few krakens, but a great pack of them. 'To business, Silent Lord,' Ed said, his voice rich with chilly pleasure, as he swept past Nita again on his way downcanyon.

She went to business. These krakens were bigger

than the last ones had been; the smallest one Nita saw had a body the size of a hearse, and arms twice that length. True, there were more toothed whales fighting this time – not only Kit, but Fang and Areinnye as well. And teeth weren't everything – what Aroooon or T!h!ki rammed didn't move afterwards.

The Celebrants also had the advantage of being wizards. Nita was terrified at first when she saw one of the krakens come at poor slow Roots – and poor slow Roots raised her voice in a few squeaky little notes and simply blew the giant squid into a cloud of blood and ink and black rags of flesh. But a wizard's strength has limits; such spells could only be worked once or twice. And since a spell has to be directed at what you see, not even the most deadly offensive wizardry does a bit of good against the choking tentacles that you don't notice coming up from behind you. So it was a slow, ugly, bitter battle, that fight in the canyon. Four or five times the Celebrants were assaulted as they made their way down between the dwarfing, twisting walls of stone; four or five times they fought the attackers off, rested briefly, and started out again, knowing that somewhere deeper down, more thick tentacles and hungry eyes waited for them.

'This is your fault!' Areinnye cried angrily at Nita during one or another of the attacks, while Fang and Kit and Ed and Aroooon fought off krakens coming from downcanyon and from above, and S'reee and T!h!ki worked furiously to heal a great sucker welt torn in Areinnye's side before Ed should notice it and turn on her.

Nita simply turned away, in no mood for it. Her face hurt from ramming krakens, she had bruises from their suckers and a stab from one's beak, and she was sick of the smell of blood and the galling sepia taste in the water. The problem, and the only reason Nita didn't answer Areinnye hotly back, was that there might have been some slight truth to the accusation. According to Carl and the manual, the same pollutants that caused cancer in human beings, that had caused the US Fish and Game Service to warn people on the Jersey shore against eating more than one ocean-caught fish a week, were getting concentrated in the squids' bodies, changing their DNA: changing *them*. The food the krakens normally ate at the great depths was dying out, also from the pollution. They had to come up into the shallows to survive. The changes were enabling them to do so. And if it was starving, a hungry kraken would find a whale perfectly acceptable as food.

Nita was startled by the sudden sharpness of S'reee's answering voice. 'Areinnye, don't talk nonsense,' she said after singing the last note of a spell that sealed the sperm whale's torn flesh. 'The krakens are here for the same reason the quake was – because the Lone Power wants them here. We're supposed to use up our air fighting them.'

T!h!ki looked soberly at S'reee. 'That brings up the question, Ree. *Will* we complete the Song?'

S'reee swung her tail in a shrug, her eyes on Areinnye's healing wound. 'I thought such a thing might happen,' she said, 'after we were attacked the other night. So I brought extra air, more than the group felt it needed. Even so – it'll be close.'

'We're a long way down the canyon,' Nita said. 'Practically down to the plain. If they're all down there, waiting for us – if these attacks have just been to wear us down—'

'I don't think so,' T!h!ki said, glancing over at Nita. 'Once out into the plain, we'll be practically under the shadow of the Sea's Tooth, close to the ancient site of the Song. And once our circle is set up, they couldn't get in unless we let them.'

'Which we won't,' S'reee said. 'Let's waste no more time. This is going to be the fastest Song on record. —Areinnye, you're hurt. How do you feel?'

The sperm swayed in the water, testing her healed tail. 'Well enough,' she said, grim-voiced. 'Though not as well as I would if this human were—' And Areinnye broke off. 'Pardon me,' she said, more slowly. 'It was an ill thought. Let me go and help K!t now.'

She went. 'You now,' S'reee said to Nita. She sang a few notes to start the healing spell going, then said, 'HNii't? Are you all right otherwise?'

The sound of Kit's battlecry came scraping along Nita's skin from downcanyon. 'No,' she said. Kit had been fighting with a skill and, heaven help him, a relish that Nita would never have suspected in him. I'm not sure it's the sark doing this, she thought. I keep thinking that Kit might actually *be* this way, down deep.

Then Nita stopped. What makes me think it matters one way or another? she thought. In a few hours, anything I think about Kit will make no difference at all. But I can't stop acting as if it will. Habit is hard to break . . .

'If it's something I can help with—' S'reee said, finishing up.

Nita brushed skin with her, an absent gesture. 'It's not,' she said. And off she went after Areinnye – into the water fouled with stirred-up slime and ink and blood, into the reach of grabbing, sandpapery tentacles and the glare of yellow eyes.

It went on that way for what seemed for ever, until Nita was nearly blind from head-on ramming. She gave up on sonar and concentrated on keeping just one more squid occupied until Kit or Ed or Areinnye could deal with it. So, as the walls of the canyon, which had been towering some six thousand feet above the Celebrants on either side, began to decrease in height, she didn't really notice it. Eventually the bitter cold of the water got her attention; and she also realized that the krakens' attack had stopped. Nita sang a few notes to 'see' at a distance, and squinted around her in the sea-green wizard-light to find out where she and the other Celebrants were.

The walls closest to them were still nearly three thousand feet high. But their slope was gentler; and the canyon had widened from some two miles across to nearly five. To left and right of the canyon's foot, curving away northward and southward, miles past sound or sight, stretched the rubble-strewn foothills of the Continental Shelf. Behind the Celebrants the shelf itself towered, a mighty cliff wall rising to lose itself in darkness. Outward before them, towards the open sea, the terrain was mostly flat, broken only occasionally by hills so shallow they were more like dunes. The rocky bottom was turning to pale sand. But the paleness did nothing to lighten the surroundings. Above it lay an intolerable, crushing weight of water, utterly black, icy cold, weighing down on the soul no matter what spell protected the body. And far out in the blackness could be seen the furtive, erratic movements of tiny lights – eerie points of peculiar-coloured fire that jittered and clustered and hung in the cold dark, watching the whales.

Nita took a sharp breath, for some of those lights were definitely eyes. T!h!ki, hanging motionless in the still water beside her, did the same. He was staring down the slope, which sank past the light of the breathing-spell, and far past echo range, dropping father downward into more darkness. '*Nothing* can be this deep,' he sang in an unnerved whisper. 'How much further down can we go?'

'All the way,' said another voice from Nita's other side. She turned, not recognizing it – and then knew the speaker very well and was sick inside. Kit hung there, with a fey, frightening look in his eye – a total lack of fear.

Nita swallowed once. Sperm whales took the great dives better than any other whale, coming down this far on purpose to hunt the giant squid; but their boldness also got them in trouble. Numerous sperm-whale skeletons had been found at these depths by exploring bathyscaphes, the whales' tails or bodies hopelessly tangled in undersea telephone or telegraph cables.

'We're a long way up yet,' Kit said, with that cool cast to his voice that better suited Areinnye than it did him. 'Barely six thousand feet down. We'll have to go down to sixteen thousand feet at least before we see the Sea's Tooth.' And he swam off towards the boundaries of the light.

Nita held still for a few moments as S'reee and various other of the Celebrants went slowly after Kit. T!h!ki went too; she barely noticed him go. *This isn't the Kit I want to say goodbye to*.

Perhaps a hundred feet away from her, Ed glided past, staring at her. 'Sprat,' he said, 'come along.'

She did. But the fighting in the canyon had left Nita so fatigued that much of this part of the descent seemed unreal to her, a prolonged version of one of those dreams in which one 'falls' downstairs for hours. And there was a terrible sameness about this terrain: a sea of white sand, here and there featuring a darker rock thrust up or thrown down into it, or some artifact more bizarre – occasionally, great pressure-fused lumps of coal; once an actual kitchen sink, just sitting there on the bottom by itself; another time, a lone Coca-Cola bottle standing upright in the sand with a kind of desolate, pitiful

222

pride. But mostly the bottom was as undifferentiated as a mile-wide, glare-lit snowfield, one that pitched forever downward.

Nor was Nita's grasp on reality much helped by the strange creatures that lived in those waters more than a thousand fathoms down. Most everything seemed to be either transparent as a ghost or brilliantly luminous. Long-bodied, lantern-eyed sharks swam curiously about Nita, paid brief homage to their Master, and moved on. Anglerfish with their luminous baits hanging on 'fishlines' in front of their mouths came up to stare Nita right in the eye and then swam dourly away, disappointed that she was too big to eat. Long, many-segmented bottom worms and vampire squid, sporting dots or stripes of pink or yellow or blue-white light, inched or squirted along the bottom about their affairs, paying no attention to the Celebrants sailing overhead in their nimbus of wizard-light. Rays fluttered, using fleshy wings to rearrange the sand in which they lay buried; tripod-fish crutch-walked around the bottom like peglegged pirates on their long stiff fins. And all the eyes circling in the black water, all the phosphorescent shapes crawling on the bottom or undulating above it were doing one of two things – either looking for food or eating it, in the form of one another.

Nita knew there was no other way for these creatures to live, in this deadly cold, but by the minimum expenditure of energy for the maximum return . . . hence all the baits, traps, hiding. But that didn't affect the dull horror of the scene – the endless crushing dark, the ear-blinding silence, and the pale chilly lights weaving through the space-black water as the creatures of the great depths sought and caught and ate one another with desperate, mindless diligence.

The gruesome power of the besetting horror

brought Nita wide awake. She had never been superstitious; shadows in the bedroom had never bothered her when she was little, and she found horror movies fun to watch. But now she started to feel more hemmed in, more watched and trapped, than she suspected she'd feel in any haunted house. 'Ed,' she sang, low as a whisper, to the pale shape that paced her, 'what *is* it? There's something down here . . .'

'Indeed there is. We are getting close.'

She would have asked *To what?* but as she looked down the interminable slope at the other Celebrants – who were mostly swimming gathered close together, as if they felt what she felt – something occurred to her, something so obvious that she felt like a moron for not having thought of it before. 'Ed – if this is the Song of the Twelve, how come there are only eleven of us singing!'

'The Twelfth is here,' Ed said. 'As the Song says, the Lone Power lies bound here, in the depths below the depths. And It will sing Its part, as It always has. It cannot help it. Indeed, It wants to sing. In the temptation and subversion of the Celebrants lies Its only hope of excape from the wizardry that binds It.'

'And if It succeeds—'

'Afállonë,' Ed said. 'Atlantis, all over again. Or worse.'

'*Worse*—' Then she noticed something else. 'Ed, the water's getting warmer!'

'And the bottom is changing,' Ed said. 'Gather your wits, Sprat. A few hundred more lengths and we are there.'

The white sand was giving way to some kind of darker stuff. At first Nita thought she was looking at the naked rock of the sea bottom. But this stuff wasn't flat, as sediment would be. It was ropy, piled-up, ridgy-looking black stone. And here and there crystals glittered in it. Scattered around ahead of them were higher piles of black stone, small, bizarrely shaped hills. Nita sounded a high note to get some sonar back, as the water through which she swam grew warmer and began to taste odd.

The first echoes to return surprised Nita until she started to suspect what they were. Waving frondy shapes, the hard round echoes from shelled creatures, a peculiar hollowness to the echo that indicated water of lower pressure than that surrounding it— That was a stream of sulphur-laden hot water coming out of an undersea 'vent'; the other echoes were the creatures that lived around it, all adapted to take advantage of the oasis of heat and the sulphur that came up with it. And now she understood the black bottom stone – old cooled lava, the kind called pillow lava, that oozes up through the ocean's crust and spreads itself out in flat, ropy piles.

But from past the vent came another echo that was simply impossible. A wall, a rounded wall, at least a mile and a half wide at the base, rising out of the piled black stone and spearing up, and up, and up, and up, so that fragments of the echo kept coming back to Nita for second after second. She backfinned to hold still until all the echoes could come back to her, and in Nita's mind the picture of the massive, fluted, narrowing pillar of stone got taller and taller, until she actually had to sing a soft note or two to deafen herself to it. It was, like the walls of Hudson Canyon, 'too big' – only much more so. 'Five Empire State Buildings on top of each other,' Kit had called it – but Empire States a mile wide: Caryn Peak, the Sea's Tooth, the site of the Song of the Twelve.

The whales ahead of Nita were gathering near the foot of the peak. Against that gigantic spear of stone they seemed dwarfed, insignificant. Even Aroooon looked like a toy. And the feeling of being watched, closely, by something of malicious intent, was getting stronger by the second.

She joined the others. The Celebrants were poised not too far from the open vent – evidently S'reee preferred the warmer water – in clear view of the strange creatures living about it: the twelve-foot stalks of the tubeworms, the great blind crabs, the colonies of giant blood-red clams, opening and closing their fringed shells with mindless regularity. No coral, Nita thought absently, looking around her. But she wouldn't need any. Several hundred feet away, there on the face of the peak, were several shattered outcroppings of stone. The outcroppings were sharp as glass knives. Those should do it, Nita thought. So sharp I'll hardly feel anything – until Ed arrives . . .

'If you're all prepared,' S'reee sang, her voice wavering strangely where notes had to travel suddenly from cold water to hot, 'I suggest we start right now.'

The Celebrants chorused muted agreement and began to spread out, forming the circle with which the Song begins. Nita took her place between Fang and T!h!ki, while S'reee went to the heart of the circle. Ed swam away, towards the far side of the peak and out of sight. Kit glided away from the circle, off behind Nita. She looked back at him. He found the spot from which he would watch and gazed back at her. Nita swallowed one last time, hard. There was very little of her friend in that look. 'Kit—' she said, on one low note.

'Silent Lord,' he said.

And though it was his voice, it wasn't Kit . . .

Nita turned away, sick at heart, and faced inward toward the circle again; and S'reee lifted up her voice and sang the Invocation.

*

'Blood in the water I sing, and one who shed it;
deadliest hunger I sing, and one who fed it—
weaving the ancientmost tale of the Sea's sending:
singing the tragedy, singing the joy unending.

'This is our shame – this is the whole Ocean's glory:
this is the Song of the Twelve. Hark to the story!
Hearken, and bring it to pass; swift, lest the sorrow
long ago laid to its rest devour us tomorrow!'

And so it began, as in song S'reee laid out the
foundations of the story, which began before lives
learned to end in resistance and suffering. One by
one the Celebrants drew together, closing up the
circle, named themselves to one another, and began
to discuss the problem of running the Sea to
everyone's advantage. Chief among their problems at
the moment was the sudden appearance of a new
whale. It was puzzling; the Sea had given them no
warning, as She had in times past, that this was about
to happen. But they were the Ni'hwinyii, the Lords
of the Humours, and they would comport themselves
as such. They would decide the question for themselves. Under whose Mastery would the Stranger
fall . . . ?

Nita, who had backed out of the circle after the
Invocation, hung shivering in the currentless water
as the Song shook the warm darkness about her. Part
of what she felt was the same kind of trembling with
excitement she had felt a hundred times in school
when she knew she was about to be called on. I'm
ready, she thought, trying to quiet herself. This is
silly. I know my part backwards and forwards –
there's not that much of it. I'll do all right.

. . . But there was also something else going on.
She had felt it start with the Invocation and grow
stronger with every passing second – that sense of

something waking up, something rousing from sleepy malice, awakening to active, alert malevolence. *It waits*, Ed had said. It was a certainty, as sure as looking up towards a lighted window and seeing the person who's been staring at you drop the curtain and turn away.

She wrenched her attention back to the Blue, who was at the end of one of his long stately passages. But it was hard.

> '—*Nay, slowly, Sounder. Slow is the wise whale's song,*
> *and wise as slow; for he who hastens errs,*
> *who errs learns grief. And not the Master-Shark*
> *has teeth as fierce: grief eats its prey alive,*
> *and pain grows greater as the grief devours,*
> *not less. So let this Stranger sing his peace:*
> *what he desires of us; there's Sea enough and time*
> *to hear him, though he sing the darkened Moon*
> *to full and back again. Ay, let him speak . . .'*

And to Nita's shock and fascinated horror, an answer came. The voice that raised itself in the stillness of the great depths was the sonic equivalent of the thing one sees out the corner of one's eye, then turns to find gone, or imagined. It did not shake the water; it roused no echoes. And Nita was not alone in hearing it. She saw the encircled Celebrants look uneasily at one another. On the far side of the circle, Kit's coolness was suddenly broken, and he stared at Nita like someone believing a myth for the first time. The innocent, gentle-spoken, unselfconscious evil in the new voice was terrifying. *'With Pow'rs and Dominations need I speak*,' sang that timbreless voice in quiet sincerity,

> '*the ancient Lords who hold the Sea in sway.*

I pray thee, Lords of the Humours, hear me now,
last, least and poorest of the new-made whales,
new-loos'd from out the Sea's great silent Heart.
No Lord have I; therefore to ye I come,
beseeching low thy counsel and thy rule
for one that's homeless, lawless, mateless,
lost . . .'

'Who art thou, then, that speak'st?' sang S'reee,
beginning the Singer's questioning. At the end of her
verse she was answered, in more soft-spoken, reasonable platitudes – words meant to lull the unwary and
deceive the alert. And questions and answers continued, until Nita realized that there had been a shift.
Rather than the Singer asking the Stranger what he
wanted, the Stranger was telling the Singer what he
knew *she* wanted – and could offer her, if only she
would take the unspecified Gift he would give her.

Nita began shaking steadily now, and not from the
cold. The insinuating power of that not-quite-voice
somehow frightened her worse than head-on conflict
with the Lone Power had, a couple of months ago.
There the Power had been easily seen in its true
colours. But here it was hidden, and speaking as
matter-of-factly as the voices in the back of one's own
mind, whose advice one so often tends to follow
without question. 'Your Mastery is hollow,' said the
voice to S'reee.

'—cold song, strict-ruled by law. From such bland
    rule
come no great musics. Singer, follow me,
accept my Gift and what it brings, and song
shall truly have no Master save for you.
My gift will teach you lyric that will break
the heart that hears it; every seaborne voice
will curse your newfound art, and wish that art

its own. Take up the Gift, O foremost Singer . . .'

Nita glanced over at S'reee. She was trembling nearly as hard as Nita was, caught in the force of the temptation. S'reee sang her refusal calmly enough; but Nita found herself wondering how much of that refusal was the ritual's and how much S'reee's own.

She began watching the other Celebrants with as much care. Iniihwit sang the Gazer's questioning and rejection with the outward attitude of mild unconcern that Nita had in their brief acquaintance come to associate with him. Aroooon's refusal of the prize offered the Blue by the Stranger, that of power over all the other whales, was more emphatic, though it came in his usual rich, leisurely manner. He sang not as if making ritual responses, but as if he rejected someone who swam in the circle with him and dared him to do something about it.

After that, the unheard voice sounded less certain of itself, and also impatient. The Song passed on to what would for the Lone Power be more successful ground: the Wanderer and the Killer and the Forager, all of whom would succumb to the Stranger's temptations and become the Betrayed – those species of whales and fish to whom death would later come most frequently and most quickly. One by one Roots and Fang and Hotshot sang with the Lone One, were tempted, and in the place of the original Masters, fell. Nita tried to keep herself calm, but had trouble doing it; for each time one of the Celebrants gave in to the Lone One's persuasion, she felt the voice grow a little more pleased with itself, a little more assured – as if something were finally going according to plan.

Nita stared across at Kit. He traded looks with her and began to make his way around the circle toward her.

The Lone One was working on the last three whales in the circle now, the ones who would become the Undecided. Their parts were the most difficult, being not only the longest sung passages but also the most complex. The Undecided argued with the Lone Power much more than did the Untouched, who tended to refuse quickly, or the Betrayed, who gave in without much fighting. T!h!ki sang first, the Sounder's part; and strain began to show as the Power offered him all the hidden knowledge of the great deeps, and the Sounder's song went from smooth flowing melodies to rumbles and scrapes of tortured indecision. *Not all that carrying on is in the Song,* Nita thought nervously. *What's happening?* And indeed, though the Sounder finished his passage and turned away, ostensibly to think about what the Lone Power had said to him, Nita could see that T!h!ki looked pallid and shaken as a whale that's sick.

The Listener fared no better. Fluke sang steadily enough to begin with; but when the voiceless voice offered him the power to hear everything that transpired in the Sea, from the random thoughts of new-hatched fry to the secret ponderings of the continental plates, he hesitated much too long – so long that Nita saw S'reee look at him in surprise and almost speak up to prompt him. It was bizarre; in rehearsals Fluke had had the best memory of any of them. He finished his verses looking troubled, and seemed relieved to turn away.

It's what S'reee said, very early on, Nita thought. *The whales picked have to be close in temperament to the original Celebrants – loving the same kinds of things. But it makes them vulnerable to the temptations too.*

And then Areinnye began to sing, questioning the Power in her disturbingly sweet voice, asking and

231

answering. She showed no sign of the unease that had troubled the others. Nita glanced over at Kit, who had managed by this time to work his way fairly close to her; he swung his tail a fraction, a whale's version of a worried headshake. Areinnye's singing was polished, superb, her manner poised, unruffled, royal. She sang her initial rebuff with the harsh certainty the Grey Lord's song called for.

> 'Stranger, no more— give me no gift.
> Power am I, fear in the water
> as my foes flee. I need no boon.
> In the Below all bow before me.
> Speak not to me. Speak not of gifts.'

The voice that answered her was as sweet and poised as her own.

> 'And do you then desire no gift of mine—
> you who have lost so much? Ah no: you have
> strength of your own indeed – great strength of jaw,
> of fluke, of fin; fear goes before your face.
> But sorrow follows after. What use strength
> when slaughtered children rot beneath the waves,
> when the sweet mouth that you gave suck is gone,
> rent to red tatters by the flensing-knives;
> and when the second heart that beat by yours
> lies ground for dogs' meat in a whaler's hull?
> Grey One, accept my Gift and learn of strength—'

That's not in the Song!

Nita stared in shock at Kit, then at the other Celebrants – who, all but Areinnye, were trading horrified looks. The sperm whale held very still, her eyes turned outward from the circle; and she shook as violently as T!h!ki had or, for that matter, Nita. The Lone Power sang on:

'—learn power! Learn how wizardry may turn
to serve your purpose, sinking the whalers deep,
taking the brute invaders' lives to pay
for that small life that swims the Sea no more;
take up my Gift—'

'There is – there is another life,' Areinnye sang,
trembling now as if storm waters battered at her,
breaking the continuity of the Song. 'Saved – she
saved—'

'—what matter? As if brutes who fear the Sea
are capable of thought, much less of love!
Even a shark by accident may save a life –
then turn and tear the newly saved!
Take up my Gift and take a life for life,
as it was done of old—'

Slowly Areinnye turned, and the glitter of the
wizard-light in her eyes as she looked at Nita was
horrible to see. 'Life,' she sang, one low, thick,
struggling note—

She leaped at Nita. In that second Fang, on her
left, arrowed in front of Areinnye, punching her jaws
away from Nita in time for Nita to roll out of their
way. But Fang didn't recover from the blow in time
to flee himself; Areinnye's head swept around and
the great teeth of her upper jaw raked frightful
gashes down Fang's side. Nita pulled herself out of
her roll just in time to see something else hit
Areinnye – Kit's huge bulk, slamming into her with
such force that she was knocked straight into the
side of Caryn Peak. She screamed; the water
brought back echoes of the sickening sound of her
impact. And then she was fleeing – out of the wizard-
light, past the boundaries of the protective spell, out
into the darkness past the peak.

The Celebrants stirred about in terrible confusion, while S'reee hurried to Fang's side and examined him. Nita stroked over quickly and brushed Fang's good side, very lightly. One of those merry eyes, now slightly less merry, managed to focus on her. 'We need you – Silent One,' Fang said.

'We do,' S'reee said. 'These wounds aren't deep, but they're bleeding a lot – and the Master-Shark's about. I've got to handle this. Meanwhile, we're shy the Grey Lord – and I don't think she's going to come back and take back what she said. K!t, are you willing?'

Nita looked swiftly behind her. Kit was hanging there, looking down at Fang. 'I'd better be,' he said.

'Good. HNii't, administer him the Celebrant's Oath. And hurry.' S'reee turned away from them and began one of the faster healing spells.

'Kit, are you sure—'

'Get going,' he said.

She led him through the Oath. He said it almost as quickly as Hotshot had, tripping in only one place: *'. . . and I shall weave my voice and my will and my blood with theirs if there be need . . .'* He was looking at Nita as he said that, and the look went right through her like a spear.

'Done,' S'reee said. 'Fang, mind that side – the repair is temporary. —Swiftly, now. Everyone circle, we can't afford a delay. Kit, from *No, I must think*—'

They sang. And if the Song had been frightening before, it was becoming frantic now. Underneath them all the Celebrants could feel some malicious force straining to get free—

Nita watched Kit closely. He didn't rehearse any of this stuff, she thought. What if he slips? But Kit sang what remained of the Grey Lord's part faultlessly; he had laid himself wide open to the Sea and

was being fed words and music directly. Nita felt a
lump in her throat – that reaction humans shared
with whales – at the perfect clarity of his voice. But
she couldn't stop worrying. If he's this open to the
Sea, he's also open to that Other—

And that Other was working on him. Kit was
beginning to tremble as the second part of the Grey
Lord's rebuff came to an end. The soundless voice,
when it spoke for the last time, was all sweet reason:

'—*strength is no use. Give over the vain strife that
saves no-one, keeps no old friend alive, con-
demns the dear to death.*
*Take but my Gift and know long years that end
not,*
slow-burnt days under the sun and moon;
not for yourself alone, but for the other—'

'No,' Nita said – a mere whisper of song.

Kit looked at her from the heart of the circle,
shaking. In his eyes and the way he held his body
Nita read how easy it would be for him to desert the
Song after just these few lines, destroy it, knowing
that Nita would escape alive. Here was the out he had
been looking for.

'No!' she tried to say again, but something was
stopping her. The malice in the water grew, burning
her. Kit wavered, looking at her—

—then closed his eyes and took a great breath of
air from the spell, and began singing again – his voice
anguished, but still determined. He finished the last
verse of the Grey Lord's rebuff on a note that was
mostly a squeak, and immediately turned to S'reee,
for the next part would be the group singing – the
battle.

S'reee lifted her head for the secondary invocation.
The ocean floor began to shake. And Nita suddenly

realized that it wasn't just the Lone Power's malice burning all around her. The water was heating up.

'Oh, Sea about us, no!' S'reee cried. 'What now?'

'Sing!' came a great voice from above them. Aroooon had lifted out of the circle, was looking into the darkness, past the great pillar of Caryn Peak. 'For your lives, sing! Forget the battle! HNii't, quickly!'

She knew what he wanted. Nita took one last great gulp of breath, tasting it as she had never tasted anything in her life, and fluked upward out of the circle herself, locating one of the sharp outcroppings she had noticed earlier. A flash of ghostly white in the background— Good, she thought. Ed's close. '*Sea, hear me now,*' she sang in a great voice, '*and take my words and make them ever law*—'

'*Nitaaaaaa!*'

'HNii't, look out!'

The two cries came from opposite directions. She was glancing towards Kit, one last look, when something with suckered arms grabbed her by the tail and pulled her down.

The moments that followed turned into a nightmare of thrashing and bellowing, arms that whipped at her, clung to her, dragging her inexorably towards the place where they joined and the wicked beak waited. No-one was coming to help her, Nita realized, as she looked down into that sucking mouth. The water was full of screams; and two of the voices she heard were those of sperm whales. *Two*— She thrashed harder, getting a view as she did so of S'reee fleeing before a great grey shape with open jaws – Areinnye; and coming behind Areinnye, a flood of black shapes, bigger than any the Celebrants had had to handle in Hudson Canyon.

She's sold out, Nita thought miserably. *She's gone over to the Lone One. She came back and broke the* circle, and let the krakens in, and everything's going to go to hell if I don't – Nita swung her head desperately and hit the kraken with it, felt baleen plates in her mouth crack, felt the kraken shudder. *Let go of me, you disgusting thing!* Nita was past working any wizardry but one. Brute force was going to have to do it. *Let go!* She slammed her head into the kraken again, sideways. It let out a shrill painful whoop that was very satisfying to her. Your eye's sensitive, huh? she thought. One more time!

She hit it again. Something soft gave under the blow, and the kraken screamed. Nita tore free of the loosening arms and swam upward, hard and fast, heading for her sharp outcropping. The whole area around the base of Caryn Peak was boiling with kraken, with Celebrants fighting them and trying desperately not to be dragged out of the boundaries of the protective spell. The bottom was shuddering harder; hot water was shimmering faster and faster out of the vent. It's got to be stopped, Nita thought. 'Kit,' she called, looking around hurriedly. There's just time enough to say goodbye.

Two things she saw. One was that ghostly white shape soaring close by, bolting down the rear half of a kraken about the size of a minibus and gazing down at her as it passed by.

The other was Kit, turning away from a long, vicious slash he had just torn down Areinnye's side – looking up at Nita and singing one note of heart-tearing misery – not in the Speech – not in the human-flavoured whale he had always spoken before – but in pure whale.

Oh, no. He's lost language! Nita's heart seized. S'reee had said that if that happened, the whalesark was about to be rejected by Kit's brain. Unless something was done, it would leave him human again, naked in the cold, three miles down.

That thought, and the echoes of Kit's cry of anguish, suddenly meant more to Nita than any abstract idea of ten million deaths. And in that second Nita came to understand what Carl had been talking about. She wheeled around and stared at the outcropping – then *chose* to do, willingly, what she had thought she'd no choice but to do. The triumph that instantly flared up in her made no sense. But she wouldn't have traded it for any feeling more sensible. She turned and fluked with all her might and threw herself at the stony knives of the peak – and hit—

—something, not stone, and reeled away from the blow, stunned and confused. Something had punched her in the side. Tumbling over and over with the force of the blow and the ever-increasing shockwaves blasting up from the shuddering bottom, Nita saw that great white shape again – but much closer, soaring backward with her as she tumbled. 'Silent One,' he said, 'before you do what you must – give me your power!'

'*What?*'

'Only trust me! Give it to me – and be quick!'

Nita could hardly react to the outrageous demand. Only with Kit had she ever dared do such a thing. To give Ed all her power would leave her empty of it, defenceless, until he finished whatever he wanted to do with it. Which could be hours – or for ever. And he wasn't even a wizard—

'Nita, *swiftly!*'

'But Ed, I need it for the Sacrifice. What do you want it for!'

'To call for help!' Ed hissed, arching away through the water toward Areinnye and Kit, who was still fighting feebly to keep her busy and away from Nita. 'Sprat, be quick and choose, or it will be too late!'

He dived at Areinnye, punched Kit out of harm's

238

way, and took a great crater of a bite out of Areinnye's unprotected flank.

Areinnye's head snapped up and around, slashing at Ed sideways. He avoided her, circled in again. 'Nita!'

To call for help— What help? And even for Ed, to give up her power, the thing that was keeping her safe and was also the most inside part of her—

Read the fine print before you sign, said a scratchy voice in her memory. *Do what the Knight tells you. And don't be afraid to give yourself away!*

'Ed,' Nita sang at the bloody comet hurtling through the water, 'take it!' And then she cried the three words that she had never spoken to anyone but Kit, the most dangerous words in the Speech, which release one's whole power to another. She felt the power run from her like blood from a wound. She felt Ed acquire it, and demand more as he turned it toward the beginning of some ferocious inner calling. And then, when she felt as empty as a shell, Ed shook himself and dived toward the lava again, driving Areinnye away from Kit.

Areinnye refused to be driven. Swiftly she turned and her fangs found Ed's side, scoring a long deep gash from gills to tail. The Master-Shark swept away from Areinnye, his wound trailing a horrid boiling curtain of black blood-smoke in the failing wizard-light.

Nita flailed and gasped with exertion – and got air from the protective spell, much to her surprise. She was still in whaleshape. And stuck in it, I bet, she thought, till I get the power back. What in the world's Ed doing?

The sea bottom around the vent suddenly *heaved* – lifting like some great dark creature taking its first breath . . . then heaved again, bulging up, with cracks spreading outward from the centre of the bulge. The cracks, or something beneath them, glowed red-hot.

The sea floor thundered with another tremor. Superheated water blasted up from the remains of the vent; rocks rained down from Caryn Peak. The red glow burst up through the widening cracks. It was lava, burning a feverish, suppurating red through the murk and the violently shimmering water. The water that came in contact with it – unable to boil at these pressures, regardless of the heat applied to it – did the impossible, the only thing it could do: it burst into flame. Small tongues of blue-violet fire danced and snaked along the outward-reaching tentacles of lava.

The wizard-light remaining in the water was a failing, sickly mist. Caryn Peak shook on its foundations. The Celebrants were scattered. Nita swam desperately upward, trying to do what she saw Kit doing – get safe above the roasting heat of the sea floor. All the bottom between her and the peak was a mazework of lava-filled cracks, broken stone floating on the lava, and violet fire.

Under the stone, under the lava, in the depths of the great crack that had swallowed the vent, something *moved*. Something began to shrug the stone and lava aside. A long shape shook itself, stretched itself, swelled and shrank and swelled again – a shape clothed in lava and black-violet fire, burning terribly. Nita watched in horrified fascination. What is it? Nita wondered. Some kind of buried pipeline? But no man-made pipeline was a hundred feet across. And no pipeline would seem to breathe, or move by itself, or rear up serpentlike out of the disintegrating sea bed with the dreadful energy of something unbound at last.

That shape was rising now, letting go its grasp on part of that long burning body that stretched away as far as the eye could see from east to west. A neck, Nita thought, as the shape reared up taller, towering over the sea bottom. A neck and a head— A huge snake's head, fringed, fanged, long and sleek, with dark-burning lava for a hide, and eyes the sick black-violet of water bursting into flame—

In the guise It had first worn after betraying the whales, and wore now again in gloating token of another victory, the Power, the many-named darkness that men had sometimes called the Old Serpent, towered over the sea bed as the binding that had held It shattered. This, Nita realized, was the terrible truth concealed under the old myths of the Serpent that lay coiled about the foundations of the world, waiting for the day It would crush the world in those coils.

And now Its moment was at hand: but It was stretching it, savouring it. It looked at Nita, drifting not two hundred feet from Its immense stony jaws – looked at her out of eyes burning with a colour that would sear its way into the nightmares of anyone surviving to remember it. And those eyes *knew* her.

She was frightened; but she had something to do yet. I know my verse now without having to get it from the Sea, she thought. So maybe I won't need wizardry to pull this off. And maybe just doing the Sacrifice will have its own power. Let's find out . . .

Nita backfinned through the thundering water, staying out of reach of those jaws, watching for any sudden movement. She drew what she suspected was a last breath – the protective spell around her was fading fast – and lifted her voice into the roaring darkness. Ed, she thought, don't blow it now!

'*Must I accept the barren Gift?*
   —learn death, and lose my Mastery?
Then let them know whose blood and breath

241

will take the Gift and set them free—'

The gloating eyes were fixed on her – letting her sing, letting Nita make the attempt. But the Lone Power wasn't going to let her get away with it. That huge, hideous head was bending closer to her. Nita backfinned, not too obviously, she hoped – kept her distance, kept on singing:

> *'Not old enough to love as yet,*
> *but old enough to die, indeed—*
> *the death-fear bites my throat and heart,*
> *fanged cousin to the Pale One's breed—'*

And with a low thick rumble of amusement and hunger, the Serpent's head thrust at Nita in a strike that she couldn't prevent.

This is it!

The sudden small shock in the water made her heart pound. She glanced downward as she sang. There was Kit – battered and struggling with the failing whalesark as if it were actually someone else's body – but ramming the Serpent head-on, near where the neck towered up above the slowly squeezing coils. Their pressure was breaking the sea bed in great pieces, so that lava and superheated water gushed up in a hundred places. But Kit ignored the heat and rammed the Old Serpent again and again. He's trying to distract It, Nita thought, in a terrible uprush of anguish and admiration. He's buying me time. Oh, Kit! The gift was too precious to waste. *'But past the fear lies for them,'* she sang,

> *'—perhaps for me; and past my dread,*
> *past loss of Mastery and life,*
> *the Sea shall yet give up Her dead!'*

Annoyed – as a human might be by a gnat – the Serpent bent Its head away from Nita to see what was troubling It. Humour and hunger glinted in Its eyes as It recognized in Kit the other wizard who had once given It so much trouble in Manhattan. It bent Its head to him, but slowly, wanting him to savour the terror. *Now*, Nita thought, and began to sing again. '*Lone Power—*'

'No!' cried another voice through the water, and something came hurtling at her and punched Nita to one side. It was Areinnye – wounded, and crazy, from the looks of her. *I don't have time for this!* Nita thought, and for the first time in her life rummaged around in her mind for a spell that would kill.

Someone else came streaking in to ram. Areinnye went flying. There was blood in the water: Ed's, pumping more and more weakly from the gash in his side. But his eyes were as cool as ever. 'Ed,' Nita said, breaking off her singing, 'thank you—'

He stared at her as he arrowed towards her – the old indecipherable look. 'Sprat,' he said, 'when did I ever leave distress uncured?' And to her complete amazement, before Nita could move, he rammed her again, close to the head – leaving her too stunned to sing, tumbling and helpless in pain.

Through the ache she heard Ed lift his voice in song. *Nita*'s song – the lines that, with the offered Sacrifice, bind Death anew and put the Lone Power in Its place. Kit just went on pummeling at the great shape that bent closer and closer to them all, and Nita struggled and writhed and couldn't make a sound.

No! she thought. But it was no use. Ed was taking her part willingly, circling in on the Lone Power. Yet even through Nita's horror, some wonder intruded. Where did he get such a voice? she thought. It seemed to fill the whole Sea.

> 'Lone Power, I accept your Gift!
>   But take my Gift of equal worth:
> I take Death with me, out of time,
>   and make of it a path, a birth!
>
> Let the teeth come! As they tear me,
>   they tear your ancient hate for aye—
> so rage, proud Power! Fail again,
>   and see my blood teach Death to die!'

And the Master-Shark dived straight at the upraised neck of the Serpent, and bit it. He made no cry as Its burning hide blasted his teeth away and seared his mouth instantly black; he made no cry as the Lone Power, enraged at Its wounding, bent down to pluck the annoying little creature from Its neck and crush it in stony jaws.

And then the sharks came.

Calling for help, Ed had said. Now Nita remembered what he had said to her so long ago, on the only way he had to call his people together . . . with blood: his own. Her wizardry, though, had lent the call power that even Ed's own Mastery could never have achieved, just as it had lent him a whale-wizard's power of song. And brought impossible distances by its power, the Master-Shark's people came – by dozens, by hundreds, by thousands and tens of thousands. Maddened by the blood in the water, they fell on everything that had a wound and tore it to shreds.

Nita found that she could swim again, and she did, fast – away from there, where all the sharks of the world, it seemed, jostled and boiled in feeding frenzy. Areinnye vanished in a cloud of sleek silver bodies. Ed could not be seen. And the Serpent—

A scream of astonishment and pain crashed

through the water. The Lone Power, like all the other Powers, had to obey the rules when within a universe and wear a body that could be acted upon. The sharks – wild with their Master's blood and beyond feeling pain – were acting upon it. The taste of Its scalding blood in the water, and their own, drove them mad for more. They found more. The screaming went on, and on, and on, all up and down the length of the thrashing, writhing Serpent. Nita, deafened, writhing herself, felt as if it would go on for ever.

Eventually for ever ended. The sharks, great and small, began milling slowly about, cruising for new game, finding none. They began to disperse.

Of the Master-Shark, of Areinnye, there was no sign; only a roiling cloud of red that every now and then snowed little rags of flesh.

Of the Lone Power, nothing remained but sluggishly flowing lava running over a quieting sea bed, and in the water the hot sulphurous taste, much diluted, of Its flaming blood. The writhing shape now defined on the bottom by cooling pillow lava made it plain that the Unbound was bound once more by the blood of a willing victim, a wizard – no matter that the wizardry was borrowed.

Aching all over, impossibly tired, Nita hung there for several minutes, simply not knowing what to do. She hadn't planned to live this long.

Now, though: 'Kit?'

Her cry brought her back the echo of a sperm whale heading for the surface as quickly as was safe. She followed him.

Nita passed through the 'twilight zone' at three hundred fathoms and saw light, the faint green gold she had never hoped to see again. When she broke surface and drew several long gasping breaths, she found that it was morning. Monday morning, she guessed, or hoped. It didn't much matter. She had sunlight again, she had air to breathe – and floating half a mile away in the wavewash, looking too tired to move a fin, the massive back of a sperm whale bobbed and rocked.

She went to him. Neither of them did anything for a long time but lie there in the water, side by side, skin just touching, and breathe.

'I got carried away down there,' Kit said eventually. 'And the whalesark started to go out on me. I would have gone all sperm whale – and then the sark would have blown out all the way—'

'I noticed,' Nita said.

'And you pulled me out of it. I think I owe you one.'

'After all that,' Nita said, 'I'm not sure who owes what. Maybe we'd better call it even.'

'Yeah. But, Neets—'

'Don't mention it,' she said. 'Someone has to keep you out of trouble.'

He blew explosively, right in her face.

One by one, finding one another by song, the other Celebrants began to gather around them. Neither Kit nor Nita had any words for them until, last of the group, S'reee surfaced and blew in utter weariness.

She looked at Nita. 'Areinnye—'

'Gone,' Kit said.

'And the Master-Shark—'

'The Sacrifice,' Nita said, 'was accepted.'

There was silence as the Celebrants looked at each other. 'Well,' S'reee said, 'the Sea has definitely never seen a Song quite like this—'

It will be a Song well sung, said a cool voice in Nita's head. *And sung from the heart. You, young and never loving: I, old and never loved—*

'—but the Lone One is bound. And the waters are quieting.'

246

'S'reee,' Fang said, 'don't we still need to finish the Song?'

'It's *done*,' Kit said.

S'reee looked at him in silence a moment. 'Yes,' she said then. 'It is.'

'And I want to go home,' Kit said.

'Well enough,' said S'reee. 'K!t, we'll be in these waters resting for at least a couple of days. You know where to find us.' She paused, hunting words. 'And, look—'

'Please save it,' Nita said, as gently as she could. She nudged Kit in the side; he turned shoreward for the long swim home. 'We'll see you later.'

They went home.

They found Nita's parents waiting for them on the beach, as if they had known where and when they would be arriving. Nita found it difficult to care. She and Kit slogged their way up out of the surf, into the towels that Nita's mum and dad held out for them, and stood there shivering with reaction and early-morning cold for several moments.

'Is it going to be all right?' Nita's father asked.

Nita nodded.

'Are *you* all right?' Nita's mother asked, holding her tight.

Nita looked up at her mum and saw no reason to start lying then. 'No.'

'. . . OK,' her mother said. 'The questions can wait. Let's get you home.'

'OK,' Kit said. 'And you can ask *her* all the questions you like . . . while *I* eat.'

Nita turned around then; gave Kit a long look . . . and reached out, and hugged him hard.

She didn't answer questions when she got home. She did eat; and then she went to her room and fell on to her bed, as Kit had done in his room across the hall, to get some sleep. But before she dropped off, Nita pulled her manual out from its spot under her pillow and opened it to one of the general data supply areas. 'I want a readout on all the blank-cheque wizardries done in this area in the last six months,' she said. 'And what their results were.'

The list came up. It was short, as she'd known it would be. The second-to-last entry on the list said:

BCX 85/003 – CALLAHAN, Juanita T., and RODRIGUEZ, Christopher K.: open-ended 'Möbius spell' implementation. Incurred: 5/25/85. Paid: 7/15/85, by willing substitution. See 'Current Events' précis for details.

Nita put the book back under her pillow, and quietly, bitterly, started to get caught up on her crying.

HEARTSONG

Neither she nor Kit got up till well after nightfall. When Nita threw clothes on and went downstairs, she found Kit sitting at the table, shoveling Cheerios into his face with the singleminded intensity he gave to the really important things in life. In the living room, she could hear the TV going, making crowd sounds, over which her mother was saying indignantly, '*Him*? *He's* no hitter! Just you watch—'

Kit looked up at Nita as she leaned on the doorsill. 'You hungry?'

'Not yet.'

She sat down beside him, carefully – she still ached all over – and picked up the cereal box, absently reading the list of ingredients on the side.

'Business as usual in there,' Kit said, between mouthfuls.

'So I hear.'

'I'm going out in a while. Want to come?'

'Swimming?'

'Yeah.' He paused for another mouthful. 'I've got to take the whalesark back.'

'Does it still work?'

'At this point,' Kit said, 'I'd almost rather not get into it and find out. But it got me back.'

Nita nodded, put the cereal box down, and just sat for a moment with her chin in her hands. 'I had a thought—'

'*Nooooooo.*'

Nita looked brief murder at Kit, then let the look go. 'We seem to have pulled it off again,' she said.

'Yeah.'

He said it almost a little too easily. 'You notice,' she said, 'that our reward for hard jobs seems to be that we get given even *harder* jobs?'

Kit thought, then nodded. 'Problem is,' he said, 'that we *like* the hard jobs.'

She made a sour face. Much as it annoyed her to admit it – her, little quiet Nita who sat in the back of the class and got decent marks and made no waves – it was true. 'Kit,' she said, 'they're going to keep doing that.'

'"They".'

'The Powers. They'll keep doing it until one day we *don't* pull it off. One of us, or both of us.'

Kit looked down at his cereal bowl. 'Both, preferably,' he said.

She stared at him.

'Saves the explanations.' He scooped out the last spoonful of cereal, glanced up, and made a face. 'Well, what *would* I have told them?'

Nita shook her head. 'We could stop,' she said.

Kit chewed, watching her: swallowed, and said, 'You want to?'

She waited to see if he would give some sign of what he was thinking. Useless: Kit would make a great poker player someday. 'No,' she said at last.

'Me neither,' Kit said, getting up and putting the bowl in the sink. 'Looks like we're stuck with being wizards, huh?'

Very slowly, she smiled at him. 'Yeah.'

'Then let's go down to the water and let them applaud.'

Kit gave the screen door a good-natured kick and went pounding down the stairs. Nita shook her head, still smiling, and followed.

It was late. The moon was now a day past full, and about halfway up the sky; its light was so bright the sky couldn't even manage to be totally black. The stars hung glittering in a sky more indigo, or midnight blue. Nita and Kit walked out into the surf, feeling the wind on them and hearing something most unusual – the sound of whales basking on the surface, some miles out, and singing where they lay. It was, as it had been on first hearing, a high, wild, lovely sound; but now the songs brought something extra, a catch at the heart that hadn't been there before – sorrow, and loss, and wonder. Oh, Ed, Nita thought, and sighed, remembering the glory of how he had sounded at the last. I'm going to miss you . . .

Nita swam out far enough to take whaleshape, then took Kit in tow until they made it to water deep enough for a sperm whale. He changed. Side by side they swam outward into the singing, through a sea illumined in a strange green-blue radiance, moon-light diffused and reflected. Dark shapes came to meet them; all the Celebrants but two, cruising and singing in the bright water. S'reee came to greet them skin to skin. 'Come swim with us awhile,' she said. 'No business tonight. Just singing.'

'Just a little business,' Nita said. It was hard to stop being the Silent Lord, with all her responsibilities. 'How are things down deep?'

'Quiet. Not a shake; and several of the hot-water vents seem to have reduced their outputs to normal levels. We're going to have some peace for a while, it seems . . . for which we thank you. Both of you.'

251

'You're very welcome,' Kit said. 'We'd do it again, if we had to.' Nita shot Kit a quizzical look, which he returned in kind. 'After all, it's our world too . . .'

They swam, the Celebrants and Kit and Nita, for a long time, a long way out – into waters bright with fish going about their business, peaceful with seaweed and coral, and warm – whether with volcanism or summer, Nita couldn't tell. 'This is the way it's supposed to be,' S'reee said from beside her, at one point. 'Not the way you met me – not blood in the water. Just the long nights, the singing, time to think . . .'

'It's so bright,' Nita said, wondering. The krill were evidently out in force tonight; between them and the moonlight, the water was dazzling. And there seemed to be more krill yet in the deeper waters, for it was brighter down there; much brighter. '*Look* at that,' Kit said, and dived, heading for the light.

At about a hundred feet down, Nita began to realize that the light in the water had nothing to do with krill. Of itself the water was burning, a harmless warm radiance that grew stronger and stronger in the greater depths. And in those depths, everything else shone too: not just reflected light, but a fire that seemed to come from *inside* seaweed, shells, branching coral. Song echoed in that water, sounding at first like whalesong – but slowly Nita began to hear something else in the music, in a way that had nothing to do with hearing. Expressions of growth, of power, of delight – but no note of limitation, pain, loss. She found herself descending into timelessness, into a blaze of meaning and purpose so bright it could have blinded the heart – had the heart not become stronger every moment, more able to bear it.

Finally there was nothing but the brightness, the water all around her on fire with light. Shapes moved in the light, swimming in it as if the water were extraneous and the light were their true medium. There was no looking at those shapes for more than a heartbeat before the eye was forced to turn away, defeated by glory. It was in the passage of those shapes near Nita that it was made plain to her, in the way the Sea gave a whale-wizard knowledge, that she and Kit were welcome indeed and had successfully completed the job they'd been given.

Kit was silent, as if not knowing what to say. Nita knew, but simply considered for a moment before singing it in one soft note that, in this place, carried as poignantly as a trumpet-call at evening.

'It hurt,' she said.

We know, the answer came back. *We sorrow. Do you?*

'For what happened?'

No. For who you are now – the person you weren't a week ago.

'. . . No.'

'No,' Kit said.

Would you do the same sort of thing again?

'Yes . . . if we had to.'

Then there's no guarantee this won't happen again. Not that we could offer you any. Hope, like fear, comes from within . . .

Nita nodded. There was nothing sorrowful about the pronouncement; it was as matter-of-fact as anything in the manual. Kit turned away from the shape, the bright Power, that had answered them. As always, Nita turned with him.

And, looking up in astonishment, backfinned hurriedly. Something was passing over. Something as huge, or huger than, the unseeable shapes in the radiant water; burning as fiercely as they did, though with a cooler flame; passing by with a silent, deadly grace that Nita would have known anywhere. *I am no wizard*, he had said. But how could he, or she, have anticipated that borrowing a wizard's power would make even a nonwizard part of the Heart of the Sea? Or maybe there was more to it than that. *What's loved*, Carl had said, *survives*. Nita's heart went up in a great note of unbelieving joy.

The passing shape didn't turn, didn't pause. Nita got just a glance of black eyes, the only dark things in all this place. Yet even they burned, a fire behind that opaque look that could mean anything.

Nita knew what it meant. And on he went, out of sight, in unhurried grace; the true dark angel, the unfallen Destroyer, the Pale Slayer who never really dies – seeking for pain to end.

Nita turned to Kit, wordless. He gazed back, as astonished and delighted as she.

'OK,' Kit said. 'Bring on the next job.'

She agreed.

THE END

SO YOU WANT TO BE A WIZARD

DIANE DUANE

Should you decide to go ahead and take the Oath, be warned that an ordeal of sorts will follow, a test of aptitude . . .

Nita's life changes dramatically when she discovers a library book on the art of wizardry! Taking the Oath to use the power wisely and well, she begins the long road of study to become a wizard. But first she must prove her worth – as does Kit, another young wizard-to-be who she meets. Together they cross over to a dark parallel world to search for an ancient book that holds the key to preserving the Universe.

On their mission, the two teenagers discover monstrous man-eating technology and wolf-like creatures who attack on sight, before finally coming face to face with the evil Starsnuffer – he who controls the ultimate power of darkness . . .

So You Want to be a Wizard is the first title in an inventive fantasy trilogy.

0 552 526452